BIO-PUNK

Stories from the
Far Side of Research

Edited by
Ra Page

For Natalie

First published in Great Britain in 2012 by Comma Press
www.commapress.co.uk

ISBN   1905583400
ISBN-13   978 1905583409

LOTTERY FUNDED

The publisher gratefully acknowledges the assistance of Arts Council England,
and the support of Literature Northwest.
This project has been supported by the Wellcome Trust.

Supported by

wellcometrust

Dilys Rose's story 'EFEMERI' was commissioned with the support of Creative
Scotland and the European Cultural Foundation, as part of International Short
Story Day 2012 and the European Short Story Network (www.theshortstory.eu)

Set in Bembo 11/13 by David Eckersall
Printed and bound in England by MPG Biddles.

Contents

CONTENTS

Introduction

COMMISSIONING AN ANTHOLOGY of short stories is rather like conducting a series of laboratory experiments. You start with a hypothesis – that the theme of the book, some burning issue out here in the non-fictional world, can have genuine, new light shed on it by fiction writers; you then establish certain experimental parameters – clarifying what the authors can and can't write about; finally, you make sure that laboratory conditions are preserved throughout – that the 'Petri dish of fiction' is hermetically sealed and the drama inside plays out *as if* it were in the real world, but with no confusion or contamination leaking between the two. The results are typically scientific too: diverse, unpredictable, sometimes even game-changing.

With this particular experiment fourteen authors were invited to respond to exciting new areas of bio-medical research so as to explore, through fiction, potential social or ethical dilemmas that might arise from them. Scientists and bio-ethicists were attached to each research area, and accompanied the author who chose it in the development of their story – from an initial consultation, through to writing an explanatory afterword to the finished piece.

The parameters given to the authors were straightforward. Firstly, the stories needed to be scientifically accurate; they had to be based on current research and stay consistent with the theory and practice as it now stands – the consulting scientists and ethicists had recourse to correct errors in the drafting process, as well as address issues of likelihood in their afterwords (see Dr Sarah Gilbert's response to Jane Feaver's vaccine trial story). Secondly, the stories had to be set within the confines of a fictional society that ostensibly had its citizens' best interests at heart.

As with all experiments, some tests fail immediately. The agar stays clear; the Petri dish a dud. Early in this experiment, one author we approached – himself a well-seasoned SF writer – responded to the commission by saying, flatly, that there was nothing to write about. His argument was with the very idea of bio-ethics – that rapidly emerging, interdisciplinary study whose set of concerns offered an umbrella concept for this commission. Bio-ethics, he argued, so often poses a series of 'ethical concerns', the answers to which are 'trivially obvious in terms of generally accepted norms of conduct and policy. Of course, these norms can be criticised and can change, but in lots of the topics [posed in this commission] the "ethical problem" only arises if the problem is posed in terms of much more controversial, and much less widely held, positions such as animal rights or Roman Catholicism.' Bio-ethics may be a growth industry, but nothing much was growing in this Petri dish.

Putting aside this respondent's considerable underestimation of what he calls 'much less widely held positions', it was a worrying start. Some of the authors invited (and some of the fictional characters they created) were indeed of a religious leaning and/or championed animal rights. Theirs may well be 'less widely held positions', and the experiment may well be rigged from the start, to get a desired 'outrage result'.

Early returns from other writers, however, suggested there was more to the bio-ethics question than the 'trivially obvious'. Fairly deep-seated dilemmas were pointed to at opposite ends of the bio-medical process. In K.J. Orr's Amazonia-set 'Elegy for a Bio-Pirate', we are confronted with a paradox at the very onset of research: should we invest in the utilization of a traditional medicine even if such 'investment' is likely to destroy both the knowledge base (shaman-led village tradition) and the environment (the rainforest) that have preserved the medicine and all knowledge of it thus far? Dilys Rose's airport-set 'EFEMERI' considers dilemmas at the other end of the spectrum: an alternative application for a technology originally developed for medical purposes (MRI brain scanning). In between these two bookends, stories returned exploring ever more bizarre consequences of 'well-meant' bio-tech: Adam Marek's 'An Industrial Evolution' considers one woman's attempt to save an entire species with the help of inter-species genetics, but asks whether preservation is always the right thing to do; Simon Van Booy's 'Flesh and Blood' examines the consequences of simply knowing too much about ourselves; Toby Litt's 'Call it "The Bug"...' considers a world segregated according to its access to life-preserving implants.

With the help of the bio-ethicists, some stories also shone a light onto apparently 'non-trivial' problems in the current legal system, either where bio-technological progress has left the statute book behind, or where the law has embraced it too quickly: Sarah Schofield's story explores the legal loophole exploited by manufacturers of over-the-counter supplements, and Justina Robson examines the grassroots phenomenon that is DIYbio – both areas where arguably more regulation is needed. Dr Jane Haley, on the other hand, notes the first case of an fMRI-based 'lie detection' conviction in a court of law (in India), and the fact that the UK has yet to test its admissibility, whilst the US has so far rejected it.

As the patterns in each Petri dish start to flower and unfurl, certain similarities present themselves. Holding each story up to the light and comparing it to the next, we notice a shared, deep-rooted contradiction in the way many characters (and arguably the society they occupy) relate to science: the rational brain appreciates perfectly well that science progresses according to the 'best methodology available to us'; but the irrational, instinctive brain still struggles to trust science, to put its faith in a process that isn't just difficult to comprehend, but inherently riddled with uncertainty. The more natural, 'human' impulse, it seems, is to fill this gap, and join the dots, not with painstaking self-education and inductive argument, but with an easy dollop of drama. As Simon Ings' character puts it, 'Any story [...] is better than no story at all.' Indeed we regularly splash 'story' all over science so as to 'humanize' it, making its players subject to all-too-human ambition. Yet, by making science more recognizable, and therefore easier to trust, we paradoxically apply to it motives and characteristics that are entirely *un*trustworthy. We prefer a single, deranged boffin to countless, anonymous lab technicians. We prefer an unlikely anecdote about a little-known natural 'cure', to peer-reviewed, published clinical trials. Because mad boffins and miracle remedies are, by definition, story elements; long, drawn-out drug trials with contesting interpretations are not.

The manifestations of this paradox are various and many-coloured. Sarah Schofield's 'Shake Me and I Rattle' examines how our love of anecdote leads to a dangerous proclivity for alternative remedies, diet pills and 'snake oil', for want of a better term. Whilst the consultant on her story, Dr Angharad Watson strives to thrust these wooly anecdotes back under the hard light of reason: 'If something is claiming to do what a drug does,' Watson asks, 'why isn't it a drug?'

Simon Ings explores the other danger of humanizing the science 'story' – that of glamourising it, expecting too much of it, becoming a fan. The problem with fans, Ings argues citing the state-led corruption of Soviet genetics, is they have no patience.

Another problem with fans is their unshiftable belief in ready-made, off-the-peg cures – magic bullets, designed by evolution, and merely waiting for us to find them. Rather like the elusive 'eureka moment' in science breakthrough stories, the characters in this collection (and indeed many real-life 'science fans') trade in past examples of the magic bullet, and convince funders and investors of the existence of new ones. Usually these bubble up from the headspring of traditional medicine: the silverfruit tree that survived Hiroshima and deters all known pests (gingko biloba), the Amazonian arrowhead poison deployed as a paralysing agent in early anaesthetics (curare), the malaria-fighting bark extract brought back from Peru by Jesuit missionaries (quinine)... these examples have a mythic status in research circles. And new candidates are always being lined up. The Linckia starfish is perhaps the latest, thanks to its ability to both regenerate lost limbs (as a newt, tadpole or axolotl might), and also generate *from* a detached limb, as an entirely new organism.

Hope is important, of course. 'Found cures' are not just myths, and bio-mimicry has become a watch-word for many areas of research (see Annie Kirby's story of a tadpole-derived 'magic cream'). After all, if evolution is the best designer, why not try to smuggle out a few knock-offs for humans to try on? But hope, as several contributors here point out, can be dangerous, damaging. And scientists are as much to blame for fuelling 'fandom' as anyone. Bio-medical scientists have two masters, after all – the funders on one side, who crave hope, respond to it and invest in it; and the general public (i.e. potential patients) on the other side, whose expectations need to be managed. The former is often served at the expense of the latter. As Dr Ian McGonigle argues in his afterword to Ings' story, an 'epistemic rift' begins to open up between what science says is possible in the lab, and what the general public realises is likely in the real world. Scientists are in danger of creating a fiction of their own, in fact, if sobriety and caution aren't sufficiently exercised in the way they communicate to the rest of us.

We called this project 'Bio-Punk' in an attempt to create a third archetype in the over-humanized science 'story' – dangerous though all these archetypes are – that is to say, an alternative to the 'science fan' and 'megalomaniacal boffin'. Unlike the fan, who allows for overzealous state-meddling, or the mad boffin, who represents the opposite – the unaccountable individual – a bio-punk is a member of a grassroots movement that organizes against an enemy far more powerful, these days, than states or individuals. I speak, of course, of corporations.

Vast, hidden libraries of coded information are currently being unlocked by genomics and, if we're not very careful, the keys to these libraries will ultimately fall into the hands of private companies – even though the secrets they contain belong to, and concern, all of us. The bio-punk believes in the common ownership of this vital knowledge, and calls on states and individuals to lobby against the likes of Craig Venter and his corporate-centipede of private investors (Celera Corp, JCVI, etc).[1]

Drawing a parallel between genetic code and computational code, the bio-punk calls for the open-sourcing of *all* genetic information, indeed all bio-knowledge, most of which remains hidden from general view in pay-to-access research journals, even when it isn't patented. (The University of Manchester's John Rylands Library, for example, spent a staggering £5,929,803 last year on subscriptions to academic journals). Dr Nihal Vrana, discussing implant technology, suggests private ownership of life-extending technology could lead to an untenable level of social segregation in the future – one that can only lead to revolution. If the secrets of the genomic libraries are privatized, an untenable level of segregation may come about even sooner than that. The best way to avoid it, we contend, is with the help of bio-punks; people like the Human Genome Project scientists who strove to beat Celera Corp to the sequencing finishing line. Whilst paying heed to the dangers of 'bio-error' (in scenarios like Justina Robson's 'Madswitch') we should also be careful not to buy into too many scare stories surrounding common ownership of research information or indeed grassroots engagement projects (like DIYbio). The media seem very quick to respond to this latter phenomenon by applying the 'anti-terror' rhetoric of the Bush-Blair era so as to convince us that the bio-punk is just another iteration of the mad

1. More on JCVI's recent work on pp. 9-12.

scientist: the mad scientist turned terrorist. In fact, this rhetoric isn't limited to the popular press. In November 2011, the US National Security Advisory Board for Biotechnology (NSABB) called on the editors of *Nature* and *Science* to censor key passages of two research papers on the H5N1 virus in the fear that the information might fall into the wrong hands – a decision that sparked immediate controversy in the scientific community, including the researchers concerned, who argued that the benefits of publishing the research in full outweighed the risks. The World Health Organisation backed the publication of the papers in full, and eventually, in March this year, the NSABB reversed its recommendation.

Individual scientists, taking up the bio-punk mantel, regularly call for open access, and free information, even to the extent of eschewing *Nature* and *Science* (subscriptions for which are over £100 per annum for individuals, and thousands for institutions) for free-access journals like PLoS One. Universities increasingly find themselves on the other side of this fence, however, and have generally dedicated intellectual property offices that continually encourage their researchers to patent everything they possibly can (with the universities themselves taking up to 60% ownership of these patents). This in turn leads to even greater secrecy within the scientific community, and the muzzling of seemingly all concerned with non-disclosure agreements. As government funding for academia declines (the UK currently ranks at only 41st in the world in terms of government funding for H.E.), universities are forced to explore other ways to generate revenue, and the exploitation of intellectual property seems the obvious route. The development of MRI – as explored in Dilys Rose's story – is a prime example of a technology that was greatly developed in UK universities, but not patented by them; indeed MRI is held up as a cautionary IP tale for UK universities.

It is in this context that the radicalism of the bio-punk – committed to the *giving away* of knowledge for the benefit of all – should be considered. Indeed it's worth remembering the words of Jonas Salk, perhaps the original bio-punk, whose discovery of the polio vaccine in 1952 has almost completely eradicated the disease, and spared humanity hundreds of thousands of infections. When asked in a televised interview who owned the patent to the vaccine, Salk famously replied: 'There is no patent. Could you patent the sun?'

Every experiment needs a control, and this one was no different. Initially we expected this role to be filled by the opening passages of Jane Rogers' story – a light-hearted canter through the prejudices, misunderstandings and snobberies that still abound in the non-science community, even in the higher echelons of academia. We assumed the 'active ingredient' being tested by this anthology in particular was the scientific input, and for much of Jane's story, common ignorance is allowed to go untouched by the consultation process, like empty agar in a control sample.

But as other stories started to come back, it occurred to us that we might have got this quite wrong. This was a commission to explore ways in which *unforeseen* ethical issues may arise from research; what we were actually doing therefore, in all cases, was testing an absence: what happens if we *don't* foresee and prevent a moral or social problem. In other words, *all* of these stories were controls. The real experiment – where the fruits of bio-ethics and social conscience will be truly tested – is taking place out there.

Dinner at High Table

or

An Erudite Vindication of Pure Research

Jane Rogers

'RICKY,' CHARLES WAS saying. 'Yes, our own dear Professor Richard Finn has this very week had the dubious honour of saving mankind from extinction.'

I rarely go in to formal hall. Once or twice a term, just to show willing. It's still a male preserve, and I always make a fool of myself. And Charles, while not yet completely plastered, was well on his way. There was a rumble of arf-arfing and table thumping. Charlie gave me a wave.

'Do go on,' I said. 'Where is Rick, anyway?' Rick being one of the few habitués of the table with a more sophisticated attitude to women than that of a prep-school boy – possibly because he's a biologist. At any rate, he understands matters of the flesh with a pleasing thoroughness. Although I had not had the pleasure, since he got hitched to wife number three.

'In the States, Cynthia m'dear, in the US of A. Saving the planet. Lend me your pretty ear and I shall reveal...'

My ear is old, Charlie. Old and bored and tired, and for all I know, ugly too. A boy brought my soup; broccoli and stilton, good. That horse-faced idiot from Ancient History was sitting opposite me, picking food out of his beard. I tried not to look.

Charlie rallied the rest of his audience. 'You've all heard of Menter? The Harvard chap who thinks he's God?'

'Don't you all,' I muttered. Horse Face stared at me, seeming to have difficulty with his focus.

'*I have created life* and all that,' said Charlie. 'Splashed across the headlines a few weeks ago.'

'Synthetic biologist,' barked Phillips. 'Frankenstein stuff. Genetic engineering on steroids; mix up your biological bits and pieces and – POOF!'

'Poof to you too,' giggled little Johnny Fraser. There's been a student complaint against him, silly boy; he doesn't know where to draw the line.

'Exactly.' Charlie reasserted his place at the top of the pecking order. 'But what you need to understand is the way some of these Yanks go about their synthetic biology.'

'They're funded by Defence,' someone chipped in. 'That's the first thing to understand about them. Funded to the tune of billions by the US Department of Defence. And what does that tell you?'

'The point is,' said Charlie, 'they want quick results. They want to hit the jackpot. There's ways and ways of creating synthetic life, and their way is corner-cutting, risk-taking, wham bam thank you ma'am!'

Much laughter from my politically correct colleagues. I put on my frostiest voice.

'So how does this manifest – in the actual research?'

'Glad you asked, Cyn. Well, they're taking stuff apart; living cells, bacteria – in fact, pathogens. Since they're the easiest. Stripping them down to get the bits they need, joining those bits together with other bits, popping them together into a stripped-out cell membrane, to try and make the thing they want.'

'I don't know what they want,' I said.

'Oh, the applications are endless. Bio-fuels. Designer drugs. Bio-remediation.'

'Which is?'

2

'Little living things – bacteria, basically – synthetically created, that eat rubbish, eat pollution. Clean-up bugs.'

I helped myself to Beef Wellington and the server brought me fresh hot vegetables. A Chinese boy, slender as a wand with long, jet-black hair and a shy smile. Delectable. They were still arf-arfing over the clean-up bugs. I told Charlie to cut to the chase.

'I'll give you an analogy. Say you wanted to make a car. Say other vehicles existed but not the car, and you wanted to make one. A sensible type might start on the drawing board. But what the Yanks are doing is taking parts of other things; the chassis, say, of a stagecoach; the wheels of a bicycle; the engine of a jumbo jet; and putting Jeremy Clarkson behind the wheel. They can separate the parts, they can recombine them in some semblance of a car, and pray they get the function they want – but –'

'It'll blow the bladdy doors off!' Horse Face's slightly surprising contribution: a passable Michael Caine impression.

'Worse than that,' smirked Charlie. 'A couple of weeks ago, their stuff started self-replicating.'

'What was it?' I asked.

He shrugged. 'What it was or was meant to be doesn't matter. What matters is, these clowns put together some clever combination of genomes in a cell which started reproducing at a rate of knots and they didn't know how to stop it.'

'Green gremlins,' suggested Johnny Fraser.

'Microscopic green gremlins,' nodded Charles. 'Binary fission. Fabulous. *We've created life!* crows Menter. Back in the Petri dish; four divisions; eight divisions, sixteen – multiple divisions, rapid, rapid reproduction. When they come in in the morning it's dripping out of the heat cabinet, it's leaking across the work bench...'

'Green gremlins! Green gremlins!' Johnny Fraser thumped the table and knocked his wine glass over. The

Chinese boy was at his elbow mopping up before it had time to spread. Great reflexes.

'And what are you going to do with it?' asked Charlie. 'Put yourself in their shoes. It's alive and has no predators. You can't flush it down the sink and let it loose in the sewers. You can't wipe it up and throw away the cloth. It's growing, all the time, growing and spreading, and you've got to contain it.'

'So what did they do?'

'The usual bio-hazard safety regs, I should imagine. Evacuate the labs; essential personnel only; steel shutters, hose down the scientists at the exits, blah blah. Of course they were trying to stop it, throwing everything at it – Menter and all his team... But what they had on their hands was an ever-growing sea of green gremlins. And worst of all from Mr God's point of view, the prospect of a media feeding-frenzy and prompt withdrawal of all funding. To be swiftly followed by the demise of the human race in a biblical flood of green gremlins.'

'D'you know they were green?' objected Phillips.

'Green gremlins! Green gremlins!' chanted Johnny, spilling his new wine down his front. The Chinese boy deftly patted his chest with a napkin and I considered spilling my own.

'Definitely green,' said Charlie. 'With the logo of his company on every cell.'

'And singing,' suggested Horse Face. 'Singing the birdy song.'

'Right,' said Charlie. 'Now you have the picture. Menter and his hapless research team pressed flat against the door and windows of his lab by an ever-increasing tsunami of green gremlins ceaselessly singing the birdy song.'

'Is this where Ricky comes in?' I asked.

'Precisely. Now what you may not know is that old Rick has been quietly doing some sterling work in this field, right under our noses. But while Menter's lot have gone at it middle-in (to use a technical term), using ready-made bits, old Rick has gone at it bottom-up.'

'Bottoms up!' cried Johnny Fraser. He flopped back in his chair and slid soundlessly to the floor. There was a minor disturbance as the Chinese boy extricated him and whisked him into the gowning room. It occurred to me that I had misread the Chinese boy, and I felt stupid.

'So what Rick has done is to start at the beginning: nothing ready-made. He asked himself, how do you make a cell? Well you have to start with a boundary. A division between cell and not-cell. You have to make the membrane, you have to find out how to make something to hold the contents in; and he's created a phospholipid bilayer –'

'For God's sake spare us the details!' barked Phillips.

'Which these American chappies never did, they got their cell walls ready-made, sucked out the insides of prokaryotic cells and put in what they wanted. So, obviously, the call goes out internationally – top secret, mind you – to those in the know: NEED HELP WITH GREEN GREMLINS.'

'And birdy song,' added Horse Face.

'And Ricky said have you considered taking the membranes apart – because then it won't be cells, and it can't replicate.'

'By Jove, he's right!' from Phillips.

'And of course they had no idea, because if you don't know how to make something you don't know how to take it apart. So Ricky flies out there and spends a few days locked in a lab wrestling with a dish of their gremlins –'

'And birdy song –'

'And to cut a long and interesting story short, at the end of the day he's found out how to dismantle their creation. More to the point, he's found out how to make it dismantle itself.'

Much arf-arfing and table thumping, causing the nearest table of undergrads to peer up at us with curiosity.

'So Rick has saved the world,' proclaimed Charlie.

'Never to be acknowledged of course. Totally hush hush. State secret and all that; but one up for the old country, eh?'

'It would be better,' I said, 'if they stopped mucking about with this kind of thing altogether. Who on Earth *wants* them to create synthetic life?'

'Ah the fair sex!' cried Charlie, and I realised I had played straight into his hands. It was the fault of the Chinese boy, who had distracted me. 'The fair sex, bless them, how they hate progress. How they dislike science in all its advances; how they love to dwell in simple mud huts, gnawing on raw vegetables, bearing a child a year, and gazing on mindlessly as these infants succumb to measles, smallpox and TB.'

'You are spouting your usual shite, Charlie,' I said. Which was not particularly witty. Though it did cause Horse Face to laugh so much he inhaled his crème brulee and had to be back-slapped by Phillips.

'If it is shite to talk of the progress made by medical science, the advances in human health and happiness, and to complain that there have always been luddites, greens, and earth mothers, often female, turning their backs on the fruits of knowledge – then I own and embrace my shite!' declared Charlie triumphantly. And loudly enough to raise a laugh and some applause from the nearest student table.

'Charlie,' I said, gathering what little remained of my dignity; 'the fruit of knowledge – which was, you may recall, an apple – was in fact first plucked and tasted by Eve, who was by all accounts a woman.'

'And look where it got you!' retorted Charlie, to thumps and chortles from his supporters. 'You've been shutting the stable door ever since.'

'And you know,' said Horse Face seriously, 'you know, the horse has bolted.'

Charlie had to have the last word. 'Trust me, darling,' he said.

'I am not your darling.'

'Nevertheless. When Rick pops out of his lab with a

6

synthetic cell that can trace and attack pre-cancerous cells in the human body, will you be saying, "No thanks"?'

They arfed. They thumped.

'Are you going to put a stop to the eradication of malaria by synthetically-engineered Artemisinin?'

I was given a brief respite by the reappearance of Johnny and his Chinese friend, both looking rather flushed. 'Thought I'd rejoin you for coffee,' Johnny smiled. 'Have you finished with the green gremlins?'

'Not quite,' said Charlie. 'Cynthia?'

'I'll tell you what,' I said lamely. 'I'll ask Rick about it. He doesn't talk as much crap as you do, Charlie.'

Charlie crowed; one-nil to him. When the Chinese boy brought my crème brûlée (which happens to be my favourite of all the excellent high table desserts) I told him I didn't want it. And I would have gone to bed thoroughly crushed, were it not for the fact that on my way back across the quad I met Rick.

'Cynthia!' he cried. 'But you're looking wonderful!'

'That's because it's pitch dark,' I told him. 'I've just been hearing how you've saved the world.'

'I wouldn't go that far,' he said. 'But it was a pretty interesting trip.'

'Will you explain it to me sometime?' I asked him. 'Charlie always makes me feel such a fool.'

'No time like the present,' said Rick. 'I've got a new bottle of duty-free in my study. Shall we?'

'Don't you have to rush back to your wife?' I blurted.

'She's not expecting me home till tomorrow.'

When he had poured me a toothmug full of whiskey, Rick explained that Charlie is an ignoramus, and that the synthetic life was *not* running riot in the lab. 'Under lab conditions they can control it – starve it of energy. Any fool knows it can't replicate without feeding on something.'

'So what *was* it doing?'

'It had got out. A pillock on their research team took some home 'in total security' to show his swotty son under his microscope how it was self-replicating. And without permission, the kid nicked out to school with it to show off the artificial life his dad made at work... They've had to close down the school.'

'It's that dangerous?'

Rick shrugged. 'You wouldn't know the knock-on effects until it was too late.'

'But you stopped it?'

When he laughs he's like a mischievous boy. 'You really want the details?'

The details were fascinating and led us, quite naturally, from the mystery of self-replicating life to the marvellous intricacies of more sophisticated forms of reproduction. Next time I go into formal hall I shall be able to tell Charlie a thing or two about phospholipid bilayers. And to look upon the Chinese boy with perfect equanimity.

Afterword:

Green Gremlins

Dr Ainsley Newson
Centre for Ethics in Medicine, University of Bristol

WHAT FIRST ENTICED me about synthetic biology – that is, the application of engineering principles to the design and construction of new biological components or organisms – was the vastness of the field; the possibilities for new understandings of biology and inter-disciplinary collaboration. The opportunities for scientific creativity using the combined techniques of biology, engineering, chemistry, physics and computer science (among others) are seemingly endless, as are the possible real-world applications. There are huge potential rewards for those researchers in synthetic biology who display open-mindedness, are open to new scientific partnerships and are adept at creative thinking. But synthetic biology is not without implications.

It is this seeming step into unchartered territory that gives rise to a role for people like me – academics who work in 'bio-ethics', a discipline that applies ethical reasoning, social science research, legal scholarship and policy-making to moral problems in bio-science and health care. With the significant potential of synthetic biology also come interesting ethical questions, which although perhaps not fundamentally new (we've travelled similar paths before with nanotechnology and genetic engineering) are vital to address for this research to be acceptable to society.

In reflecting on Jane's witty and illuminating story together with the research that inspired it, what jumps out to me, as an ethicist? The work described in the piece, 'Menter's' Green Gremlin bacterial cells, seems to have been inspired by work at the J. Craig Venter Institute that was published in

2010. JCVI scientists created what was termed the first self-replicating synthetic bacterial cell. This was not a fully 'synthetic' cell in that it was a modified replication of a real-world bacterium. The host cell wasn't synthesised in the lab but adapted from an existing bacterium. It also wasn't, obviously, made of plastic or any other unnatural material. But they did put it together from scratch in that they first artificially synthesised all the parts of the genome they would need, as opposed to the cutting and pasting approach of genetic engineering. It also shows that functional genomes can be made (synthesised) in the laboratory and then put into an empty host cell to continue replicating. This same team is now working to make a 'minimal cell', an artificial organism that will contain only those genes needed to sustain simple life – nothing else.

The central character in Jane's story asks: 'Who on Earth *wants* them to create synthetic life?' Well funding bodies, for one, and governments. They have ring-fenced significant research funds for this type of work and the more basic science that supports it. And surveys and other conversations with the lay public have also shown broad support and enthusiasm for synthetic biology.

The drive to create synthetic life might better be understood if we see where it could lead us, which is to new, better and cheaper pharmaceuticals, new medical diagnostic tools and treatments, new ways of cleaning up the environment (bio-remediation or toxin detection) and new, cleaner, greener fuels. In addition to these applications, synthetic biology research is also expected to help us to understand more about the fundamentals of biological life; how it works and what can go wrong and when. The systematic approach of synthetic biology will help to unlock some of the secrets of biology that have hitherto remained elusive. In an increasingly application-driven research culture, the value of this intrinsic knowledge should not be underestimated.

It's also important to point out that we are not talking

here about Frankenstein-style artificial sentient entities. Synthetic biology could lead to the creation of an entity not previously found in nature that is capable of sustaining and replicating itself, but this will be a micro-organism. And while synthetic biology does lead to interesting discussions about what it is to be 'alive' and what, if any, moral obligations we may owe to the entities that are created through this research, in the short to medium term we are not talking about creating new, complex creatures. So just as we use anti-bacterial sprays to control germs around our homes, so too will we treat early synthetic entities. If synthetic biology does one day lead to more complex entities, once they do arise we can look to the moral capacities they might have. We would then consider the question: what is it about a life that is valuable and ought to be respected? If a new life-form had certain capacities, for example sentience or the ability to feel pain, then this may give rise to certain moral obligations towards it.

Does this mean that researchers in synthetic biology are 'Playing God'? And if they are, does this matter morally? It is true that creating a new form of life (if this is ever achieved) is about the farthest from 'natural' that you can get. However, this is what decades of scientific research, particularly research in health, have been all about: trying to overcome the inherent problems that nature lumbers us with. Objections about 'Playing God' seem to assume that Nature, or the corresponding God-like entity, gets it right all the time, which of course it doesn't. Nature is neither harmonious nor stable. But we do need to be careful and cautious about what we create.

Is there money to be made in synthetic biology? Certainly. And there are already patents, which concerns many (including me). There is, thankfully, a ground-up attitude among many synthetic biology researchers to ensure that the benefits of this research are accessible to many rather than few. The main way this is being achieved is by using a collaborative, 'open source' approach to research, to try and innovate ahead of those who only have commercial gain as their aim.

But what of the green gremlins? Will we need Rick to save 'mankind from extinction'? Synthetic biology, like any form of biological research, cannot be entirely without risk. And for this reason, attention to the bio-safety and bio-security aspects of synthetic biology has been a focal point since the field first emerged. In a European context, it is currently considered that existing rules and regulations more than adequately cover synthetic biology risks. Yes, there is still a risk of a rogue scientist synthesising smallpox in his garage, but such problems are not unique to synthetic biology. Moreover, although there are concerns over the creation of novel life-forms, if we simply cease to do any activity because it carries a risk, then we would not only deny ourselves the benefits of synthetic biology, we would stymie the whole field from developing. What this precautionary approach is saying is that we should keep things as they are, just because we can't trust ourselves to keep doing the right thing in the future. Taking this reasoning to its logical conclusion would mean we would never be able to do very much at all. And, as Rick points out in Jane's story, lab conditions can also be put in place to control the green gremlins, namely by starving them of energy.

Synthetic biology and the entities that researchers create from it may well change how we understand life, but it will not reduce how special we think it is. Rather, I hope that it will inspire greater awe for life's complexity.

An Industrial Evolution

Adam Marek

'I AM JOSTLING *for position, trying to find a view in the gaps between elbows and bodies. I cannot miss it. This moment. Ellie gasps and grunts and groans. One of the surgeons shifts, and then... there it is. Pulled from her roughly, it seems to me, its orange fur dark and slicked down against its tiny frame. The world has just become a different place. Another genie is out of the bottle.'*

Caspar Stak, *Black Window*, June 2024 Issue.

Even though the road from Kapas to Perjan Tungul is now so smooth that the bus glides with barely a bump, ten minutes into our journey a man in the back row gets travel sick and lays a Duty Free carrier bag on the floor to cover it. I spend the next four hours with a t-shirt tied round my face, my headphones in, and my eyes closed.

I arrive just after three in the afternoon, and am surprised to see here a big café with parasols, cushions on the chairs, waiters in white shirts, a fountain, and a bar made entirely from glass with an enormous fruit and flower arrangement in the centre. This is not the Sumatra I remember.

To step out of the bus, I must break through a wall of heat. It seems to roar in my ears. Eleanor has arrived on an earlier bus, and is sitting on her suitcase in the shade of a palm tree. Three young boys crowd her knees. All four are talking and laughing.

It has been 20 years since I saw her, and even though she has aged considerably during her exile in Canada, she is instantly recognisable: the conspiratorial hunch and sideways tilt of the head, the nodding, the emphatic hand wringing. Like her beloved orangutans, she is thick in body and long in limb. Her hair a comb-shy tangle of white weeds.

I can delay this moment no longer.

Eleanor doesn't notice me, or doesn't appear to, until I'm right by her side when, making a demonic shape of her face, she says to the children, 'This is one of the most evil men in the world. Don't even look at him. It will bring you nothing but misery.'

The boat we take is a public transit, holding about 20 people, and depositing them one or two at a time on the jetties that poke out of the riverbanks like a parade of eager tongues. Banau Batong is the last stop, more than an hour on from the penultimate drop off, and we are the only ones travelling there. Eleanor sits in the front of the boat, chatting with the captain, him letting her steer where the brown river runs straight. She has one leg crossed over the other, and has let her sandals slip off. The soles of her feet are leather, her toenails turquoise.

I sit at the back, in the panel of sunshine, growing giddy on the nostalgic pleasure of petrol fumes, enjoying the sun against my closed eyelids, listening to the engine, the water sloshing against the hull, and the few bird calls. When I made this journey, aged 23, I was enthusiastically pointing my phone this way and that, trying to film the gaudy sunbirds that flashed between the trees, and the crocs that crossed the river like zippers. I had wanted to capture the sounds, so I could spend time back at my desk in England describing faithfully the thrum of life, intoxicating in its richness, an aural assault from 10,000 throats and stridulating insect legs. Now, the sense of loneliness here is so eerie, I give up the sun to move to the front of the boat and sit on the cushioned bench close to the captain and Eleanor.

'It was a good idea to take the scenic route,' I say.

Eleanor nods.

'It's so quiet though,' I say, 'isn't it?'

Eleanor raises her eyebrows. She has the most remarkable eyes. Amber, flecked with gold. A toad's eyes. Quite beautiful.

'I barely recognise it,' I continue. 'It must be even stranger for you.'

She licks her lips. 'Strange is what used to make this place special. Now it's…'

She stares at the ripples we leave behind us, maybe searching for the right word, but doesn't find it.

The Banau Batong base camp is surrounded by a moat. A slimy, green mosquito nursery. A man is painting the wooden drawbridge that crosses it white. On the end of the bridge closest to us, there is an orangutan. This limp-limbed wookie is the first I've seen in 20 years, but unlike any I've ever seen.

The orang is standing upright, leaning on the wooden rail looking down into the moat. He is wearing a pair of cut-off denim shorts, and a baggy yellow t-shirt that has a bib of berry stains and is stretched long around the neck. He has on a red baseball cap with the Banau Batong company logo – two black B's placed back to back, like a butterfly.

'Is it safe to cross?' I call to the man, pointing at the orang.

The man seems puzzled. He gestures with a sweep of his paintbrush in the air that it's okay to go.

Eleanor has already taken the initiative and is walking towards the ape with a kind of droopy body posture and her head flopped down, chin almost on her chest. The man stops painting to watch as she gets closer. The orang turns his glassy black eyes to her, then gives an eerily human upwards nod in greeting, and holds his fist out towards her.

Eleanor is confused. She looks across at the man, who smiles and comes over to demonstrate what we should do. He holds out his own fist and gently knocks knuckles with the orang.

'This is Homer,' he says.

Homer, we are soon to see, is not unusual here.

Base camp is a village of wooden cabins on short stilts, home to almost 60 workers and their families. When we arrive, most of them are out on the plantation, and the place feels deserted, but there are three old men on foldaway seats watching a Brazil versus Argentina match on a huge screen on the side of the largest building. Above them looms a water tower, and painted on its side is a cartoon orangutan face.

We are met here by Adhi Perkasa, the Banau Batong Manager. He wears chinos, a pink polo shirt, white leather shoes and a white flat cap. I am relieved that his English is quite good, and that he seems pleased to see us. He gives me a two-handed handshake, and then kisses Eleanor on the cheek — it leads me to suspect that he doesn't realise who she is.

It is now 6pm, and the humidity has turned the air to soup. Grey-brown clouds churn above us. There is nothing I want more than for them to break so I can stand here and rinse off the last 48 hours. They rumble, teasingly.

Adhi takes us to the cabins where we'll be staying, on the way explaining that he has worked at Banau Batong since he was 16, working his way up through the ranks of harvesters and supervisor levels. He is now 29 and manages the whole plantation, an area of more than 90,000 hectares. This is the third largest oil palm plantation in Sumatra.

'A big responsibility,' I say. He raps on his chest with the side of his thumb, and gives a confident wink.

Two young girls, both wearing baggy dresses cut from the same floral fabric, run to him, calling out 'Adhi! Adhi!' and stretch up to slap his slightly protuberant belly, demanding sweets. He pinches both of their noses, and then reaches into his pocket and takes out two hard-boiled mints in plastic wrappers.

'How many orangutans do you have here?' Eleanor asks.

Adhi looks confused. '*These* are not orangutans,' he says, ruffling the girls' hair. 'These are our *children*.' He pauses a moment before breaking into a big laugh that exposes the whole cavern of his mouth and all of his bright teeth.

Eleanor and I have our own cabin with adjoining rooms. The rooms are small, but surprisingly well kitted-out. I have a big plush bed, and the curtains match the bedspread – a tasteful pattern of overlapping orange, white and red circles. When Banau Batong was still a rainforest reserve, I had to share a shed with two volunteers and a pink tarantula, and I slept on a stinky camp bed.

'There's an insectocutor!' I note with delight. 'I was dreading getting eaten alive again.'

'We look after you,' Adhi says.

Eleanor and I are to share a bathroom that is sandwiched between our rooms. I notice that neither door to the bathroom has a lock.

'We'll have to whistle when we're in there,' I say.

'I can't whistle,' Eleanor says. 'But if you open the door while I'm in there, I'll scream.'

Adhi loves this. 'She'll scream,' he says, thumping me on the chest with the back of his hand. Even as he leaves us alone to unpack, he is still laughing about this. 'She scream!'

We eat dinner in a big dining hall with the workers and their families. I'd been hoping there would be lots of orangutans at the base camp, but Adhi tells us Homer is the only ape that lives away from the main colony, a kind of mascot.

'I take him from poachers when he was a baby,' Adhi says. 'My father was a boxer. He teaches me.'

Adhi's father was one of 14 people killed trying to control a fire that ripped through part of Banau Batong ten years ago. High up on the wall behind the serving counter, there's a memorial collage of these people made from leaves and seeds.

The residents of Banau Batong bash elbows as they eat, talking over the top of each other. Their children sit on the tables, under the tables, run between the tables. The air conditioning in this room is set high and I am now kicking myself for not bringing a jumper.

I wish that I spoke a little of the language. My ignorance excludes me from most of the conversations. Eleanor's tongue finds the words she hasn't spoken for 15 years as if it were only 15 days.

Dinner is fried tofu with sticky rice, shredded cucumber and a spicy peanut sauce.

'You like it?' Adhi asks.

'It's actually really good,' I say. He smiles and pats me on the back. When I've finished, he says I should follow him to the kitchen. Here, the larder shelves are stacked with hundreds of plastic gallon-bottles of dark red palm oil, all bearing the Banau Batong label – the same cartoon orangutan that is painted on the water tower.

'We have this in England, too,' I say. 'You can't eat or wash without using something that has this in the ingredients.'

Adhi looks genuinely moved by this.

On the first night, Eleanor and I slump in canvas deck chairs beside a fire in a metal drum. Above us is the big screen, which is now showing tennis. The clouds continue to rumble overhead but do not break. My eyes are stinging because I sprayed too much mosquito repellent on my face. It makes every sip of beer taste a little bit like lemon, and a little bit like poison. The repellent was not even necessary, as I've now noticed insectocutors, like blue lanterns, on every post around the moat.

'I was surprised when my editor said you'd agreed to come back,' I say. 'Pleasantly surprised, I mean.'

'I nearly didn't.'

'Well, I'm glad you did.'

She stares at me, maybe wondering if I'm being serious.

'My little girl begged me not to come,' I say. 'She's inherited a fear of planes from her mum.'

'I didn't know you had children,' Eleanor says.

'Just Hattie, she's eight.'

'That's nice.'

'How is Michael?'

She shrugs.

'How long has it been?' I ask.

'Even when I left a voicemail about my cancer he wouldn't call.'

'I didn't know. Is it... one of the bad ones?'

'I've already had it chopped off,' she says, indelicately flipping her remaining boob up from underneath. 'They caught it in time.'

'I'm so sorry.'

'Cancer's one thing you're not responsible for.'

We don't say anything else for a long time, but just sit there and listen to a far away radio playing the Rolling Stones' 'Paint it Black', and to the riot of cicadas – about the only wildlife that remains here in profusion. I'm exhausted after the two days' travelling, but I don't want to leave Eleanor out here alone. She sits there for so long, unmoving, that eventually I can't bear it any longer. I'm about to say that I have to go to bed when she starts snoring. I crouch beside her and gently shake her arm. She wakes with a violent start, horrified to see my face so close.

The storm breaks during the night. Thunder and rain make a warzone of my dreams, and I wake exhausted.

Breakfast is rice with curried vegetables and a fried egg on top. Eleanor and I shovel the food into our mouths, both of us eager to get our first glimpse of the plantation, and especially the apes. Adhi takes us in a brand-new chilli-red jeep. He proudly strokes the cream leather upholstery and the glossy walnut dash. 'It's a work of art,' I say, and this pleases him. The road through the plantation is so straight and flat that he has all the control of the jeep he needs with just one finger on the steering wheel.

The scale of the plantation is terrifying. We drive for maybe an hour before we reach the area where harvesting is happening today, a whole hour of exactly the same view, unchanging, identical tree after identical tree, perfectly spaced apart. It has a hypnotic effect, which seems to dilate time and make this journey torturous.

Finally, mercifully, I see an orangutan dragging a palm leaf across the orange dirt. 'I see one!' I call out, the way I used to call out 'I see the sea!' on trips to the beach. And then there are more. Lots more. Dozens of them.

'Exactly how many orangs do you have here?' Eleanor asks as Adhi stops the jeep.

'Exactly is not possible to say,' he says. 'Maybe, in whole plantation, seven, eight hundred.'

Eleanor's mouth drops open. At the peak of her orangutan reserve, she had around 90 apes, and they were spread over an area half the size of Greater London. Here, in ten times the number, and all working within a square mile, the sight is overwhelming. Beneath the canopy of palm fronds, the air is filled with the sound of their soft-hoot conversations and the hum of the buzz scythes that they wield. These industrious orange apes lurch to and fro, a sense of orderliness to their activities. There is co-ordination, co-operation. This is a factory floor, a production line, each ape engaged in his or her task but mindful of its neighbours, constantly reassuring each other with nods and an incredible array of elastic expressions.

The orangs all wear clothes, even the young ones clinging to their mothers' stomachs while they work, t-shirts at least – most of them orange and bearing the Banau Batong logo. It's easy to tell how old the orangs are, relative to each other, from the colour of their t-shirts. The older the ape, the more the sun has bleached the dye.

They all walk upright, lumbering in a kind of drunken

way that makes the hairs on the back of my arms stand up, because most of them are carrying highly dangerous tools.

Adhi makes a 'give me' gesture, and the orang nearest us gives up his buzz scythe. This is a seven-foot pole with a wicked-sharp sickle on the end that vibrates when a button on the handle is pressed.

'When my grandfather worked in the plantation,' he says, 'he had a long pole with flat blade and he have to jab jab jab at each leaf to prune the tree, then jab jab jab, ten times for each fruit. It takes him fifteen minutes to harvest one tree. Now...'

He gives the buzz scythe back to the orang and makes a gesture, clapping his fingers against his thumb.

'How many sign words do they know?' Eleanor asks.

Adhi shrugs. 'We have signs for everything we need to say.'

The orang responds by going at the tree with quick, accurate pulling motions, hooking the scythe round the thick stem of each leaf and pruning it away to reveal the red fruit balls that sprout from the top of the trunk like monstrous half-metre raspberries. The ape chops seven leaves in 30 seconds, then severs the short stem of the first fruit. While we have watched this, another orang has come over to stand at the base of the tree. It seems to practise the act of catching a couple of times in the air, and when the actual fruit topples, it clutches the heavy ball against its chest, wrapping its impossibly long arms around it, then sets the fruit gently on the ground and waits for the next one to fall.

'Before apes,' Adhi says, 'the workers let fruit hit the ground. They get bruised. We lose many fruit this way. Now, all is perfect.' He grins proudly and pinches his thumb and forefinger together to make a loop. The universal symbol of perfection.

Working together, these two apes strip the tree down to a bare nub, pile the six fruits in one of the many trailers, and stack the discarded pine fronds in a cage, all within about three minutes. Adhi says the trucks take the fruits to a processing factory at the northern edge of the plantation.

'Are they engineered to be like this?' I ask. 'You know, so dextrous?'

Adhi doesn't understand, but Eleanor interprets, and he responds in English that they are 'normal apes'.

'At the centre,' Eleanor says, 'we always had to be careful about the behaviours the orangs picked up from us, so they could still act like wild apes when we released them onto the reserve. The orangs were always inquisitive about what we were doing, but these apes here, this is...'

'It's amazing,' I say.

Eleanor looks sour. 'Is that what you're going to write in your article, that this place is AMAZING?'

'We don't teach them,' Adhi says, 'they teach each other.'

'Monkey see monkey do,' I say, and Adhi laughs.

'Those cutting tools look very dangerous,' Eleanor says. 'How do you ensure the orangutans' safety?'

'We have ape hospital,' Adhi says.

Eleanor and I both want to see where the orangutans live — Ape Town, as Adhi calls it — but he insists that there isn't enough time, and the apes won't be there now anyway. He promises to take us there tomorrow. I sleep most of the drive back, and wake to a fire-gold sunset so beautiful I send my wife and daughter a picture, along with one of the shots I took of an orang with a buzz scythe, and one of my tired face, with the message, 'Perfect sunset. Clever monkey. I am miserable without you.'

After a long hot shower, I go to the dining hall for dinner. Eleanor is already there with Adhi. Tonight, dinner is a prawn curry that is so hot I sniff all the way through it. A teenage girl sitting beside me takes a hard-bound sketchbook from her canvas bag, and a little hand-stitched roll of pencils. She draws me in profile, licking the tip of her finger to

22

smudge the soluble graphite, and complains whenever I turn my head and talk. I am a disobedient model for maybe 15 minutes, during which I discover that her name is Ndari, she was born in Banau Batong, that her father was also one of the men killed in the great fire of 2034, and her ambition is to work on a ship. Nothing specific. Just any kind of work on a ship. Her drawing is not flattering, but her sketches of the orangutans are something else. I ask if I can buy one, a portrait of an old female that must have taken her hours. She tears it out of the book and refuses payment. So wrapped up am I in this sketch and questioning Ndari about her terrific gift that I miss the beginning of an argument between Eleanor and Adhi. I only become aware of it when I see at the edge of my vision Eleanor waving a dirty spoon at him in a threatening manner.

'Come in my office,' Adhi says to her. 'I'll show you my prizes.'

'I don't want to go in your office,' she says. 'They're obviously idiots. You've not *saved* anything. You've ruined them.'

'To be fair,' I say, picking up the gist of the conversation, 'these apes were never *purely* wild. Most of them will be descended from your apes, won't they?'

Eleanor flushes white. I realise too late that maybe I shouldn't have said that.

'What?' Adhi says. 'You're Ellie *Lundgren*?' He laughs out loud, claps his hands together, addresses the rest of our table in Indonesian, points at her. There is laughter that spreads infectiously. Her surname passes from mouth to mouth. Soon it seems the whole room is in hysterics, wiping coffee from their chins with the backs of their hands. It is a loud and ugly sound that drives Eleanor from the room, slamming the door shut behind her.

I leave shortly afterwards. Heading back to my cabin, I see Eleanor outside with Homer the orangutan, helping him fill a tin cup from a tap on the side of the building. The news is on the big screen, shining blue light onto them, but no one is watching it. This TV stays on all day and all night, the fire that never goes out.

I know I should go and apologise, but this moment doesn't feel like the right one.

Back in my cabin, I try making some notes but cannot concentrate, so I stop and put my head on the pillow, leaving the lamp on. After an hour or so of restlessness, I hear Eleanor brushing her teeth in the bathroom. I get up and knock on the door.

'I'm sorry,' I say to the closed door. 'You know, the whole reason I agreed to do this article was to try to make up for whatever part I played in how everything went before. I guess I'm failing at that.'

The bathroom door opens, and Eleanor is wearing a tight-fitting, long-sleeved t-shirt tucked into some kind of long-johns, which are tucked into her socks. She has a toothbrush clamped in her mouth, and a little white foam on her knuckles.

'This really isn't all about you,' she says. Flecks of foam fly in my direction.

'Why *did* you agree to come back?' I ask.

'It was a mistake.'

The door behind her opens and Homer stands there looking into the cabin, silhouetted by the bright light outside. His shaggy fur makes a brilliant orange aura. 'Off you shoo, you big brute,' she says, but he is reluctant and takes some physical pushing.

I tell her to lock her door, and she scoffs at this.

'These aren't the apes you used to know,' I say.

A few minutes later, when I'm lying in bed, I hear the click of her door lock.

We have to set out for Ape Town at 4am. Adhi says that at 7am, all the trucks arrive to take the orangs out to whichever part of the plantation they'll be working.

'Today we see your babies Ellie,' Adhi says, making his characteristic belly laugh that after 36 hours here is grating.

'Be kind,' I tell him, and he smiles, holding up his hands and bowing his head a little in deference.

Again the drive is long, 90 minutes through dismal monoculture. Every hour I spend here, the monotony of it depletes me a little more. My eyes ache for variety.

In my imagination, Ape Town would be a shanty town, reeking of garbage, the apes bundled together in nests they'd crudely constructed from the detritus of the palm oil industry. As we reach the outskirts, I realise how wrong I am.

The sun is just rising, and against the yellow sky are hundreds of cabins on stilts in long, straight lines. Row after row of them. Adhi drives slowly through this grid of open-front cabins. Eleanor and I wind down our windows and hear the most extraordinary sound, the accumulated sleep noises of 800 apes. It's like purring, like an old engine, like something bubbling up from underground.

In each of the cabins, sleeping orangs are heaped together. It is impossible to say how many are in each one, so enfolded are they, but I would guess at about four or five. Sleepy faces turn towards us. They make enormous yawns, stretch their long arms, shuffle for comfort and settle again.

'There are males there too,' Eleanor whispers.

'They all sleep like this,' Adhi says.

I ask what the significance of this is, and Eleanor says that in the wild, orangs didn't form groups. Young apes stayed with their mothers for eight years until maturity, but the males were absent wanderers, seeking the company of females only to mate, occasionally fighting with another male for territory.

'What about the senior males?' Eleanor asks.

'No top apes,' Adhi says. 'Listen, you will hear.'

We're all quiet for a moment. From far away, we hear a series of drawn-out, throaty calls. This, I come to understand, is a recording of an alpha male. The sound inhibits the release of hormones in the males, keeping them subservient to this facsimile ape, and even stops their wide cheek flanges from developing. This is not a trait that has been engineered into these clones. Adhi is simply utilising a natural tendency within the apes.

'There's nowhere for them to climb,' Eleanor says.

'They don't like to climb so much.'

'You've got a hell of a set-up here,' I say.

With her fingertips, Eleanor rubs her temples, her eyes, and then her whole face with both hands.

The hospital is a big wooden building at the edge of Ape Town. Like the base camp, it is surrounded by a moat and connected to the mainland by a drawbridge.

A young woman wearing khaki shorts, white linen shirt and green wellington boots comes out to greet us. Her hand is soft and sticky. She looks harassed, but happy to see us. Her name is Mariana. Originally from Brazil, she has worked at the Banau Batong ape hospital for two years now, managing a team of just two nurses. She shows us round the four wide rooms that comprise the treatment centre. This place reminds me of a children's A&E department. Plastic boxes of toys are stacked up against the walls. Simple clouds are painted on the ceiling. Hanging in canvas sorters designed for shoes are vacuum-sealed packs of medical paraphernalia – bandaging, scissors, plastic devices the purpose of which I cannot guess. The whole place smells of pine.

On the day that we visit, there are 17 orangs in the hospital with a mixture of maladies and injuries all the way from flu to severed limbs. On a blanket on the floor of one room is a young male ape called Lennie who flicks through a children's board book with his one long arm. The other arm terminates before the elbow in a bulge of bandage.

A female ape totters through the doorway (again walking on two feet – I've yet to see a single dragged knuckle) and holds out her arms to demand a hug, which Mariana readily gives her. 'This is Bonnie,' Mariana says. 'She's going to be a mommie, aren't you Bonnie?'

Eleanor gasps, and kneels down to hold Bonnie's hand. I feel silly for not noticing the ape's enormous pregnancy bulge right away.

'She's so *young*,' Eleanor says.

'She's eleven. We find eleven to thirteen is about average here,' Mariana says.

'My goodness, and how long in-between births?'

'Usually three years.'

'*Three?*' Eleanor says.

'Why the speed up?' I ask. When Banau Batong was seized by officials, and Eleanor dragged in front of the ethics panel, she insisted she'd had to breach the conditions of her cloning permit, and risk her own life, because of the eight-year gap between orangutan pregnancies. If she hadn't, the last few orangs would have died nearly two decades ago. This is a fact.

'We're not sure,' Mariana says, 'but it may be because they don't have to face the same challenges that a true wild ape would have.'

'Do you have any young ones here?' Eleanor asks.

'Oh yes,' Mariana smiles. 'Our nursery is through here.'

Eleanor comes to life in the nursery, as soon as she sees the little ones, three of them, sat on a fleece jumper in a wooden crate together. And they *are* impossibly cute. Their big black eyes and their dopey wide grins. Their wild orange hair that sticks up all over the place. Their lovely fat bellies. Their comical inquisitiveness. Cute in a way that makes human babies look boring. They are utterly adorable, and even I am down on my knees holding out a finger for one of the three to grip.

Eleanor coos over them, blowing their faces, and they love it, closing their eyes and wobbling. Eleanor asks Mariana a stream of questions about their care, about their mothers, about how long they spend socialising with mature apes, their diet, weight and whatnot, but I barely listen because one of these gorgeous little things has crawled onto my lap and is hugging me and I am giggling, enchanted.

We eat wedges of pineapple for lunch, flatbread and tall glasses of rice milk. Afterwards, Eleanor stays inside while Adhi and I walk the perimeter of the moat. We absently begin kicking an orange forward whenever we come to it again, and soon we organize ourselves into taking turns, passing it from one to the other.

I ask him about the future of the Banau Batong project. The ape population here now outnumbers the human population eight to one. It's hugely successful. Where does he go from here?

'Forty years ago, there were seven thousand orangutan in Sumatra,' he says. 'Now about eight hundred. We have a long way to go.'

'So Ape Town will continue to grow, with more orangs working in the plantation every year?'

'It is early days,' he says. 'But apes make good economy. They eat small. They like work. They make no complaint. What we have here, other places can have. Everyone profits.'

'Franchising?' I say.

Adhi smiles and raps the side of his thumb against his chest.

When we've finished a full loop of the moat, and Adhi has kicked the orange into the water, it is time to go. Eleanor and Mariana are outside. They have all three baby chimps in a half-barrel filled with soapy water, and are making hats and beards on the babies with bubbles. The orangs' fur is flattened against their bodies. One of the apes slaps both hands into the water, sloshing a wave over the edge and right into Eleanor's lap. She giggles. She is sparkling with joy.

I stand and watch them from a distance for a few moments before going over.

'You're not coming back, are you?' I say.

Eleanor shakes her head.

'These apes are barely apes any more. Someone has to teach them how to be wild again,' she says. 'They need me here.'

She picks up one of the babies, wraps it in a towel and cuddles it against her belly, resting the side of her face on the top of its head and rocking slightly. Deep down, I suspected she might stay. I *hoped* she would. I've always blamed myself for everything that happened here. This was my chance to make amends.

I stare at them, enjoying this sight for a few minutes, before noticing that Adhi has an expression of discomfort on his face. He is scratching the back of his head.

'I'm sorry, Ellie,' he says. 'But you cannot stay here.'

Eleanor looks up at him. She withers, loosening her grip on the chimp ever so slightly.

'What's the problem?' I say. 'You couldn't get a better orangutan expert anywhere in the world.'

'We don't need an expert. We don't want wild apes. They are good now. Everything works.'

Eleanor hides her face against the baby orang. None of us speaks. We look at the ground. And then, I see she is shaking slightly, sobbing. Despite all my intentions to make things right, I brought Eleanor back here after 20 years to break her heart all over again. She was right about me.

Caspar Stak, *Black Window*,
25th Anniversary Issue, August 2044.

Afterword:

Chimeric Animals and Inter-Species Breeding

Professor Bruce Whitelaw
The Roslin Institute, Edinburgh

ANIMAL BIO-TECHNOLOGY IS still a relatively young area of biological science. With this status both excitement and seemingly large leaps forwards in our understanding and capability are possible. Perhaps this was best illustrated when in 1996 Dolly the cloned sheep was born at Roslin. But there have been other dramatic animals produced, for example the goat-sheep chimera or 'geep' produced about a decade earlier.

Within an experimental context the production of chimeric animals, still predominantly rodents, is a powerful way to tease apart the factors that control how tissues, organs and body fluids are formed and function. Though the majority of chimeric animals that have been produced are intra-species, for example, a mouse that comprises cells from two different mouse strains, there are examples of inter-species chimeras. The geep and a recent study describing a mouse that has a pancreas-derived from rat stem cells have stimulated much thought. Furthermore, there are also examples of chimeric animals that contain human-derived cells. The vast majority of such studies utilise rodents and are proving valuable in rapidly advancing our understanding of biological function, most specifically within the context of blood formation. There are examples, however, of larger animals – goats – that have organs containing functioning human cells. It is expected that future cell-based therapies can be evaluated for their biological safety using these chimeric animals.

So, to make distinctions. Cloning produces a genetic

copy of an animal. It can produce many such copies or clones, and this methodology has been applied to many species – laboratory, livestock, companion animals – and monkeys by the related method of embryo splitting. But in all of these studies, the species born was the same as that of the surrogate mother. In Adam Marek's intriguing story, a great ape is born from a human. This is science fiction but certainly thought provoking, exposing the reader to a range of dilemmas; species conservation, deforestation, man's relationship with animals and in particular our interaction with the evolutionarily closely related great apes. Although studies are pushing the boundaries, the ability for one species to give birth to another is still, so far, science fiction.

To achieve the orangutan birth from a human female that underlies Adam Marek's story the developing ape foetus would need to be 'hidden' from the human womb. The womb would need to know that a foetus was developing but not sense the foetus as not-human. Otherwise the foetus would be aborted. This biological 'trickery' has not yet been achieved. If such methods were to be developed the potential to apply them in a species conservation scenario could be attractive. There are, however, big biological barriers to be overcome; and even a scientific optimist would limit the imagination to methods that would only work between closely related species. An example proposed by my colleague Dr Bill Ritchie would be the birth of a Scottish wild cat from a domestic cat.

The closest science has managed to get to this scenario are the chimeras I described above. In these animals, non-host cells are introduced either at a time when the host immune system is not yet fully functional or into animals that have an impaired immune system. The immune system is designed to recognise non-self cells and destroy them. The potential of utilising chimeric animals to accelerate the advance of scientific knowledge and the preclinical evaluation of new drugs and other strategies to treat disease is now an exciting area of bio-medical research.

At Roslin, like many other research organisations, we have been generating chimeric mice for many years. This is a standard procedure. We are now exploring the formation of chimeric animals by introducing cells – usually stem cells – to the developing embryo. We are working with experimental animals including mice, rats, chickens and sheep. This is achieved by introducing stem cells into the preimplantation embryo which is an established technique in mice and extensively used worldwide to produce transgenic mice. We are now exploring this practice with livestock. We aim to increase our understanding of the interaction between the placenta and the developing foetus, the role of specific immune cells in this process, and the role of cells in the early embryo. Our longer term goal is to characterise the network of interactions that enable the development of a healthy foetus. This is all purely academic research. The output of which is greater knowledge of biological processes.

The production of chimeric animals also offers potential bio-medical applications. The possibility that animals could be used as bio-reactors is being investigated. In addition, there is considerable current optimism that stem cell therapies can be developed sufficiently to offer new surgical intervention strategies. Stem cells may be able to provide missing function, for example insulin production for those suffering from diabetes. But these stem cells possess characteristics which if not controlled resemble that of tumour cells. Therefore, if such cells are to be delivered to human patients a robust evaluation of their tumour-forming capacity is required. We are exploring approaches that utilise chimeric animals to perform this assessment.

So, back to Adam Marek's short story. Thought provoking science fiction, but a story that builds from what is currently an area of active scientific research.

EFEMERI

Dilys Rose

IT IS SUNDAY evening and Alyssa has spent an energetic day in bed with her new boyfriend. At least she thinks of Lars as her boyfriend, though she has only met him twice before, both times on a Sunday. She has decided that from now on she will only meet him on Sundays because she likes to keep things clear and simple, to know what's happening when.

So he's good in bed but is he on the level? asks Moll. They are in the staff changing rooms, tying back their hair, buttoning up their uniforms.

I can see right through him, says Alyssa.

You shouldn't take your work home with you.

I can't help it.

Sometimes it's okay not to know, to pretend everything's fine.

Not for me, says Alyssa.

No, says Moll, maybe not.

Alyssa is incapable of pretence and due to her inability to offer praise where it isn't due, she goes through boyfriends fast. As far as sex goes, she certainly won't say she's done when she isn't. Lars has copious sexual stamina despite being skinny as a stick insect; Alyssa sees this as a plus.

After they've been through the staff security checks, Moll and Alyssa click their tooled-up belts into place and make their way across the processing hall to the checkpoints. The vast, glass building is an echo chamber of squeaking trolley wheels and rumbling walkways against a never-ending backtrack of bleeps. The queues are long and slow moving. The air is stale, heavy.

There's Leon, says Moll. Gate Nine. He's looking good.

No he isn't, says Alyssa. He's looking as fake as ever.

Leon Bass, the division controller, is in his early fifties. He has a meaty swagger, a mane of freshly highlighted gold brown hair and a habit of tossing his head like a lion about to roar. Leon likes to live up to his name, though roaring, rumour has it, he confines to the bedroom. In a work situation, a low growl usually suffices.

Come on, Alyssa. Don't spoil my sex-with-the-boss fantasy. It helps me get through the night shift.

Doing your job properly will help you more.

What's bugging you?

I don't know. Yet.

Keep me posted.

Maybe I will, maybe I won't.

People on the receiving end of Alyssa's bald pronouncements find her rude, brutal. She says exactly what she thinks, when she thinks it, and can't comprehend why jaws drop in shock, shame or outrage.

Leon clocks Moll and Alyssa and gives them a brisk little salute.

Why, says Alyssa, would you want to have sex with that grizzled old git? You'd be better off paying for a robobonk. No risk of infection and guaranteed to last the pace.

It's a fantasy, says Moll. A mind game.

Fantasies are pointless. Unless you can eventually act them out.

As usual, Alyssa strides across the concourse, followed by Moll, who is shorter and stouter, and struggles to keep up. Alyssa never fails to get a buzz at the beginning of her shift. She's eager to get started, to root out the liars and cheats. She likes her uniform, its epaulettes, button-down pockets, its dark, heavy-duty fabric and red piping. It makes her feel taller, more purposeful. If it weren't against the rules, she'd wear her uniform all the time.

Before they enter the processing hall, people often pause

to do one last mental cleanout. Some close their eyes and do some deep breathing, as if they were about to plunge into an abyss, or turn tail and bolt back the way they came, before they pass the sensors which activate the shatterproof doors. From there on they are in the hands of the security guards.

Leon's on his way over, says Moll. How do I look?

Your eyebrows need plucking.

Do they? D'you have any tweezers?

Here? says Alyssa. Of course not.

Are they really bad?

Yeah.

In the business of false compliments, Alyssa is ahead of the game; if the new border controls, rushed through parliament after the last presidential assassination, can really be described as a game. Whereas others are finding it difficult to rethink their thoughts, to make them innocuous and transparent, Alyssa's thoughts have always been transparent, if not innocuous. In the past, her thoughts have got her into trouble; now everybody's thoughts are getting them into trouble. Especially in Alyssa's line of work.

Evening, ladies, says Leon. I trust you had a relaxing day.

I had a lovely lazy Sunday, says Moll.

I had a totally knackering day in bed, says Alyssa.

Too much information, says Leon, stretching his lips into a mirthless grin, then moving on to inspect staff changeover all the way down the line.

Alyssa enjoys her work and is considered to be one of the best. She can pick up on the slightest flicker of irregularity, is shit hot on body language but what really sets her apart from the others is that old, disputed and unquantifiable chestnut: intuition. Given the spectacular advances in psychological profiling and neuroscience, Alyssa's reliance on being guided by a hunch is considered a hokey throwback, irrational and irrelevant as a rabbit's foot or a red sky at night.

After the day staff have logged out from Gate 13, where the functional magnetic resonance imaging (FMRI) scanner is located – Moll and Alyssa key in their ID codes and signal to the first in line to step inside the cubicle. There's always a bit of hassle when the shifts change, especially at Gate 13. Those who have been singled out to go through 'EFEMERI' – as security staff have tagged the scanner – are tetchy enough without having to be kept waiting. Rumours go around that some guards are easier to get past than others, that some have a price. The rumours are true.

Neuroimaging at border controls is still cumbersome and costly: as yet it is only used for spot checks, a mixture of random and overtly suspicious characters, but the leaders are calling for the scanning of all travellers, and research into developing cheaper, more compact scanners. The decimated human rights movement is opposed to this development. *Our thoughts are our own!* the campaigners cry, though even the most ardent of them know that the battle is already lost.

Many religious groups, on the other hand, including Moll's all-singing, all-dancing ecumenical church – support the use of neuroimaging. Some consider it a godsend: a sin contemplated is no less than a sin enacted; prevention is better than cure. But what of those whose brains contain the most dangerous thoughts, who wipe them clean on a regular basis? The more people have to hide, the greater the lengths they will go to to hide it.

Moll and Alyssa's first case of the evening is a distracted-looking woman in her mid-sixties. It may be the cheap facelift or the gin she reeks of which makes her eyes pop and her words run away with her:

It's so long since I've travelled. I don't know how many years it is but it was before independence. I did vote for independence but I didn't expect all this extra fuss just because I want to visit my grandchildren south of the border. That's surely not a crime is it?

Step this way, please, ma'am, says Alyssa.

Is something the matter? Is something showing up on your screen? Can you really tell exactly what I'm thinking right at this moment? I bet you can't. I bet you can't really tell anything at all from all those fancy images. I bet it's all a trick, to intimidate people, to put people off travelling. I bet that's what it is.

The woman casts around, hoping for support from others in the queue but everybody just looks bored and irritated by the time she's wasting. Alyssa sighs loudly and pointedly. Moll scrunches together her untidy eyebrows.

Nothing's the matter, ma'am. Stand still please. And don't speak until the questions come up on the screen. And then you should answer *briefly*. You do know what that means?

Of course I do, slurs the woman. I wasn't born yesterday.

No, says Alyssa. You were born sixty-five years, three months and seventeen days ago.

Pshhhhh! Didn't anybody ever tell you that a lady's age is her secret?

We don't do secrets here. Pass.

Is that it? Can I go?

Pass through the doorway, ma'am. Immediately.

The woman flounces off, tutting and blowing out her cheeks.

Next.

Well in advance of travelling, people prepare for the checkpoints. Encephalic modification clinics offer innovative hippocampal procedures and claim high success rates; at a price. If the top end of the modification market is beyond your funds, there are other avenues to explore: a wide range of drugs available over and under the counter; traditional therapies like meditation, hypnosis, yoga and juggling; puzzles and tasks geared towards cognitive realignment; a smörgåsbord of dietary regimes.

Alyssa prefers the night shift. How people behave when

they are half-asleep and disorientated is more interesting: their guard is down; they forget to approach the barriers wearing determined, forthright expressions; they don't try to curry favour with chummy comments about how hard the guards work, and so on. Alyssa has no time for pointless chit-chat.

It has been a shift much like any other: a few awkward customers, a few idiots, wise guys, drama queens, pains in the arse, a few anxious souls with nothing to hide, convinced that EFEMERI would pick up some imaginary thought crime. Towards the end of the shift, as day is beginning to break and the processing centre becomes infused with rosy dawn light, Alyssa is distracted by a nearby commotion. A lanky young man in an eccentric, anachronistic get-up, involving a deerstalker, spats and goggles, which dates back to the early days of flying machines, is refusing to remove his eyewear and twirling a Malacca cane in a reckless manner.

If you don't do as you're told, sir, says Leon, you will be refused passage.

Damn it man, says the lanky young man, in an affected, antiquated accent. Who *do* you think you're talking to?

I don't care who I'm talking to, says Leon, his voice deep and thick and threatening. You do what you're told or you stop right here.

You jest. I've had my fill of this *bagatelle* of a country.

Leon's face goes dark: he's a dyed-in-the-wool nationalist. He buzzes for back-up and immediately a phalanx of armed guards approaches.

Gate 13, sir. Move along if you know what's good for you.

My dear man, are threats part of your code of practice?

There are heavy fines for obstructing officers from carrying out their duties. And plenty witnesses who'll say you're doing exactly that.

Oh, very well then, says the young man, whose name, he claims, is Brenn. Do your worst! Scrutinize the catacombs of my grey matter. I assure you, you'll find nothing amiss.

The silly grin on his face might suggest that Brenn is high on some mood enhancer but up close Alyssa sees a clear, challenging glint in his eye. He's planned to be picked out, to subject himself to EFEMERI.

So this is your truth machine, is it? says Brenn. Oh, the wonders of science! To spy on the most private domains of *homo sapiens*. What progress we've made! Now everybody's secret self can be revealed. We've killed off mystery once and for all. And what good will come of it?

Step inside, sir, if you please.

My pleasure entirely.

Leon nods to Moll and Alyssa. It's a nod that means: give him the works. Which they do. Moll goes through the full version of the questionnaire. Section headings include: purpose of visit; contacts at destination; physical and mental health; sexual orientation; religious and political affiliations; alcohol and drug consumption; education and social background; leisure activities; languages spoken; history of previous travel.

Alyssa checks the screen as Brenn responds to each area of questioning. Not a flicker. His brain waves are as consistent as stitches on a sewing machine.

He's clean, Moll keys into the textbox which only she and Alyssa can see.

No, Alyssa replies. Know in my bones.

Passed all. Bones not evidence.

Brenn emerges from the capsule, his grin still intact.

Did you find me interesting, ladies? Did you find my answers revealing?

Wait there, sir, says Alyssa.

She buzzes for Leon who is standing nearby with the guards, picking out more candidates for Gate 13.

So? says Leon.

Room V, says Alyssa. Moll looks askance. Room V, Alyssa repeats.

My, my, says Brenn. First Gate 13 and now Room V!

Come this way, says Leon.

Brenn is escorted to the interrogation room. Alyssa is struck by his bravado, his arrogance, his bare-faced cheek. He has been relieved of his cane and flying goggles but seems all the more amused by the proceedings, as if this development had also been part of his plan. His jaunty walk reminds her of Lars, whom she last saw a few hours earlier, fresh from the shower, a tiny towel wrapped modestly around his waist. When she asked what he'd be doing while she was at work, he said he was going to visit his mother. It was a regular arrangement. She'd cook him dinner and pour out her woes over the roast chicken and gravy. Alyssa believes Lars. She doesn't believe Brenn.

Alyssa becomes restless. She'd like to see what's happening in the interrogation room but only upper level security deals with the background checks, the up close and personal intimidation, the mind games. How will Brenn fare and why is he putting himself through this?

Alyssa was one of the first to volunteer for the user testing of EFEMERI and blazed through the tests. This didn't make her popular with her colleagues. *We're not going anywhere,* they whined. *We stay here and watch people go in and out. What we think about doesn't matter.* But of course it does. EFEMERI is only as good as the person observing the results. There's always a permissible margin of error, a rise or dip in the readings which is open to interpretation.

We should call Leon for this one, Moll keys into their private text box.

The woman in question is middle-aged, well-dressed, tight-lipped. There are concerns over her place of origin and her final destination. She has language problems and her scores on politics and gender issues are over the limit.

No, Alyssa replies. Clean.

You blind?

Not the bigger picture.

Calling Leon. End of.

But Moll doesn't have to call Leon because he is already approaching the gate with Brenn ambling freely beside him.

No guards and Brenn is even more bumptious than before, twirling his damn cane and swivelling his goggled head like some street entertainer. People are laughing. There's even some muted applause.

Let him pass, says Leon. And Alyssa – my office after your shift.

Farewell, my lovelies! Brenn declares, practically prancing through Gate 13, blowing Alyssa and Moll a kiss as he continues towards the exit, and the freedom to do whatever it is he has planned.

Afterword:

Magnetic Resonance Imaging and Security Applications

Dr Jane Haley, Prof Stephen Lawrie,
Prof Burkhard Schafer and Prof Joanna Wardlaw
Edinburgh Neuroscience and School of Law,
University of Edinburgh

FOR CENTURIES THE brain has been a mystery; while it was possible to look at its structure post-mortem, it is only more recently that we have been able to view both the structure and function of the *living* brain. Magnetic Resonance Imaging (MRI) typically uses magnetic forces 60 million times more powerful than the Earth's magnetic field to temporarily realign the protons present in the hydrogen atoms within water. Feeding that information through a computer algorithm can reveal the structure of tissues that are high in water content, such as the brain. It is now very widely used as a tool for diagnosing pathology in the living brain, such as seen in strokes and tumours, and to monitor treatment response. So important is the discovery of this technology, and the resulting clinical applications, that MRI developers have been awarded the Nobel Prize for Medicine twice – in 1952 and again in 2003.

Over the last 20 years the technique has developed further and the intrinsic magnetic properties of haemoglobin can now be used to measure tiny changes in blood flow. These relate to the electrical activity (and metabolic use) of neurones without the need for the injection of radioactive tracers. This 'functional MRI' (fMRI) technique allows the activity of specific brain regions in the human to be visualised as coloured picture elements ('pixels') superimposed on a structural scan.

Being able to see 'the brain in action' has become a powerful research tool permitting scientists to probe the workings of the mind; it is now commonly used by neuroscientists, psychologists and psychiatrists trying to understand how the brain functions and what happens when things go wrong. All of this is tremendously exciting, but it might also be leading us in directions that are not quite what the inventors imagined. So, how close are we to the 'extra-curricular' fMRI capabilities such as 'lie detection' and 'mind reading' found in the world that Dily's Rose's Alyssa inhabits? If current newspaper coverage is anything to go by, we are almost there!

The most obvious problem for routine airport-style scanning is one of scale, cost and safety. An MRI scanner is large, very heavy, expensive to run and the magnetic forces used so strong that large metal objects such as chairs and trolleys would get dragged into them, not to mention the potentially disastrous consequences of disturbing the surgical plates, pins and clips found inside many people these days. But technology advances so quickly that perhaps these issues will also be rapidly resolved. So, how reliable are the actual data collected? Lie-detection, for instance, seems like a straightforward, possible application and could be useful. Except that lie detection isn't straightforward. It probably relies on the perpetrator understanding at some level that they are lying (perhaps not so easy with a psychopathic person), that there are clear regions of the brain involved with deception (rather than the general stress of a procedure), and there is a level of reliability in the detection procedure that is robust enough to be useful. One can imagine that the agitated lady wanting to travel to England to see her grandchildren (Scotland is independent in this version of the future!) is highly stressed and may become confused about what she should or should not reveal about what is her subjective reality, as opposed to actual fact. The question is, which version of the truth would the brain scan reveal – the 'real' truth or what she believes to be true? In the world of the present day researcher, subjects are tested under controlled experimental conditions:

groups of volunteers might, for example, undergo scanning as they deliberately lied or told the truth, as instructed, and by comparing the activation profiles seen it might be possible to see differences with some degree of *statistical* certainty. Repeated several times by different research groups, it might be possible for neuroscientists to reach a consensus about the approximate activation profile for lying. What this could tell you about lie detection 'out in the field' when examining one stressed, agitated grannie is even less certain.

Despite the high levels of uncertainty surrounding the robustness of the technique, fMRI as a lie detector is already being tested as potential evidence in courts of law around the world and commercial companies are springing up in the wake of this. India has the 'honour' of having the world's first conviction based on an fMRI scan (for murder). In the USA, despite multiple attempts to introduce this evidence, the courts have resisted, partly because they have robust criteria for admissibility (which neither Scotland nor England have in place yet). But, it isn't just in the courts where this is an issue; there is currently no law in the USA (or, as far as we know, elsewhere) preventing the use of fMRI in determining employee truthfulness, and companies are happy to provide this service for a price.

Most of us may feel that none of this is relevant, since we believe we are truthful and law abiding and so have nothing to worry about. But lying is in the eye of the beholder – the dividing line between the banker who is a successful go-getter, risk taker, pillar of the economy and the community, and a feckless violator of the banking guidelines, fraudster and wrecker of lives is indeed all in the mind – not in the mind of the perpetrator, but of the lawyers who draw these distinctions. fMRI is, however, already encroaching on every-day activities. Companies who used to rely on focus group feedback are increasingly turning to fMRI technology to find out how people respond to their products. It seems focus groups haven't been providing accurate feedback, resulting in lost profits and waste when product lines have to be ditched. So, can science provide a solution? Can fMRI indicate what product packaging you prefer, even if you don't know yourself? Neuromarketing companies believe so and are using fMRI to examine activity in regions of the brain involved in emotional responses to different marketing material. Whether this form of 'mind reading' is reliable is debatable, but does it really matter if large corporations want to use their money in this way? Maybe not, but it is a short step from product selection to employee selection.

So, you think you are the perfect candidate for the job? You have the right qualifications and experience. But will your brain scan agree? Increasingly, employers are subjecting potential candidates to a barrage of psychometric tests and then a health MOT before they are employed. What if this also involved a brain scan – to assess whether you might develop a mental health condition and/or to determine whether you have the right set of skills or personality type for the job? Although this is not current practice, it is potentially very close. In the USA it is illegal to use a polygraph as part of pre-employment screening, but not fMRI, and there are companies now openly discussing this application. Companies will be quick to capitalise on this and, in the vacuum of regulation that currently exists, you may find you will have to comply to get the job you want. Apart from the ethical implications of refusing someone employment because they may develop an illness in the future, or might not quite be the person they present to the world, can this actually be done at the moment? Well, yes and no. Methods to tell who is at high risk of schizophrenia or dementia, or who is autistic or depressed, are emerging in research studies, so it may well be possible to predict some mental illness using fMRI in the near future. Can we tell someone's personality type and skill set? No, not to the extent that would be required to be useful in interviews, so you can relax... for now! These limitations will, however, probably not stop people promoting MRI for such purposes.

Amongst this slightly disturbing view of the future glimpsed in 'EFEMERI' by Dilys Rose, we shouldn't forget that there is some remarkable work being done with brain scanning technology. In addition to pioneering experiments that are genuinely trying to understand how the brain works and how we can help when things go wrong, there are some astonishing outcomes. The last two years have seen the advent of fMRI being used to help people who survive major brain injury in a persistent vegetative state. A worse predicament is hard to imagine – a still-functioning brain trapped in an unresponsive body. For years people in a 'vegetative state' have been assumed to have no higher brain function and to be unaware of themselves or their environment. fMRI has shown that a small percentage of these patients have appropriate brain activity in response to questions and some of these patients now seem able to communicate via fMRI with basic yes or no answers. Which then raises the difficult question of whether we should be asking them if they want to live or die.

Further Reading
1. 'What are you Thinking? Who has the Right to Know?'
http://www.scottishinsight.ac.uk/Portals/50/BrainImaging_Report_final.pdf
2. 'Neuroimaging in Society: Legal, Corporate, Social and Security Implications'
Joanna M. Wardlaw et al. *EMBO Reports* (2011) 12, 630 – 636
http://www.nature.com/embor/journal/v12/n7/full/embor2011115a.html
3. 'Can It Read My Mind? – What Do The Public And Experts Think Of The Current (Mis)Uses Of Neuroimaging?'
Joanna M. Wardlaw et al. *PLoS One* (2011) 6(10): e25829
http://www.plosone.org/article/info%3Adoi%2F10.1371%2Fjournal.pone.0025829
4. The Royal Society: Brain Wave Publications
Neuroscience, Society and Policy (module 1); *Neuroscience: Implications for Education and Lifelong Learning* (module 2); *Neuroscience, Conflict and Security* (module 3); and *Neuroscience and the Law* (module 4)
All can be accessed from: http://royalsociety.org/policy/projects/brain-waves/
5. *Cortex* (Special Issue), Volume 47 (10) Nov/Dec 2011
http://www.cortexjournal.net/issues

The Challenge

Jane Feaver

WE'VE BEEN ON our own since Mark was nine and his dad left. Ten years ago, 2002. Bruce was in the army when I met him. Mark has the picture of him in uniform face down in his top drawer. I was left with the house – which was mine in any case from Mum – but that was it. No maintenance, nothing. Last we heard he was in Wakefield, running a pub. Good luck to him.

'I bet it was the uniform,' Mark said. We were watching an old DVD, *An Officer and a Gentleman* – though his dad was neither of those things. This time last year Mark and me weren't getting on so well either. It had been two years since he'd chucked in school and apart from scraps of work – a stint in Morrison's – he'd showed no real sign of wanting to do anything.

I kept telling him, it's not that I thought he should move out, it's just he had to take some responsibility. He couldn't slouch about the house all day, could he? I'd come home after work and he'd not have moved from that couch, crumbs, crisp packets, buckled-up cans everywhere.

'Smells like a rabbit hutch in here,' I'd say, opening the curtains, even if it was already dark, just to get some circulation.

I missed him, course I did, when he went off for his training. But I was dead proud the day of his passing-out parade. 'My God,' I said to him, when we met up afterwards for drinks, 'what have they done to you?' It was like they'd put him in one end of a machine, rubbed and scrubbed and polished him up. 'I hardly recognise you,' I said. 'Come here!'

He smelled how my dad used to smell, spick and span of coal tar soap.

'How many years have I been trying to get you to cut your hair?' I said, poking him. 'Look at you!' He was like the little boy in his school photograph again. 'I forgot you had ears,' I said.

It's given him a sense of direction, definitely. The way he holds himself now. Confident. Like he's found his back-bone. Makes me well up to think of the change there's been in him.

8 til 3.30, Windmill Road. And I've been there – hard to believe it – eleven years; seen half a dozen classes right through from reception into year six, thinking they're big boys now with their hair gel and their mobile phones. There's a couple of them every year will always remind me of Mark, just that age. 'Miss,' they call me, just like they call the teachers, some of them on their tiptoes, holding onto the ledge. 'Miss, can I 'ave a dinner ticket?'

It was one of the teaching assistants told me about the trials: Emma Hatfield – she was in Mark's year at Cheyney. Her mum's a cleaner at the Warneford and she said they were desperate for volunteers, did it herself last year and it paid for the holiday.

'A round of drinks,' she says, 'I'm not joking, it's like half a day's work.'

'You get paid?' I asked.

She nodded, enthusiastic. 'You could, like, go on your lunch break,' she said, 'if you're not frightened of needles, which I am, but Mum isn't.'

'I'm not mad about them,' I said.

'Mum says you don't have to look.'

Holiday: that word stuck.

– 'Mum?'

'Mark? Is that you?'

– 'Who did you think it was? Howayadoing?'

'What about you? How are you?'

– 'It's boiling out here, Mum. You wouldn't believe it. Stick your head in the oven one day. That's what it's like.'

'How hot is it?'

– 'Roasting. Ten times as hot as it gets at home. I swear, I'm sweating like a pig.'

'You drinking lots, aren't you? You must drink, it's good for you.'

– 'Yes, Mum, I'm sick of it. You sweat it off in a minute... It's doing my head in.'

'You all right?' I had to control my voice.

– 'Yeah, surviving. Look, Mum, I gotta be quick. Can you send Q-tips? And toothpaste – not that shit stuff?'

'Course I can.'

– 'And razors?'

'Hang on, love. Let me write it down.'

Hearing his voice churned me up. It was ever so close, hard to think he was half-way across the world.

'Is it sandy out there?' I asked him.

– 'We're in the bloody desert, Mum. Yes.'

It was an effort to believe. It reminded me of my brother and me, out the back with soup tins and string. 'Over and out,' he would shout and he'd make me say it loudly back, '*Roger*. Over and out.'

I imagined Mark in some sort of wooden booth, boxed in.

'You're keeping your head down, aren't you?' I asked.

– 'Yes, Mum.'

'You be careful, won't you – sweetheart?'

– 'Mum. I'm gonna have to go now. Things to do.'

'Look after yourself, Marky. You will, won't you?'

– 'Love you too.'

– Clunk: so abrupt when it ends, the sound of a fat fly, bang into my ear.

Every now and then you see something on the news. Course it's there all the time in the background, but then, with no warning, it rears like a monster, ready to upset everything.

'If you hear it first on the radio or on the TV,' the Major had told us, 'you can rest assured it will *not* be your son or daughter.'

So then you'd have this terrible sense of relief. Terrible, because you'd be thinking: *How can I be relieved?* Some other mother in her black suit, who's cried her eyes out. I would home in on that mother's face – or the girlfriend's or the wife's – and know it could just as easily be mine.

And yet it wasn't, I'd tell myself. Thank God, I'd think. It isn't me.

Funnily enough 'challenge' was a word Mark used. 'I need a challenge,' he said, as if he had to persuade me. 'I'm sick of being bored.'

I was pleased for him. I thought he'd reached a turning point; I thought, *All will be well.* I knew in my bones that he'd come round, if I could only let him be and didn't nag. And he'd proved me right. But as soon as he went out to Afghan, from the morning he left, I wasn't able to sit still. I felt useless.

He'd been out there a month or so when Emma's mum sent her into school with a flyer. *If you are aged 18 to 50 and in good health, get in touch...* Why not? I was the right side of fifty, not quite on the scrapheap yet. And then, when I went along to the Churchill for that first meeting, and they'd sat us down with the pros and cons and used the very same word – 'The *challenge* involves a day in London,' they'd said – it seemed meant. Not just the money, but a challenge too – that's exactly what I needed. What's more, hearing the lady talk – a million dying from it every year, babies most of them – I began to feel that in some small way I would be doing my bit.

I give permission that my medical notes and data...

I agree investigators may contact my nominated next of kin if

I fail to attend for a follow up after the challenge.

I understand that should I fail to return for review as stated above, I may become seriously ill and die.

I agree to take part in this study.

Signature of Volunteer:

As I finished ticking the boxes and signed my name, it gave me a lift to think that Mark must have done something similar. MARK BRADLEY. He always writes his name in block letters.

It was during those five weeks' leave, before he went off that he told me he'd got to write his 'death letters'. I admit, it took the wind out of my sails.

'What a name for it!' I said. 'They don't mince their words.'

'Who should I write to? I hate writing,' was all he said. He'd chewed the top of that biro until there was a hole in it.

As far as I was aware, he'd never had a proper girlfriend. The closest he'd come was Joanne.

'Jo,' he'd said, pushing her through to the kitchen to meet me – 'Mum.'

It was the first time he'd ever introduced anyone like that. She had a long flop of dark hair that hung across her face. I caught Mark looking as if he'd brought me home a present. 'Lovely,' I'd said.

'Make a list,' I said to him now.

'A list?' he asked. 'How am I gonna make a list?'

'Joanne?' I suggested, testing him, though my stomach was turning over. And then, 'I wish you wouldn't do that – I hate chewed pens!'

There were going to be six of us in our group, the 'control' group, which meant we'd have the challenge but not the new vaccine they were testing. So, although we wouldn't earn quite so much as the others, it didn't involve as many visits to the hospital — fewer needles and bloods. The day before London, we had to go in for a final check-up, five tablespoons of blood, which is not pleasant. They had to test that the females of us weren't pregnant — which I couldn't help tell them, in my case, would be a miracle.

'Don't wash in the morning,' we were told. 'No soap, no perfume or aftershave.' It puts the mosquitoes off.

'The great unwashed!' the big fireman said, clapping his hands as we grouped together. We'd been told to gather by the vending machine outside M&S on platform one. For the 8.06. There must have been nearly twenty of us in the end, with the medics — a bit of a party atmosphere. I noticed then how bubbly she was, the small girl in our group, and how she seemed to know everyone already.

On the train, I was relieved to be sitting next to a man who had nothing whatsoever to do with the trial, a businessman. He had his laptop plugged in. Bubbly girl and the fireman were behind us. I shut my eyes.

'Graham,' I heard him tell her and the rustle of his anorak.

'What made you do it?' she asked.

'Couple of lads at the station came along last year,' he said. 'I want an iPhone.'

'I work at the Institute,' she told him. 'Research.'

'Oh? What does that involve, then?'

'TB at the moment. We're testing mice. I want to go out to Africa.'

'Wow.'

'If they can find vaccines — for things like TB, Malaria — it would be like all the aid anyone's ever given rolled into one.'

'Wow. I never would have known that. Really?'

'People don't. It's like a knee-jerk reaction to send the money out there — half the time it doesn't get into the right hands. But pictures from Africa I suppose are far more sexy than pictures of men in white coats.'

Sexy. She was bold. I felt myself blush for him; I heard him unzip his coat and try to slip himself out of it.

'It's a vicious circle: poverty, disease... But if you can break the cycle,' she went on, 'then people start to get educated, to look out for themselves – things like that.'

He grunted, folding and pressing the anorak into his lap.

'Sorry,' she said. 'I sound like a lecture.'

'No, not at all. It's interesting. You don't think about it, do you?' Then he said, lowering his voice so that I had to keep very still to pick it up, 'Bit weird, that 'Malaria Man' stuff – I looked it up after, did you?'

'All of us knew,' she said. 'It got in the papers.'

They'd mentioned the man in our first session as a warning to us: he'd run off at the crucial point without telling anyone and without treatment.

What would we feel about being tagged? they'd asked. *Would it put us off?*

Yes, we all agreed, it would. It would make us feel like criminals. But I'm sure I wasn't the only one who felt pleased to be consulted, pleased to be able to say 'no' and have attention paid to it. That was the unexpected part: being made to feel special.

'We need to emphasise how serious it is that you keep in touch,' the doctor had said. 'We've had hundreds of volunteers and never had a serious problem. But if you don't come in, there's nothing we can do. In the end – in that particular case – we had no option but to call in the police. Not that he was a danger to anyone else, but if you contract the disease and don't receive treatment then, yes, there is the possibility of fatality.'

'He must have known the cops were onto him,' Graham said from behind me.

'And he was a nurse,' the girl said. 'It was weird. He knew the risk.'

'It's unbelievable. You wouldn't think a nurse would behave like that, would you?'

Imperial College is in the west of London, but it could have been anywhere — we didn't have a chance to look around. Soon as we arrived, we were whisked from the reception and taken upstairs, shown straight into an open-plan office. There were sandwiches out on the tables already, and jugs of orange.

'Tuck in,' someone said, because we all held back.

They had sprigs of parsley and brown bread — *healthy* I was thinking, though the crusts had been cut off. I was hot already. Hot from the journey and hot from being in a strange building. I worried suddenly if I was the only one who'd taken them at their word and not put on deodorant. I grabbed a couple of egg sandwiches and took myself off to one end of an empty table. The girl and the fireman were queued up. It was almost comical, seeing them next to each other, Little and Large. She was the sort of girl who'd always have been popular — popular since she was born. She had lovely hair, cut perfectly straight along her neck. A doll-like figure: it made you want to pick her up, look after her.

'Helen,' she said, smiling as she came over. She nodded at the chair next to mine, 'Can I join you? By the way, I know plenty of people who've done this before,' she said, sorting herself out — her coat, her plate of food. 'They've all been fine — promise.'

I tried to smile, to stop looking worried. 'Have you?' I asked.

'Not this one. I've done psych trials, drug trials — but not this.'

'Do you work at the hospital?'

'The Institute,' she said. 'I like the trials — you get to meet people.' She took a small bite, swallowed it down. 'And,' she said, 'I get to find out what it's like on the other side — being a volunteer. I'm hoping I'll be running trials of my own one day,' putting the palm of her hand to her head, 'touch wood.'

The fireman came and hovered over us.

'Graham,' Helen said, and, turning to me, 'I'm sorry, I don't even know your name?'

'Maureen,' I said. 'Mo.' The orange juice had made my teeth sticky. 'Pleased to meet you,' I said.

The 'challenge suite' was a small room off a laboratory and, after lunch they told us, we'd be led in there one by one.

'Take a seat,' the nurse said when my turn came, following me in. There were two chairs either side of a small square table and a young man in a doctor's coat standing in the corner, wearing the same blue rubber gloves as the nurse.

'It won't hurt,' she said as if she too thought I was a mouse.

I sat down as she waited by the window through to the laboratory – what in our house was called 'the hatch' and opened from the kitchen to the lounge. It was the thing about the new house my mother had been most proud of. 'Use the hatch,' she'd shout, 'that's what it's for.'

In a moment the glass shutter was slid to one side and a sleeve and a blue hand appeared holding a small plastic cup. The nurse was ready; she took it, holding it at arm's length like it was full to the brim, set it on the table. There was a gauzy material across the top, kept in place with a thin rubber band.

'There's five of them in here,' she said, peering over the top and tapping the sides of the cup very gently. I found myself straining to hear, expecting a hum – the sort of hum we get round us at the end of the summer, loud enough to make me turn the light on and sit up in bed with a rolled-up magazine. But I couldn't hear a thing. Perhaps they didn't hum, the ones that had malaria?

'Slip your jacket off,' she said. As soon as I did, I was

aware of the heat rising from my top, musty-smelling like an old radiator.

'Roll up your sleeve, if you would,' she said. 'I'm going to turn over the pot and place it on your arm. I doubt you'll feel a thing. Five to ten minutes, we'll give it, all right? If you could just rest your arm on the table, make yourself comfortable? Relax.'

I did as she asked, laid out my arm. She tipped the cup carefully and set it against the skin, pressed as if it were a glass to a wall and she was going to listen in.

'We'll put a cloth over; they like the dark, that's when they feed – it'll encourage them. There,' she said, 'that's right,' as the young man brought forward a dark duster-cloth, laid it over my arm and knelt down to straighten it, adjust the corners. Although it's been years since I've been to church, him kneeling and us sitting there in silence reminded me of it – the cloth over the sweet wine.

Perhaps I expected a pinprick or a sting? The silence made me ten times more nervous.

'You never notice you've been bitten, do you?' I said. 'Not until afterwards and it begins to itch?'

'That's right. You may not feel a thing,' the nurse said, keeping an eye on her upturned watch.

And then it began to tickle. As if a feather were trapped in there, floating just above the skin.

'It's tickling,' I said, making an effort to keep still.

'Good,' she said. 'Let's hope they're biting!'

I looked it up: *Falciparum malaria*. It was like the doodles we used to make from the insides of felt tips – prints of little circles, a pretty mauve colour. I was off work in any case because of half-term. We had to report in at the Churchill the following Tuesday, six days later – seven days was the earliest incubation, they told us. After that, it would be twice a day for check-ups, bloods, so that the doctors could treat us as soon as they saw the slightest sign.

It would have been quite possible for me to fit the follow-ups around my job, but I'd already decided that I'd take that next week off as well. I was owed the holiday.

The morning after the challenge – still half-term – I gave myself ten minutes extra in bed. I was a bit tired, nothing else. I switched on the bedside lamp and had a look at my arm: the swelling from the night before had gone down to five distinct peaks. 'Perfect,' the doctor had said, examining me and patting my arm, 'Ready to go.'

As soon as I saw the bites I wanted to itch, but I resisted. We'd been given a tube of antihistamine, which I reached for, squeezing the cream directly onto the spots. I decided it would be best if I got up and was busy. After breakfast, I'd do the kitchen cupboards, knowing it would take me all day.

I was standing on a chair in the kitchen when the doorbell rang. It's hard to remember now if I had an inkling, because I've been over it so many times, enough to convince myself that I had. Who rings at that time, mid-morning? The postman? I hadn't ordered anything recently, not that I could think of. The electric?

There's frosted glass the length of the door frame. I could see it wasn't a child, and by the broad shape, the height, it was probably a man, a man wearing a cap, some sort of uniform.

Even as I knew exactly who it was, I squashed the thought. It was the Salvation Army, I told myself, collecting for jumble; a traffic warden lost in a back street. My tongue was like a rag. I took hold of the catch and pulled open the door. The man had half turned and he revolved back smartly on his heel, reached up for his cap and drew it off, held it pressed under his elbow.

'Mrs Bradley?'

Mark had a computer, a great big lumpy thing that took up half his bedroom. Although we've got one in the school office, it was Mark who, four or five years ago, first showed me how to get online. We used the telephone extension on the landing, the sound it made, chirping like a bird; he'd shown me what to look for at the top of the screen, the bar that filled up like a syringe.

Since then, all my clothes I buy online, eBay mostly. I like to get a parcel in the post; I like the notes that people sometimes put in. *Hope you enjoy wearing this as much as I did! Take Care J.* And lately, because of the money, I was looking up holidays for us. Mark was due back before Christmas and it would be a surprise.

It was years since we'd been away together. By the time he was a teenager Mark had lost interest. He must have been seven or eight the last time we went as a family, all three of us. We'd hired a caravan at Weston. Two bedrooms it had, plus a shower and a loo. Mark loved it. We bought him one of those little surf boards with a shark on. Half the time his dad was like a little kid too, took it into his head that they were going to build a fortress, a proper castle, not a poxy thing from a bucket. I remember how clear and blue and hot it was that day, me stretched out in the one deckchair. They'd got a tower from a piece of driftwood, a fence most of the way round from razor shells. Ingenious, I said. It wasn't until we got back to the caravan that I realised how burned I'd got: I'd lashed the cream on Mark but not bothered with myself, wanting, I suppose, to get brown. The sun was like acid, worst along the line of the swimming costume; I could see it in the mirror, the skin in blisters, peeling off. I lay on my front along the thin length of the couch and groaned. It was Mark with his soft hands who helped to pat the Nivea on my back.

'Gently,' I said, putting my head to one side. 'Be gentle.' And he was: so soft I almost cried.

'Mrs Bradley?' the Major said.

If I had denied it then and there, it would have been the truth. As if what truly revolted me was the sound of my own name.

'May I come in?' he asked.

As soon as his shiny, cherry-black shoe stepped over that threshold, I knew.

He spoke as if he had a check-list, about arrangements and how the army'd sort it all out if I wanted them to, to which I nodded, because then it wasn't happening – it wasn't my problem or my mistake.

'It'll go out on the news,' the Major explained. 'Be prepared for that. In a day or two. We can give them his passing-out photo, if you'd like, unless there's one you prefer?'

If I didn't answer him; if I could just manage to say nothing...

'There's no need for you to say or do anything at this moment in time,' he went on. 'You'll need a while to let it sink in. But I'm going to leave you with the number of a very nice lady, a counsellor, who'll talk it all through with you, when you're ready. We'd strongly advise you to speak to her.'

'Next of kin' is what I was to Mark and 'next of kin' was exactly how I put him on the form at the hospital: with our home address, his mobile number (which, even as I wrote it down, I knew – out there – couldn't work).

It was the second time recently I'd thought about God. Because it felt as if someone were watching me, someone high up. Someone who knew there was a design to it. Either that, or I'd brought it all on myself. When the Major left he took everything with him, ransacked the house, raped and pillaged. All without lifting a finger. I sat on the couch in the thick air and undid myself from everything I had ever learned that kept me on the straight and narrow. Like a great harness, I took it off.

Everything's online nowadays or easy enough to find. I put in 'caravan site' and 'Weston-Super-Mare'. Three or four down the list, there it was, the exact, same place: Sea View Caravan Park. Est. 1978. A phone number.

'I've been before,' I told the lady who answered, 'about ten years ago.'

'Oh?' she replied. 'And when were you thinking?'

'Something small,' I said, 'Friday, if you've anything free.'

'This week?' she said, taken aback. 'Let me check. Bear with me.' I couldn't help thinking she took her time on purpose. 'You're in luck,' she said. 'We've a two-berth, free at four o'clock Saturday. Do you want it for the week?'

'See how it goes,' I said.

We agreed, as it was short notice, I'd pay when I arrived, at the office. I'm not stupid. They can trace things on computers, on credit cards. And I'd given her my maiden name, Harris. Up in Mark's room, I was proud of myself, covering my tracks, looking up B&B's in Brighton, Weymouth, Bognor Regis, anywhere I could think of, onto the machine. I even looked up Wakefield, and 'pub', and 'Bradley' (not for the first time, either). It would be natural, they might think, that I'd want to track his father down: 'Your son, if you're interested, he's been blown sky high.'

The bed in his room was stripped. Mark had taken the SpongeBob duvet with him. I lay on the shiny mattress, my head, where his head would have been, where, at eye level, there were cut-outs from magazines, Sylvester Stallone, Bruce Willis, Britt Ekland – a gun tucked into her bikini.

'Do you know how old she is now?' I'd once asked him. 'Way older than me, way more wrinkly.'

There were greasy spots of Blu Tack all over the walls I'd once painted, from where he'd pulled a lot of stuff down. The calendar had disappeared from the back of the door, pictures I'd turned a blind eye to – there are certain things a mum doesn't dwell on. He'd cleared up a few months before he went away, on account of his meeting Joanne I assumed, which, though nothing appeared to have come of it, made me think at least he thought about such things.

I have never done anything wrong or anything out of

the ordinary in my life. Not if you don't count the divorce. I have always done exactly what I've been told. I was perfectly well behaved at school, got through my exams, didn't give my parents any kind of grief. Apart from when Mark was little, I've worked, earned my own way. If it had been up to me, I'd have had more kids, but Bruce was never keen. Leave it a year or two he kept saying until he left himself and it was too late. There's nothing to say that, by now, Mark doesn't have a dozen little brothers or sisters out there. He's asked me that directly once or twice. 'Who's to say?' I told him; I'm not going to lie.

'Wanker,' Mark said.

'Don't say that,' I said. 'He's your dad. Nothing's going to change that.'

'I didn't choose him, did I?'

'None of us has a choice,' I said.

'Fat lot of good he does,' Mark said.

We were able to agree on that.

But there was no time for this. The next day, I acted like I was on a mission. I would do it all in cash; took out £400 from the big post office in town, the most I'd ever taken out. 'It's for a deposit,' I said, though I had no reason to explain.

On Saturday morning I set off with my small red case, took the bus as far as Carfax then walked out towards the station. I was like a ghost – as if I'd been away for years and come back at some dim point in the future. There was a load of students on the pavements with their bicycles. The way they spoke: *Yaaah*, like cowboys. I was invisible to them, same as the other ghost whose eye I caught in the windows of the cafes and restaurants, all the way down George Street.

'Weston-Super-Mare,' I said through the holes in the ticket office. 'Single, please.'

It was only a couple of hours away on the train, change at Didcot, Bristol Parkway. The minicab – another fifteen minutes – dropped me off at the entrance to the site and, by that time, I was so fingers and thumbs that I managed to give him a £5 tip.

The place was drabber than I remembered, but it might have been the weather, the season. The path was churned up and muddy all the way to the green prefab.

'I'm early,' I said, pushing the door. 'Sorry.'

The lady behind the desk was plump and middle-aged.

'Mrs Harris? Not to worry,' she said, as we sorted out the money. 'The other people left nice and early. I'll show you down.'

'It's quiet,' I said, as we walked along a line of caravans and awnings.

'You've come at the right time, if that's what you're after,' she said.

I wasn't used to returning anywhere that wasn't home; it was like a dream. I followed the lady, lifting the wheels of my case from the ground. There was sand on the path, dirty, trodden in. I wondered if it was the same sand as the sand in the desert? The sand Mark complained of so bitterly. 'It gets bloody everywhere,' he said. 'You wouldn't believe it.'

'Path to the beach,' the lady said, nodding towards a bin for dog dirt. 'Here we are.' She unlocked the door and put her nose inside. 'You should find everything in there you need: bed's made up. Anything else, just ask. 9.30 to 4, someone's in the office. We've bread and milk in there, tins, the basics.'

'Thanks again,' I said as she handed me the key, shutting myself in as soon as she turned away. I had a headache, which I put down to the excitement, the adrenalin. I wasn't used to journeys. I ran the tap until the water cleared, filled a glass and took a sip. It tasted of perfume. The two stainless rings of a hob. Baked beans, that's what I remember, and corned beef hash, which was Bruce's favourite – he used to get it on exercise. I opened the cupboard next to the sink. There was a set of three saucepans, an enamel frying pan. I'd polished them before we left last time with a wire scourer until they shone because I didn't want anyone thinking I didn't do the same at home.

On the counter there was a tray with a teapot, a cup and saucer set out, a jar with complimentary tea-bags. I put the kettle on, then went through and sat down on the corner couch. On a ledge opposite, there was a portable TV. I went over and pulled out the little plug: I had half an idea that I might be traced.

It was definitely smaller than the caravan we were in last time. There were twin doors at the kitchen end, with the toilet and the shower and just the one tiny bedroom off the lounge. I took my case through and sat on the edge of the bed. The curtains were shut but by the light of the open door I unpacked: wash-bag, a couple of Mark's old t-shirts, knickers, and the thick, long-sleeved nightdress I'd had from Mum – a 'passion-killer', according to Bruce – which I liked to wear when it got cold. At the bottom of the bag, there was the pad of lined paper with the long brown envelope I'd tucked inside. MRS BRADLEY, 6 BAKER CLOSE, HEADINGTON, OX3. The kettle started a shrill whistle.

I got up to make tea, taking my time, letting it brew. Into the cup I emptied the two tiny pots of UHT. When it was done, like an egg and spoon race, I carried the full cup through on its saucer, clicked on the lamp.

Dear Mum

I'm hoping you dont get to read this because if you do then its curtains for me! You know I'm no good at writing. What would I want to say to you – that's what the padrey said for us to write.

You have always been there 4 me. Anything that is good in me comes from you. Not the bad stuff, the good. Your doing.

If I think about dyeing I think anyway you might get run over by a bus or blown up even on a bus or be born with a dodgy heart or something – any day it could happen to you, your time is up. It's the same thing to me and I'd rather cop it doing SOMETHING. See a bit of the world thrown in. You can die of bordom I bet.

Your the best mum. Brilliant!! I know I havn't always been

the best son. I want to make it up and be someone you can be proud of one day to call your son. Love you mum,
Mark
P.S. If you see Jo say hi. I didn't write her a letter, will you tell her I'm useless at writing.

I turned off my phone though it was three days before they'd start looking for me. Dear Mark. Dear Mark. Dear Mark. I threw down the biro – couldn't get any further than that. I pulled up my sleeve to look at the bites, then brought it down again and began to scratch through the material – I didn't care – hard as I could, up and down, side to side, like rubbing sticks, until my arm was on fire.

As it got dark, the rain came in off the sea. The noise it made: I'd heard nothing like it since that summer before; it came in waves, handfuls of grit against the walls and the roof.

Bruce had been on Carlsberg for breakfast. 'Don't nag,' he'd said, before I said anything. 'We're on holiday.' He'd done his bit, he said. 'Off you go, Markie, why don't you go and see if you can find a mate?'

'He can't go out in this?' I said.

'Will you come?' Mark asked.

'They've table football in the Clubhouse,' Bruce said. 'Don't be a pussy, go on. Be a man.'

'Don't go off the campsite, will you Mark?' I said. 'Or with strangers? Come back for your dinner?'

'Go on,' Bruce said after him. 'Go on, mate.'

I'd watched him in his seaside shorts pick up speed and run as fast as he could, dodging the rain like he was dodging bullets.

Day Seven. Writing it down takes up the time. With no telly, no radio, alone in a place that isn't your own, what else is there to do? I've been out once or twice for milk and biscuits. I've even tried the beach. But it's so flat and wide and empty – I don't need that.

10.30. A second missed appointment. They'll be ringing for me now, jumping up and down.

Day Eight. Safer indoors, except I'm afraid of the fire: the gas explodes with a bang when the pilot catches. So I've kept my coat on. Beginning to notice things going on *inside*: prickling in my wrists and fingers, throbbing under my arm and in my neck. If I lie back and shut my eyes there's a rainbow of colours like disco lights.

'All right, mouse?' Bruce says, pulling me backwards from the door.

'Do you think he'll be OK?' I say.

'Course! What's gonna happen? Come here. Stop fussing.'

He's got his arm around me from behind, pulling me in towards him.

'Why not?' he says.

'It's a goldfish bowl, that's why.'

'Not in the back, it's not. Come on mouse, do as you're told.'

'Let me clear up,' I say.

'We're on holiday,' he says again, hurting my wrist as he pulls me into the bedroom, 'in case you hadn't noticed.'

Day Nine. The sea. It's louder today. All through the night the breathing doesn't let up, as if there's someone under the caravan, waiting. It crosses my mind: it could be Bruce. *Bruce?*

'It's ten tomorrow,' she says, 'unless you've decided to stay on?' The lady at the office is at the crack in the door. She has to look up and round.

'I'm going to sweat it out,' I tell her. 'Sod's law. I'm OK, really. It's just the time of year.'

I hand her the cash through the gap and she folds it

discreetly, without counting it. 'If you're sure,' she says, but she's not certain. 'You'll let me know if there's anything…'

'I'll be right as rain, I know it – in a day or two.'

Ten. There's people out there who let themselves be wrapped up – explosives hung on them like a life-jacket. What would make a person do that? Wires crossed, wire-snippers, a detonator either side: This is what it feels like.

Eleven. Hotter every minute. I can hear them looking now, through the hatch, under the couch, the stairs, round the back of the shed. *Bruce will be back*, I tell them, *in no time, he'll come back*. But they're like the ugly sisters, you can't fob them off. I know exactly what they're after: slipper-shaped, pink, pulsing. They can't wait to get their hands on it. No knocking, no manners, as if they own the place.

There's another couple in the corner, been there since last night, rolling about on the floor, fighting, spawning – no difference. It's filthy, this place. I should have got out while I still had the chance, while I still had legs. There's sand chock-a-block in my throat. And the wailing. Like a siren. How long can a baby keep that up? *Pick him up*, I want to say, though the words won't come out. *Pick him up for God's sake*. Little mite, wailing his heart out, from where the sea breaks up, backs off.

Afterword:

Vaccine Trials

Prof Sarah Gilbert
The Jenner Institute, University of Oxford

THE ERADICATION OF malaria from the world has been under discussion for more than 60 years. The *Plasmodium falciparum* parasite causes around a million deaths each year, many times that number of severe illnesses, and has a major impact on the potential for economic development in malaria-endemic areas. Controlling the mosquitoes that carry the disease has some beneficial effect, but to finally eradicate this disease, vector control will need to be coordinated with effective use of anti-malarial drugs and the widespread use of a vaccine. Unfortunately, malaria is a very difficult disease to vaccinate against, and as yet, there is not a highly effective vaccine that can be used. However researchers in several institutions are working hard to develop a vaccine that would be suitable to use.

New vaccines must be tested on volunteers in clinical trials, to find out if they are safe, immunogenic and effective. The first safety studies involve using a very low dose in one closely monitored volunteer at a time, gradually increasing the dose in subsequent volunteers. Blood samples are taken to study the immune response to the vaccine, and to find out if the vaccine is producing the desired effect. If these early studies are satisfactory, it is then time to find out if the vaccine is effective; does it stop people from becoming ill with the infectious disease that it is designed to protect against?

In some cases this may require very large and lengthy studies to find out if the vaccine works, as is the case for HIV vaccines. But for a few diseases, it is possible to deliberately infect volunteers with a disease under very carefully monitored conditions to find out if the vaccine works, and *Plasmodium falciparum* malaria is one of these diseases. It is not a simple matter to set up this type of study. The strain of malaria that is used has been maintained in laboratories for many decades and can be treated with any anti-malarial drug. The studies have been carried out so many times that there is now a well-established protocol for infecting the volunteers, monitoring them afterwards and treating them when necessary. The volunteers have to be young and healthy, and undergo an extensive screening procedure to assess their suitability to take part.

Lots of different types of people volunteer to take part in these clinical trials, for many different reasons. Some are medical researchers who are keen to see new vaccines moving towards the point when they can be used to provide health benefits, even though their own research may be in a very different field. For anyone studying medicine, taking part in a clinical trial can add to their education, giving them first-hand experience of the process of informed consent. Some volunteers are mainly interested in the money they will be paid for the time they spend taking part, but others, such as the volunteer who told me 'I wanted to make a difference' have more philanthropic reasons.

Jane Feaver's story 'The Challenge' approaches this type of clinical trial from the volunteer's point of view, and does a good job of painting a picture of what it's like to take part. We spend a lot of time talking to the volunteers about what will happen to them, what they need to do, and above all, how to get in touch with us whenever they need to. They may be 'guinea pigs' in one sense, but we don't treat them like 'lab rats'. They know that they are free to withdraw from the study should they wish to, and since they don't need to be kept in quarantine they are able to stay in their own homes and come to the clinical trial centre for planned follow up appointments, which can fit in with their working day. As Jane mentions, we ask them for feedback on the way we conduct the trials, and take their views into account. But we need to make sure they understand that if they are taking part in a malaria challenge trial, it is vital to come to every follow-up appointment. Before they can take part, they have to agree to provide us with information to help us find them if we need to, and they know that if necessary we will contact the police and the news media to help us find them.

Is this safe? Is it ethical to infect someone with a disease that could kill them, even though they have agreed to it? Ethical committees in many places, all including experts and also lay members, have reviewed these studies in detail and think they are well justified. The studies are very carefully planned and conducted to minimize the risks to the participants, and the study design as well as the information that is given to volunteers has to be approved by a recognised research ethics committee before any study can start. The procedures and the risks are carefully explained before volunteers are asked to give their consent, and the researchers reserve the right to exclude any potential volunteer who, in their view, has not understood the implications of what they are volunteering for. Are we likely to attract people who see this as a means of committing suicide? It's possible that such people might ask to take part in these studies, but they would have to wait until a challenge study was planned (once or twice per year), fulfill all the criteria for inclusion in the study, pass the health screening, convince the researchers that they were mentally stable, and then go into hiding for up to three weeks after the infection had taken place. The chances of all of that happening are extremely small, and if someone really wants to commit suicide, there are many surer ways of doing it. In reality over 1,000 people have now taken part in challenge studies to test vaccines, across several countries, without any serious adverse outcome.

What happens to Maureen Bradley in Jane's story? We leave her suffering alone, slipping into delirium. But that is probably not the end for her. Malaria fevers peak every two days rather than get steadily worse, so Maureen should still have some time left to be found. In reality even before she became ill, the police would have been looking for her and her photograph would be on news bulletins and in the newspapers. In a clinical trial setting she is most likely to be found, and not end up as another of the million deaths caused by malaria every year.

Xenopus Rose-Tinted

Annie Kirby

I TELL SOPHIE I want to leave. *I'm old, things change, I want to be free.* She sighs and gives me an indulgent smile but does not respond. The first time I met Sophie, she was repulsed by me. Now she doesn't want to let me go. I have always thought she is beautiful.

Sophie sits on the sofa bed smoking, as Evie dances and sings around the flat in her underwear. Sophie is weary, I can tell, as though the coming day is already behind her, settling its weight into her shoulders. As Evie whirls, Sophie stares into space, not watching the sunset of scar tissue on Evie's chest. The smoke obscures Sophie's guilt. There was a time when Sophie would have had a mug of tea with her cigarette, but now she can't bear it, so she nourishes herself only with the smoke, inhaling it instinctively in steady breaths.

Rainy sunlight leaks in through the bay window, catching in their hair. Evie's hair is a cheerful cloud. Sophie's is pale and liquid, spilling out from its hurried fastenings, its restlessness accentuating her inertia. It's time for Evie to get dressed. Sophie scrunches up woollen tights and unrolls them over Evie's feet and knees. Evie puts her arms over her head to thread into the sleeves of her sparkly jumper, wriggles into the skirt Sophie holds open for her. Evie's clothes all appear pink to me, but they might be a different colour. Finally, her coat with ladybird patches and wellie boots tugged on with a giggle. Evie is unusually compliant, obeying Sophie's calm instructions. Evie loves to go out in the rain. I like to think she gets that from me.

Evie waves me bye-bye in her charming way, opening and closing her plump hand from a fist to a star and back again. Sophie doesn't say goodbye, she rarely does. From my place in the window, I watch them through the steamy glass as they cross the road, Sophie hunched beneath a dark umbrella, Evie splashing into puddles, a slippery little tadpole in her shiny coat. I catch just a glimpse of them – my sight is poor – before they melt into a pink, watery haze. The rain is fragile and misty, rose-coloured; it struggles weakly against the sunshine. I remember a time when Sophie would have run through rain fiercer than this, laughing with her arms outstretched. If Sophie would set me free, I could feel the mist and the rain on my skin. I think I would like that. I spread my fingers into a star against the glass. *Goodbye Sophie. Bye-bye Evie.*

Evie's not a tadpole anymore; she hasn't been for a long time. They have left me alone again. I cry out, but there is no one to hear me. There is nothing to do except be still and float and drift into the colours of a dream.

My people have a word to describe Sophie's people, a concept not present in her culture and unpronounceable in her language. In one sense, it means primitive, in another, a culture fractured, laid bare by its own stumbling, imperfect evolution. The closest word in Sophie's language to describe this condition would be *desolate*. The desolation of Sophie's people is most discernible in their lack of ancestral dreams. It is almost inconceivable that they do not dream the dreams of their ancestors, nor even their descendants, but years of dreaming both Sophie's and my father the scientist's dreams have convinced me this is true.

When I dream, I see the world in the colours my ancestors saw. Cool, brown mud stirred up by my feet, cloaking me. A kingfisher that carries the orange sunrise on its chest and the purplish black of midnight on its wings plummets beneath the surface, breaking free in a cloud of droplets, a glittering fish in its beak. The lowing of cattle thrums through the yellowish-green reed beds into my hiding place. This is the world my ancestors dwelt in for millennia, a world of beautiful, unequivocal colours. These ancestral dreams sustain me. But poor Sophie is alone, cut off from the ones who came before her and has only the pale, snaking smoke of her cigarette for comfort. When Evie grows up, she will be desolate too.

I was conceived *in vitro*, in a bright, shining lab, but don't assume that just because the process was clinical it was without affection. My father, the scientist who made and raised me, who I think of as my ancestral father, is one of Sophie's people. Reflective and wistful by nature, his pensive demeanour often brought to my mind the frail but beautiful stand-up-white-bird that waded by the shores of the lake where my ancestors lived. As well as being a scientist, my father was a storyteller, as I am a storyteller. My earliest memory, not long after I was born, is of drifting in a tepid, amniotic-like bath with my brothers and sisters, as my father loomed above us, concentration engraved into his eyebrows, whispering, *I have to get this story out. I have to get this story out.* There was a hallucinatory rhythm to his words and I floated into my first ancestral dream, to a world where Sophie and my father's people had barely begun their tainted evolutionary journey, and I could submerge myself in the shallows of the lake as dragonflies with transparent wings and shimmering bodies flitted above the surface.

When I awoke, ascending the silted layers of my dream one by one into consciousness, I discovered that my father had cut me in half.

Evie is flushed and sleepy from her bath. She curls up on the soon-to-be-unfolded sofa bed in her pyjama bottoms, sucking her thumb in the fluttering light of the television. Sophie switches on the naked bulb that sways from the ceiling, the intrusive, brilliant light reminding me of days spent in the lab watching my father work. The overhead light means it's time for Evie's magic cream. Her face crumples and flushes and she jams her thumb further into her mouth. If Evie were still a tadpole, she wouldn't need the magic cream.

Hush, hush, baby girl. Let me see. Sophie is on her knees, her eyes level with Evie's chest. It is during this daily ritual that my fondness for Sophie is at its greatest, when she wipes the self-imposed filter from her vision and stares head-on into her shame. Sophie's face is composed as she studies Evie's scar, her eyes flickering faintly. The scar is like a map, marked with the contours of Sophie's guilt. *It's getting better, Evie-Boo. The magic cream is kissing it all better.* Sophie has never kissed Evie's scar. She's thought about it, considered touching her dry lips to the ravaged, melted skin, pressing them down again and again until it heals through sheer force of will. But she has never been able to bring herself to do it because deep inside, deep where she locks away her darkest dreams, where only I can see them, Sophie is disgusted by Evie's scar, by that blemish on her once perfect daughter.

Sophie's right about the scar healing. Even with my compromised vision, I can see that Evie's skin is smoother in places, and that the outline of the scar has shrunk, like a lake receding in a drought. Evie is not mollified by Sophie's words. She doesn't remember ever not having the scar. The scar is part of her. She doesn't like the cream because it's cold and smells like medicine for grown-ups. It's very new, she hasn't got used to it yet. Evie sniffles, shields her chest with her arms and twists her body into the corner of the sofa. Sophie unscrews the lid from the tube. She squeezes the cream onto her fingers, allows the warmth from her own body to seep into it. *Be a good girl, Evie-Boo, and you can have sweeties.* Evie hovers on the cusp of a tantrum, then the moment is past and she grudgingly offers up her torso to her mother. Sophie stifles the shiver of revulsion that runs through her as she massages the cream into the scar tissue but I feel it. I feel it through Evie.

Later, with Evie asleep in the made-up sofa bed and Sophie stretched out on the other side, watching television in the dark with the sound turned down, I beg her again to set me free. She doesn't reply.

I have watched my own conception a hundred times through my father's dreams and it's a beautiful thing. My father thinks of it like music. First, he learns the musical notes of my people, committing to his mind each quaver and semi-breve's precise location on the stave, all the while humming to himself. He remembers when he was a child, lost in his piano practice, floating on the sweet, bitter arpeggios of Chopin's nocturne in C sharp minor. He recognises my people's music as a nocturne of shadow and light, haunting in its own way, but he wants us to be special so he adds another bar, his own composition, a smattering of jazz, fizzing and popping in red and green, that burrows into the melody like a ragworm burrowing into sand.

An interlude, so that the essential parts of my anonymous biological father's newly modified sperm can be incubated in a solution that began with eggs being spun and washed like dirty laundry. More eggs, gently expelled, crammed together, the steady rhythm of a twisting dial, a needle penetrating egg after egg. The jazz-contaminated nocturne gets inside and switches on a light.

This is when I begin, when my cells start to cleave. Carefully, lovingly, my father uses a pipette to move me to a Petri dish.

A mug of tea. Sophie had a mug of tea. She liked to drink tea in the mornings. By then I thought of Evie as if she were a granddaughter. Sophie? It's more complicated. A daughter? A mother? A lover, perhaps, although there has been just one brief moment of intimacy between us. Evie's father was in the flat, passing through on his way to a demonstration, a breakout, a strategy meeting somewhere more exciting than here. Sophie was annoyed with him for turning up unannounced, annoyed that she wasn't wearing any make-up, annoyed that she wished she were wearing make-up. Evie, oblivious to her relationship to the man with the big cloud of hair just like hers, sat on her play mat, banging square pegs into round holes and babbling to herself.

Evie's father put his feet on the coffee table. He gave me a long, narrow stare, over at my place by the window. *I can't believe you haven't let it go.* He drank dark, hissing liquid from a can, scrunched the can in his fist. *Sophie, you've changed. I can't believe you'd be so cruel.* Sophie sipped her tea impassively. *I have changed. I've got Evie. She loves him.* He scowled. *You shouldn't encourage her. She needs to learn what's right.* Sophie bit her tongue, not wanting to argue in front of Evie. Her bun was haphazard, unravelling into soft helixes. *You look tired,* he said, touching his fingers to the hollow between her jaw and neck, a place where he used to kiss her. *Well, aren't you just like Superman, swooping in with a compliment to cheer me up.*

He brushed his fingers up to her cheek, catching wisps of her hair. *Don't be angry.* Sophie stopped being angry. I felt her anger dissipate, like spitting phosphorous put back in its jar of calming oil. He stroked his thumb against the corner of her mouth. Sophie balanced her mug of tea on the arm of the sofa. *We can't,* she said. *Evie.* He said, *Be a good girl Evie, stay on your play mat.* Things happened fast then, Evie's father and Sophie entwined like twisting DNA, shutting the bathroom door behind them. *Ma-ma?* Evie looked up from her pegs. *Ma-ma?* She could hear Sophie laughing in the bathroom. She clung to the edge of the sofa and pulled herself up onto her toddler legs. I cried out, tried to stop her, but she didn't hear me. I couldn't stop it, couldn't get to Evie from my place by the window. She started to scream.

If only Evie had still been a tadpole.

My father closes the blackout curtain and shines a light on me. The light is special. It can see the pathways of fluorescent jazz notes around the place where my father cut me in two. My father thinks the illuminated trails are beautiful. They remind him of the time he stood on the beach at Gardur, near the old lighthouse, during a stopover in Reykjavik with Marie, inhaling salt and coldness, watching the luminous-green striations of the aurora borealis wax and wane. Marie had kissed him, pushing her cold tongue into his mouth and he was irritated because he wanted only to stand, a speck on the beach, watching the lights pulse their mystical patterns across the sky. He was a little closer to his ancestors that night. Now, Marie is married to a man who prefers kissing to geomagnetic light shows and my father is alone, squinting into his fluorescence microscope, patiently observing the aurora borealis of oxidisation in my regenerating tail.

Sometimes, I dream the lives of my descendents. For many, their world is mud, waterways choked with plastic food cartons and drinks cans and the dreams of their ancestors floating with them on the oily surface of the city. Others live like I once lived, stacked up in windowless rooms, in a state of perfectly still meditation, or calling out to each other above the ceaseless electric hum. Some, like me, see the world through a rose-tinted filter, their red eyes a genetically inscribed label that reminds our father which of us he gifted with the fluorescent jazz notes.

Life in the lab was dull, especially as I grew to adulthood, absorbed my tail into my body and new siblings arrived to steal my father's attention. Still, I had plenty of time to dream, floating back to the hazy African wetlands of my ancestors, or permeating my father's dreams as he studied the channels of light that illuminated the tails of my younger brothers and sisters. Then I met Sophie, and everything changed.

It was night, my favourite time; I liked the tranquillity, the darkness. The lab was deserted, except for my brothers, sisters, and I. I retreated into a dream where I sank my feet into muddy shores and listened to the music of my people calling to one another across the lake. I was woken by a crash and a brilliant, blinding light. I froze. There was giggling and shushing. *Oh my God, are they toads? The labels say Xen-o-pus. Frogs, I think.* Ripples of alarm radiated from my brothers and sisters, stacked up on shelves along the walls. *Poor things, what a terrible life in these tiny tanks. Let's take them. It's not what we came for, Chris. We can't get what we came for, so we might as well do some good. Not cute and fluffy enough for you?* Dark, pink-tinted shapes moved towards me. *What is going on with their eyes? Is that natural? Of course it's not natural; they've been testing on them. Carry them in this. Come on, come* on!

The tank I had called home for half a lifetime of dreams was wrenched from the shelf and I found myself swimming with my brothers and sisters in a container with solid sides that shut out the light. There were more thuds and bangs, crunching noises, the water whipping up as if in a storm. Some of my siblings panicked, crawling on top of one another as we were sloshed and thrown around, but I remained calm.

Get in the back with it, hold the lid. Why can't you do it? Go, go. The noise that came next was indescribable – a thunderous roar that pulsed through our bodies. The pure intensity of the vibrations shocked the fear out of my siblings, and they clustered with me on the bottom, occasionally jolted into the sides of the container and each other, waiting for the noise to end. When it did, the relief was so intense that I almost didn't notice the sliver of light opening up above me. The light flooded down to where I crouched, like the moon sliding out from behind a cloud. Why I did what I did next, I can't explain. An instinct for self-preservation, perhaps, or an association of bright lights with the familiarity of my father's lab, but I would have been safer huddling with my siblings. If I had stayed with them then, I would be free now. Or dead. Who knows? The winters have been cold. Whatever the reason – fear, stupidity, bravery – I jumped towards the light.

I landed in darkness – a dry, warm place. It was not what

I expected. I scrabbled around, disorientated, but could not free myself. There seemed to be barriers in all directions, walls with soft contours, but impassable all the same. I heard sloshing water, the cries of my siblings, birds calling, mud squelching. Splash, splash, splash. *Swim away froggies. Swim away.* I realised, with a sense of dread, that my siblings were gone and I was alone.

My sanctuary, during that long, terrible journey, was a dream of my father sitting at his computer, frowning and composing strings of words like musical notes. He was writing a story of jazz notes, hydrogen peroxide and the aurora borealis in the regenerating tails of tadpoles. *I have to get this story out*, he muttered, his fingers soaring across the keys as if he was playing the melancholy arpeggios of his childhood. He was not one for speculation, my father, but he was cautiously eager, excited to see where his results would lead – a treatment for scar tissue, the renewal of damaged spinal nerves, the regrowth of a human limb. *I have to get this story out.* I slipped into another dream, where I drifted sedated in a Petri dish, kingfishers and dragonflies darting and weaving above me in the bright lights of the lab as I descended into sleep.

When I awoke, still cocooned in the warm place, the darkness had diminished. Voices floated above me, the words indistinct. Jostling, rustling, I shrank back. A human hand brushed against my parched skin. There was a scream, laughter. I froze, was thrown around again, then tipped out of my cocoon into a cool, shiny place that reminded me of my father's lab. *Ugh, I can't believe there was a frog in my bag. And that you put it in my bath.* Water flowed, rising up over my body. *It's only a frog, Soph. We'll set it free in the morning. Oh my God, that was so gross. C'mon babe, let's go to bed.* The lights went out. I waited, dreamless, until morning.

Well, look at you with your red eyes. I have to pick you up now because I need my bath back. The voice was female, soothing. *I can do this.* A hand scooped me up. *You're not so bad, not really. Poor thing.* I sat on her palm and looked into her face. *What does the world look like to you? Do I look like a big, red monster?* She was one of my father's people, like him, yet not like him. My body quivered. *Poor thing. You're terrified.* From that moment, Sophie was my kin, and I could see into her dreams. I knew that they had broken into the lab with a stolen key card and an alarm code hacked from a carelessly stored email. That they had been looking for mice, rats, maybe monkeys, but there had been another layer of security, for which they didn't have a card or a code, and so they stumbled on us instead, the *Xenopus Rose-Tinted,* with our red eyes, jazz-infused nocturne of DNA and the ability to dream one another's dreams. I knew that she thought she loved a man named Chris. I knew that she, like my father, never ate the flesh of animals. I found a tadpole, too, floating snug in her belly. She didn't know about it yet, because she was desolate and the tadpole was very new. *I'm going to put you in a washing-up bowl and God help you if you crap in it. Do frogs crap? Never mind. Later, I'm going to take you to the ponds and set you free.*

Sophie never did set me free. She fell in love with me instead.

I thought I would never see my father again and it made me sad. But I did see him, just the once, in a dream of Sophie's. It was the barest, fleeting moment. In Sophie's dream, she was in a place where my father's and her people congregate, to feed, drink, search for mates. Sophie sucked up sweet liquid through a tube. The liquid made her warm, nebulous around the edges, like the anaesthetising solution my father placed me into when he wanted to study the lights in my tail. A man, his long, angled body leaning into a counter, moved into her peripheral vision. It was my father, a little older, and not squinting into a microscope or muttering to himself about stories or designing musical codas for frog DNA. Sophie watched him drink, attracted by his height, his reflective manner, the placement of his wristwatch which drew the eye to his large hands. He must have felt her eyes on him because he turned and smiled at her. I had never seen him smile. Sophie's body grew warmer. She returned the smile. She thought about Evie, at home with the babysitter, and Chris who-knows-where, and withdrew into her customary inertia, shrinking back into the crowd. I was disappointed. I think they would have liked each other.

Evie's scar is fading, a little each day. My father's and Sophie's people are not so different to my people. Only the smallest twist of DNA separates us, our nocturnes composed of the same notes in a different key. I wish we could cure them of their desolation. I wish Sophie could have protected Evie in her belly forever, safe from steaming mugs of tea, absent fathers and that cold, antiseptic scented cream.

My jazz-infused, oxidising, aurora borealis nocturne is almost at an end. Like my father, I am a storyteller and I have to get my story out. Sophie is not going to set me free, so I can only trust that my descendents will dream of me. Sophie and Evie are crossing the road outside the flat. *Goodbye Sophie. Bye-bye Evie.* I watch them from my tank in the window, as they disappear into the rose-tinted sunlight.

I lie still, and drift into a dream filled with the colours of my ancestors.

Afterword:

Tadpole Tissue Healing

Dr Nick Love
Faculty of Life Sciences, University of Manchester

HUMANS CAN TRAVEL to the moon, dive the deepest depths of the oceans, and set up camp at the frigid South and North poles. Humans can build super computers, construct bionic arms, and decode almost any creature's DNA. However, despite our technological feats, following bodily injury, humans are still largely at the whims of our somewhat inefficient wound healing biology. Even relatively minor surgical procedures can result in lifelong scars, or worse, turn into life-threatening infection and other complications.

In other words, the human body cannot perfectly heal large wounds or regenerate complex appendages following injury, and the tissue repair process can result in scarring, disfigurement, and impaired function. Chronic and difficult-to-heal wounds pose a huge challenge to hospitals and cause significant physical and emotional suffering to individuals and their families. For this reason, a major goal of biology and regenerative medicine is to develop methods to more efficiently heal wounds and rejuvenate damaged human tissue.

Towards this aim, scientists study the biology of organisms that possess admirable capacities to regenerate body parts following removal. One such organism is the Xenopus tadpole, which has the ability to regenerate its tail appendage (and also its eye lens) following removal. The regenerating tadpole tail is especially interesting to scientists and clinicians – it demonstrates the somewhat rare instance of vertebrate spinal cord regeneration. Because tadpole tails heal without scarring, scientists are now racing to translate such regenerative abilities into a therapy, a 'magic cream' if you will, that might one day help heal human wounds. It is with this goal in mind that Annie Kirby in 'Xenopus Rose-Tinted' explores the role of fluorescently modified Xenopus frogs in bio-medicine's quest to develop a scar-tissue-rejuvenating 'magic cream'.

Xenopus frogs have a special place in the story of modern biology. Xenopus was the first vertebrate organism to be 'cloned', and later, the first amphibian to have its genome sequenced. In the 1990s, a procedure was invented that allowed the creation of genetically modified (also called 'transgenic') Xenopus frogs and tadpoles. This technique, combined with advances in fluorescent protein technology, enabled scientists to create transgenic frogs (and thus tadpoles) that express fluorescent proteins in their tissues. Some of these fluorescent proteins have been engineered to change light-emitting properties depending on cellular chemical states (for instance, cellular hydrogen peroxide or calcium levels). Hence, transgenic Xenopus tadpoles expressing these fluorescent proteins give scientists a direct window into the biological and cellular mechanisms that underlie and promote vertebrate, scar-free healing and tissue regeneration.

In 'Xenopus Rose-Tinted', we encounter the story of one such transgenic frog that expresses two very different fluorescent proteins in its body. One of these fluorescent proteins is expressed all over the body and changes fluorescence properties depending on the oxidizing effect of hydrogen peroxide (H_2O_2), an important signal chemical found within cells. The second fluorescent protein, a simple bog-standard red fluorescent protein (RFP), is expressed only in the frog's eye lens. During the frog genetic modification or 'transgenesis' procedure, the fluorescent RFP eye lens functions as a 'marker' and gives scientists an efficient way to screen for 'founder' or 'F0' transgenic organisms. An unintended result of this genetic modification marker is that these frogs and their progeny go on to see the world through a ruby-red eye lens i.e. their vision is always 'rose tinted'. Following transgenesis, these precious founder frogs are then pampered by their scientist creators, and only the frog's tadpole progeny (who are also transgenic for the fluorescent proteins) are used for experimentation.

In 'Xenopus Rose-Tinted', we consider the life of one such hypothetical ruby-lensed transgenic frog that has been 'rescued' and now lives with Sophie and her daughter Evie, who bears a large scar on her chest. Prior to this rescue, the frog had been living in a research laboratory where its vegetarian scientist 'father' had been working on a scar-reversing 'magic cream'. One interesting point for us to consider is that during the liberation, the laboratory interlopers are disappointed to find frogs – they had hoped to free cute and cuddly mammalian or primate species. This brings up the intriguing fact that we humans feel more empathy and sympathy towards mammalian creatures such as dogs, cats, horses, and primates, yet will seemingly rejoice at the deaths of worms, mosquitoes, spiders, snakes, rats, and other 'pests'.

The frog in 'Xenopus Rose-Tinted' has the added ability to dream the dreams of its ancestors, allowing it to understand the colours that it has never seen due to its red eye lens. Moreover, the frog is omniscient, and can comprehend the seemingly silly follies of its human owners. It should be noted that Xenopus frogs are not known for their ability to dream or read human minds! However, Xenopus most certainly can recognize the difference between fellow Xenopus frogs and humans – this recognition, sometimes referred to as 'conspecific recognition', is often held as evidence that most animals indeed do have at least some sense of 'self'.

Ultimately, the scientist in the story hopes that better understanding the regenerative properties of transgenic Xenopus tadpoles and their 'fluorescent jazz' will more quickly bring about a 'magic cream' that will enhance human wound healing and thereby reduce human suffering. Such a feat (which very well may be possible) would add yet another notch to bio-medicine's achievements, which include (i) the near-eradication of the viral diseases small-pox and polio via vaccination, (ii) the harnessing and neutralizing of bacterial infections via antibiotics, and (iii) the development of modern medical procedures like bone-marrow transplantations. These were clear victories for humankind that in some way or other relied on live animal research.

However, whether it is indeed 'right' or 'ethical' to create genetically modified animals (like transgenic Xenopus frogs that see the world in a strawberry-red hue) is less clear. In any argument, the ethics of using, raising, and creating animals for medical research should always be viewed alongside the other human uses of animals: the testing of cosmetics on animals (for human vanity) and the factory-style raising and slaughtering of animals for the meat industry (for the human palate). From a frog's (and possibly a human's) point of view, it may be more desirable to be a well-fed laboratory frog than a spoonful of frogs' leg soup. This last point is not intended to trivialize the plight of animals housed and used in medical research facilities, but is important to keep in mind as humans (and their animal partners) travel towards an undetermined and malleable future society, whose rules cannot yet be seen or read.

The Modification of Eugene Berenger

Gregory Norminton

To: Erlking, Goldie, Leopardgurrl, Horny Bob.
From: Fr. Terence Mode

GREETINGS — AS THE priest of an old faith might have begun a letter to colleagues in the world gone by. It's status orange here in San Francisco, the storm belts having passed with only minimal damage, and the Seminary exudes a sense of purpose as we await the arrival of a fresh intake. I imagine it must seem a long time since the beginning of your novitiates, yet to me the process of renewal is like the seasons of old, a cycle of change which embodies the mystery of regeneration. I look forward to encountering new and startling permutations: the diversity of forms which only the young seem capable of. Yet I confess to some trepidation, for the mind seeks what is known and established, and even those of us who belong to the pioneering generation crave, as we get older, a kind of stasis, a settling into established norms, so that we can travel without further dislocation to the final transformation of death.

It is difficult to be a student of flux. We set our hearts against change; we long to be frozen when everything flows. Yet I have witnessed the thaw many times, and wish to share one instance with you. It's a story of struggle, of needless resistance and pain. It's the story of my old university friend, Eugene Berenger, and his attempt to swim against the tide of the world. I did not go looking for his story: it came to me.

87

Mine was the task of advancing it towards the only possible outcome. Sometimes that's all we are called upon to do. We are ferrymen, my brothers and sisters. We are guides leading the blind to the fountain of sight.

I had known Eugene Berenger, on and off, for fifty years, ever since our young days sheltering from the Great Recession in the groves of academe. Our friendship had waxed and waned over the decades, and when I received his email last year it had dwindled thinner than a crescent moon. I had, however, gotten to know his wife, Marie, after she came to me for guidance along her path to Eclosion. The joy of her conversion had in turn reconciled their daughter, Sally; whereupon Eugene moved out of the marital home to a one-bedroom apartment in Portola. He informed me of this himself, in an email full of intemperate exclamations. He would remain true to himself, he wrote, even at the expense of family and friends. I recognised at once the symptoms. We must think of them not as faults but as patterns, neither to be dismissed nor condemned but alleviated with care. For compassion is our watchword: the liberation of imprisoned forms must be done tenderly, using all the tools of science and revelation.

I decided to pay Eugene a visit. I wasn't sure what state I would find him in. Even when we were freshmen I had noticed the morbid cast of his thoughts. He used to obsess about his grades and would gnaw like a dog at the bone of some grievance: the sarcasm of a tutor, the scorn of a beautiful classmate. We headed, after Berkeley, in different directions – me towards the sacraments, he into the dusty and, being done, reassuring obscurity of European history. The past and its memories were a place of safety for him, as they remain for many of my contemporaries. Your generation, of course, has never had that luxury.

Eugene Berenger was hiding out in a squalid apartment block on Burrows Street, where I arrived by cab and searched for his number. He buzzed me in and, after refusing my hand, which he regarded with undisguised horror, admitted me to a disordered room that smelled of pizza and synthetic olives. I could tell from the set-up that he had been sitting, before my arrival, among consoles that were streaming several newsfeeds at once. I thought of an addict gorging on what sickens him. (You will recall, from your training, that an unhealthy preoccupation with current affairs is a classic symptom of Aversion). I looked about for evidence of previous visitors. There were no photographs of Marie or Sally, and I commented on the fact while he coughed and cleared a place for me to sit.

'I can't bear to contemplate what I've lost,' he said. He straightened to look at me and there was defiance in his eyes. 'I didn't think you'd come after what I wrote.'

'How could I not? Your email had the force of a summons.'

'Or a curse,' he said, and sat down amidst the dismal footage. 'Is Marie all right?'

'I've no idea. Why don't you ask her?'

He gave no reply, merely huffed sarcastically and muted the sound on his monitors.

'I'm sure she would appreciate hearing from you,' I said.

'Did she tell you that herself?' It was my turn to meet a question with silence. 'It's like,' he said, 'the old narcotics trade.'

'What is?'

'The reversible stuff – those gels they put under their skin – that's the gateway drug. Get the kids used to looking like mutants and they'll move on to permanent upgrades. Like the ones – Christ, Terence, what if your mother could see you now?'

I laughed at this: it was such old world talk. 'My mother taught me to be true to myself.'

'By doing *that* to your face?'

My instinct to make light of his complaint faltered at

the sight of tears in his eyes. 'Oh Eugene,' I said, 'there's no need for that.'

'I can't help it!'

'You're nostalgic for a world that's gone.'

'At Berkeley you were so good-looking I could hear people catch their breath when we walked into a room. I used to hang out with you just to be near all that promise. You seemed to embody the beauty of the world.'

'Well now everybody can. Think of it that way.'

'That isn't *beauty*. Beauty's natural. What you and your cultists do –'

'I can't allow you to use that word.'

'– what you do is *wrong*. I know I must sound like I'm from Alabama or Utah, but nothing will change my mind that body modification is a sin against nature.'

'I think we all know,' I said, 'what sins against nature have been committed. Mammon was the god of the *old* religion. Don't tar my Church with that brush.'

Eugene blew his nose and dabbed at his pale, red-rimmed eyes. 'I'm sorry. It's just I take things hard. The loss of Marie... and now Sally...'

'They're not dead, Eugene.'

'Don't tell me I haven't lost them.'

'You haven't.'

'They're *gone*.'

'Only to Modesto. There's no reason to hurt yourself like this. To hurt them.'

I could have saved my breath. Eugene was not in a place to hear me. 'You know,' he said, 'she never told me who talked her into it. Who brainwashed her.'

'Why do you suppose it was brainwashing?'

'Oh, come on. This is my wife we're talking about. I *knew* her.'

'Did you? Isn't it perhaps the discovery that she wasn't the person you thought she was –'

'She was kidnapped. I don't mean literally but she was

taken away from her life. They all are.'

'Was I?'

He faltered. 'You have a talent for sounding reasonable.' I was careful not to soften the scrutiny of my gaze. 'Am I a bigot, Terence? Am I just some throwback – a reactionary who's outlived his time?'

'Your emotions are entirely understandable. The task is not to reproach yourself for them. It is to change them for the better.'

'I guess it must have been like this in Rome,' he said. 'When the Christ cult took over. The empire was dying and the old beliefs with it. People must have felt dislocated. They must have despaired.'

'Do you despair, Eugene?'

'Yeah, you'd like that, wouldn't you? It would give you something to work with.'

I let him know, with a chromatic shift in my corneas, that I would not be unsettled by his hostility. He cleared his scrawny throat – so different from my own, though we were of an age.

'Maybe I'm getting old,' he said. 'I *am* old. So are you.'

'In body perhaps.'

'I guess when Marie did... that to herself and Sally followed... I blamed you. I mean that it was your, uh, face that came to my mind. The face you used to have.'

'Which one?'

'That serene smile of yours. Like a Buddha. Beaming at the mutilation of those I love. Oh I know that word's taboo – it's an obscenity to describe an obscenity. But what else can you call the warping of a woman's natural body?'

'We call it Eclosion. Like the emergence of a butterfly from its chrysalis.'

'I call it a flight from reality.'

'We're not escaping reality, we're outflanking it.'

'But changing our bodies like this, altering our nature. It's a failure of solidarity with the past.'

'The past failed in its solidarity with the future. Why should we be nostalgic for a place that made us homeless?'

Eugene was not easily persuaded. Morphing, he said, was the result of human arrogance. Our bodies having evolved over millions of years, who were we to promote ourselves above all other life?

'That, if I may say so, is a classic misapprehension. You must have noticed the forms we take – the sources of our inspiration. By embodying our kinship with other species, we have not dethroned humanity so much as democratised creation.' I told him how Morphers across the globe have made their bodies living memorials to the species which our forbears extinguished: the Rhino Boys of Botswana, Pandaoists in China, the clawed and banded women haunting the ruins of Ranthambore in honour of the tigers that used to roam there. Eugene seemed affected by these instances: I could see him grimace as he fought to tamp down something in his chest. I asked if he would take some water but he shook his head.

'How many of the freaks you mention,' he said softly, 'have corporate sponsors? And don't think I won't see you lying. I know about your corneal implants.'

'I have no reason to lie to you, Eugene. The Church is consistent on the matter. We oppose the commercialisation of Morphing – commerce being the lifeblood of the domination system.' I reminded him how that system had revealed its true nature in the enhancement scandals that brought down the Olympics.

'And how!' he said with boyish glee. 'I could never figure out how you guys survived that shit storm. Of course you blamed commerce for hijacking something beautiful.'

'Body dissatisfaction had always been a weapon in advertising's arsenal. It was the most obvious step in the world to link morphing to fashion, body modification to self-improvement. For corporations it was like pushing an open door. The new generation, raised by virtual moms and housebots, inured themselves to norms that meant little to them. By adolescence, daily immersion in the Pornstream ensured that a young person felt out of the ordinary, was frankly something of a freak, not to possess at least a basic Dejina or meatotomised cock. Cupid, you know, is a coercive cherub. If electrocleansing your pubis is what it takes to be admitted to love's banquet, how many will choose to starve? If, by painless immersion, you can rid yourself of the taint of pigment, why would you remain in darkness?'

'And you *approve* of this?'

'On the contrary! The repression of melanin is a deplorable phenomenon. It's conformism of the worst kind. The Church goes in the opposite direction: away from homogenisation into diversity, with many colors added to the few naturally available to us. You'll find no gene silencers in our hydrogels. We believe not in a common *process* of revelation but in its individual *manifestation*.'

I watched Eugene consider these words. For a moment the weight seemed to lift from him. Perhaps it was the beginning of grace. I felt a door open, just a fraction, in his guarded soul and reached out with a comforting hand. The movement was misjudged.

'Can't you see,' he cried, 'I don't care about these distinctions! I don't give a damn whether you're motivated by profit or prophecy – the net effect's the same. Morphing's what I object to, not the motivations behind it.' A sob escaped from his throat. 'It took my wife away from me. It took my baby girl. Everyone I love.'

He stood up, jolting the monitors, and staggered to the bathroom, where I heard him heave and gasp. I hesitated, wondering whether I ought to go to him; but I figured he would hate me for seeing him in his distress. There was a flush from the air cleanser and he returned, pale with determination.

'I think you should leave,' he said. 'I wrote because I wanted to see you – to witness what you'd done to yourself. I needed a good laugh.'

'Did I provide one?'

'Maybe you think I'm crazy to strike out alone. I don't care. I wanted you to see me refuse what no one else can resist.'

'You speak to me as if I were your enemy.'

'Are you not?'

I got up to leave; but the pressure of his gaze goaded me to a candour that may have been incautious. 'I don't think you're crazy,' I said. 'I believe your soul is in torment for resisting what it most longs for.'

I left the apartment with his curses ringing in my ears.

And that might have been the last I saw of Eugene Berenger. I had not succeeded in helping him; if anything – I told myself as I returned to the seminary – I had turned away from one in Aversion. Yet I felt disinclined to start over, in view of what had passed. Little did I know that the working of grace had not yet finished with my friend of old.

Two weeks after our encounter in Portola, I was meditating in my office when Father Funhouse announced on the intercom that an acquaintance of mine was being shown to my door. I opened the same a fraction of a second before my visitor knocked. Perhaps it was merely surprise that left his fist trembling in space a foot from my heart.

'You look exhausted,' I said, as I in my turn cleared a place for him to sit. He declined to take it. 'Have you spoken to your wife since we met? To your daughter?'

'Oh, you'd like that. That would fit your plan.'

He was trembling in all his extremities. I asked if he would care for a toke.

'God knows I've tried. I really have. To understand why they did it. To look at them without wanting to throw up. But I can't turn my mental world upside down. I can't reject what is scientifically normal.'

'Science has changed,' I said, sitting down to take some of the tension out of the air. 'It serves *us* now. For centuries, science gave us means at the expense of meaning. Once upon a time we were made in God's image, with the cosmos revolving around us. Now we're denizens of a rock in space, spinning on its axis towards extinction. This demotion made us mad. We plundered the Earth's resources to plug the meaning gap; we buried ourselves in a mausoleum of stuff, until we could no longer bear the daylight that revealed us to ourselves. The biosphere, it turned out, was our only source of meaning. And look what we'd done to it.'

'Denatured it,' said Eugene, 'like you want to denature me.'

'The Church wants nothing of the sort. We're not monsters.'

'Oh no – what would you call *that*?' He pointed at the picture of Father Ghoulish on my desk.

'You know I was speaking metaphorically.'

Eugene folded his arms across his chest to quell their shaking. I pretended not to notice. 'Historically,' I said, 'the forces of coercion worked the other way. Abstainers forget the prejudices we had to overcome before we went mainstream. There was resistance everywhere. A mermaid was drowned in Nantucket. Lizard boys were lynched in Tennessee. But we stood firm, convinced of our legitimacy. And we helped to transform medicine on the way. For example, tracheal implants used to feel to a lot of patients like an invasion, a mutilation. As lifestyle morphing became common, the mental stigma attached to medical procedures faded away. The shame went. The fear abated.'

'You pretend to love humanity – you talk all peace and love. But how can you love something when you want to alter it out of all recognition?'

'Elevate,' I said. I reminded him about our Foundational Creed: the fruit of our deliberations, that terrible hurricane year when everything changed. As the world altered, warping faster than our hearts and minds could adapt, we came to feel that the only way of reaching an accommodation with change was to run ahead of it, to make an adventure of transformation, to inscribe as it were on our flesh the startling dynamics of the Anthropocene. We bent science to a new and spiritual purpose. We used its discoveries to discover our potential. We became alchemists of the flesh, every Morpher his or her self-creation.

'That sounds like pride,' said Eugene.

'Not in the sense you intend. We don't worship ourselves. That would be anthropolatry.'

'Gesundheit!'

'We morph in order to transcend the self,' I said, 'to escape, at first in form and thereby in spirit, the egocentricity that led our species to this unhappy pass.'

Eugene was not really listening. Like a man bent over a conundrum, or sounding in himself the first murmurs of a gastric complaint, he stood by the window viewing the sidewalk.

'Are you sure,' I said, 'I can't persuade you to sit? You're setting me on edge, standing like that.'

'I think I'm done with sitting.' Eugene pulled a folded sheet of paper from his pants and tossed it across my desk. I took it up and read the contents. I put the paper down.

'I hope you know we would never endorse this.'

'No you wouldn't. But you're the high priests of a tribe. And tribes need enemies to cement their identity. They need outsiders, non-members. People like me.'

'That,' I said, 'is a deplorable document. You should take it to the police.'

'You think they give a shit about Abstainers like me? For all I know, it was a cop who put that in my mailbox.'

I tried to assure him that this was wide of the mark. I offered to take up the matter myself, with the DA if necessary.

'The DA,' Eugene laughed. 'That bastard speaks with a forked tongue.'

'He can't very well help that.'

'Nobody can protect me. Nobody would even *want* to.'

'I want to help you, Eugene.'

'You? You're the original freak police. How could I turn to you for help when you're my enemy?'

'Please. How can you call me that after all these years?'

'It was you who advised my wife.'

My desk was really most extraordinarily dusty. 'Excuse me?' I said.

'You were her rabbi – confessor – whatever the heck you call it.'

'To my knowledge,' I said slowly, 'Marie and Sally came to Eclosion after making up their own minds.'

'You brainwashed them.'

'I did not.'

'You helped them fuck themselves up.'

'I had – absolutely and categorically – no part in fucking them up.'

Eugene shook his head. 'Wrong answer,' he said, and it took me a moment to recognize the revolver for what it was. The air drained from the room. My hands lifted of their own accord. That deadly aperture was all I could see, and it wasn't until he began pulling at the latch of the window that I guessed his intentions.

'What are you doing?'

'Enough with the lies. I'm letting some light in.'

'It's maximum UV out there. I don't think you should –'

'Hah!' he cried and, having released the latch, pulled up the windowpane. The heat blasted our bodies. I tried to get to him but the revolver kept me at bay. He waggled it a couple of times as he heaved a leg over the sill. My fingernails made contact for an instant with the belt of his pants. Two of them split to the quick with his momentum. I heard the impact of his body as it connected with the sidewalk. I was alone in my wind-shaken room.

You will share with me, dear friends, my horror at what had come to pass. Yet I determined, in the days that followed Eugene Berenger's attempt on his life, not to let his suffering be in vain. As it was for my Roman namesake, nothing human is alien to me – not even an aversion so intense that it prefers annihilation to the transformation it so needlessly dreads. When Marie and Sally, now Tinkerbell, Berenger asked me to attend them at their loved one's bedside, I refused to allow the trauma of what I had witnessed to distract me from my duty.

The injuries sustained by Eugene were extensive: you will recall from your ordination how many flights up is my study. It would be an indiscretion to share with you specific details of the damage done; suffice it to say that he had contrived, in his fall, to strike face-first the seminary railings. Eugene was put in an induced coma – would remain there for several weeks – and I endeavoured as best I could to console his wife and daughter. Marie Berenger, having power of attorney, was able, with my advice and blessings, to oversee the preliminary stages of reconstructive surgery that would ensure for Eugene a return to something resembling the life he had enjoyed.

Subcutaneous biosensors had been fitted, as a matter of course, on first admission to ER. The decision was then taken to fit an intrathoracic assist device that would pump oxygen to his damaged lungs. A nano-endoscope would allow his future carers to monitor his pathways. Nobody missed the irony that Eugene was being kept alive by the very technologies whose spiritual purpose he had so despised. Yet how could his loved ones have elected to replace a pulpy mess with the mere fleshly simulacrum of a nose when rhinoplastic alternatives are available that will not only replace but upgrade the usual functioning of the sense organ? It was not possible, even had it been desirable, to replace myopic, faded septuagenarian eyes with equally senescent grafts; what sense would there have been in trying when UV-resistance comes as standard in the most basic ocular implants? The surgeons set to the task with their customary aplomb. And slowly, over weeks, Eugene Berenger returned to wakefulness. I ensured, after lengthy deliberations with hospital staff, that Eugene's resurfacing was managed at such a pace that Marie and I were able to introduce him gently to his altered condition. A shock at this early stage might have been fatal. His mental and somatic systems were protected by finely calibrated doses of morphine, anxiolytics and SSRIs. The decision was taken to control his serotonin receptor levels until such time as staff could be confident there would be no further attempt to act on his suicidal ideation.

We prayed over my old friend and wept, his wife and daughter and me, to see his resistance ebb away. He began not just to hear but to listen to us, and to see with eyes made new in both a literal and a metaphysical sense. He was equipped with an admirable set of new teeth. His auditory capacity was enhanced and the bone structure of his broken face extensively remodelled. It was a small step, in the end, to go from being reconciled to his palliative implants to embracing – as a Choice and a Way – the skeletal, muscular and dermal modifications which, his wife and I persuaded him, would make a virtue of medical necessity. 'There is nothing more sacred than life,' I used to remind him while he moaned assent from beneath his plaster casts.

When the time came for Eugene's transfer from the ICU, I employed all my powers of persuasion, and called in favours going back to the earliest days of the Church, to secure a place for him at the Panta Rhei hospice up in Washington. I know what sterling work they do there to repair the links, so easily broken, between body and soul, life and hope, mere existence and spiritual joy.

You will note, my brothers and sisters, that the case of Eugene Berenger should not be taken as a practical instance of assisted transformation. It would be deplorable to steer an Abstainer towards self-harm in the hope of achieving what pure reason cannot. Instead, I share this story with you to illustrate not only the dangers of leaving a pathology untreated, but also by what extreme means fate, or what we properly call the Essence of Flux, may break through the hardest carapace to grant liberation to one who feared it. Having, in his obstinacy, left himself no other escape route, Eugene Berenger had had to break himself and thereby break with the Inner Parent of his phobia. Despair and destruction allowed him, against the odds, to slough off the Exuvium of his old self – to emerge with iridescent wings from the chrysalis of denial. His Eclosion, for which daily his adoring wife and daughter give thanks, is a demonstration *in extremis* of transformational grace. For the news I receive on a regular basis from our colleagues at Panta Rhei is most encouraging. Only last week, he consented to the anointing of his brow with RNA-silencing chrism: thus wearing the first sign of his reconciliation to change – the bindi of the true Heraclitean flame.

Now I leave you to clamber into my ceremonial robes. It is that happy time of the year when I must read the ordinal for missionaries passing out of my care, and receive into the same a fresh consignment of polymorphous beings. Accept, dear brothers and sisters in transfiguration, my loving salutations.

Terence

Afterword:

Body Modification

Dr Nihal Engin Vrana
Division of Health Sciences and Technology, Harvard MIT

BODY MODIFICATION IS quite abundant in nature. Some animals and fungi go through several stages of life that do not resemble each other at all. The human experience is not quite like that: we grow steadily and reach an adult form which is more or less a larger version of the child's. The need to change is part of the human psyche and we often do so by modifying ourselves with ornaments. Although we have a popular culture of body modification (tattoos, piercings, etc), most of it is just a continuation of established traditional practices, while scientific body modification is mainly related to necessity and reconstructive surgery.

Current body modification therapies include prosthesis for amputees, retinal implants for the blind, skin grafts for burn and skin ulcer patients, and tracheostomy operations. In most cases, these inelegant solutions compare poorly to healthy tissue and entail a decrease in the quality of life. But this is changing fast. With the advent of tissue engineering and more sophisticated biodegradable implant designs, modifications are no longer stop-gap solutions. Currently, we can develop many tissues on the 'bench-top' and design implants that can degrade within the body and integrate with it in such a way that their presence will cease after a time to be discernible.

When our search for successful tissue and organ substitutes ends, as this story suggests, the turn of attention to other uses seems inevitable. Just as, over time, glasses and lenses – inventions of necessity to restore our vision – turned into accessories, so it is plausible to think that biomedical developments such as hydrogels, which are used for regenerative medicine as scaffolds for cell growth, or biosensors developed for diagnostics, can become fashion items for personal use. Current systems developed for replacing organs can also pave the way for new developments in reconstructive surgery, and can even make the process so easy that individuals with no medical expertise can perform the necessary operations – just as you can get a piercing or tattoo today. When this point is reached, we may see an exponential growth in the daily use of body modification and implant technology, which might also create a sub-culture just as advances in communications technology did. Which brings us to Gregory's vision of a cult assigning religious meaning to body modification, in a world already rocked by disaster.

A large-scale society make-over may indeed result from such implants, but we should bear in mind that their predecessors did not have such altering effects. For example, coming back to glasses, their presence did not create a push for 'better vision', where sophisticated glasses give their users superior senses. Do we have the technology to make such a device? Most probably, but it didn't happen. So there is a possibility that biomedical devices will not spill over too much beyond their intended area of usage. They might turn into fashion items, perhaps, or become voluntary necessities, the way the internet has done. Isn't the internet a must of our daily life? How many of us couldn't work efficiently without a mobile phone at the moment? Consider, for a moment, our global addiction to these communication technologies; it's not hard to picture a similar world-wide compulsion for other technologies.

Today, as far as sophisticated body modifications go, several full face transplants have already been made, and the design of artificial limbs has been enhanced for better performance in running. There has already been controversy over the utilisation of such artificial limbs in this year's Olympics, as they are considered to provide unfair advantage. We have subcutaneous devices that can release drugs on demand and techniques like collagen injections and Botox to re-shape our features. However, there remains an important obstacle to more widespread use of such technologies. The problem is that our bodies are not as willing to accept these changes as our minds are and they can respond to implants with a mechanism called foreign body response. Even though methods of controlling foreign body response constitute an active research area with important breakthroughs, this and other problems such as allergies, infections and permanent damage to the body, make high-scale body modification a fringe activity. Although, as I searched for background for this story to help Gregory, I came across some extensive modifications that I would never have imagined!

Developments in society may bring other changes to our bodies. After obsessing about beautification, our next obsession may very well concern functionality. We are currently able to build complex 3D implantable systems with live cells and materials, and to inject biomaterials into our body that can be controlled with outside stimuli; we have developed smart materials which can react to their surroundings, including inner-body environments. Moreover, these systems have reversible natures, which can circumvent the risks of current protocols that necessitate extensive intervention. As our understanding of the basis of the biological molecules has improved, we have developed synthetic materials from natural building blocks which can easily be better than their evolved counterparts. Developments in microfluidics and miniaturization have also brought in systems where diagnosis and sensoring can be done in very small volumes with extremely small devices.

Gregory's story catches the essence of such changes, exploring how the necessity of change can distort our values and beliefs until they become articles of faith. How possible is it to live in our age without believing in money or mortgages? When our body becomes the next landscape to build upon, why *shouldn't* we believe in the necessity of such alterations? What will happen to those who resist? Will they be just shunned or forced to comply, like poor Eugene Berenger, brought back to a life he dreaded by the technologies he despised? I find myself questioning my position as a developer of such technologies. I think that the greater the invasion on daily life allowed by such research, the more concerned the research community should be about the possible ramifications of its innovations. Otherwise, the sufferings of Eugene Berenger will be upon us.

Elegy For A Bio-Pirate

K. J. Orr

THORPE HEARS THE rumour scouting at a conference.

Recession-era conferences are something else; desperation in the air – ever more familiar faces gone and everyone trying to make their mark. That said, he is no different, and he stays close, skirts the edges, skulks by the refreshments tables outside meeting rooms waiting for the remaining players to re-emerge. He drinks so much coffee from the large silver urns that he gives himself heartburn.

In the evening, two pints and a chaser down at the hotel bar, a young researcher, Alex, starts talking.

Afterwards Thorpe goes back to his room – fills the pad of hotel paper that sits beside his bed with ink from the hotel pen; everything Alex has said. And then he does a giddy barefoot dance around his room, a solo conga across the carpet and onto the bed, looping around again, his socks brought into the mix, shaken to the right, to the left, the *Sha-Sha-Sha* of maracas in his head.

His notes, when he finds them in the morning, are an exuberant, barely legible scrawl. His lettering, in this moment of triumph, is large and expressive. His numbers – he has jotted projected revenue; a ten-year plan – are inspired flourishes that might even be described as poetic.

Prescience is what it was.

'Things are looking up,' he had said to one of his investors just the morning before, knowing it to be a bald lie, but needing more money, more time.

'Things are looking up,' he had said to his wife as he left

for the conference – as he backed out of the driveway of his double-mortgaged home. 'No need to worry anymore,' he had said. 'Everything is going to be just fine.'

New addiction treatments. Anti-virals. Not even half the story.

★

Two men and a girl.

When he finds them, at the falls, at Kaiteur, they are watching the water, and look like they are sculpted, they are so still. Small figures sitting on jagged cubes of rock close to the lip. When they notice him, they fling out their arms and beckon.

They are all younger than him by a stretch. The men are rangy, wearing shorts only. They are unhealthy looking, the line of their ribs showing under the skin, red welts covering their legs. Both have sun-bleached, white-blond hair, and are pale, could be twins. The girl is attractive, freckled, mid-thirties perhaps – older than them.

One of the men reaches out a gangly arm and slaps a clammy welcome onto Thorpe's palm. 'Hey man!' The other squints at him through a long fringe. 'You English?'

Thorpe nods. 'Just flew in from London. You're the first people I've seen since Georgetown. This country's deserted.'

Ahead of them, from the foot of the gorge, the river winds its way through the forest. Behind them, among reeds, at the head of the falls, the water slows to the point of stasis, looks as if it is barely moving, all silence, all stillness, before tumbling headlong.

'Fuck. Long time since I've seen London,' the man with the fringe says.

The girl gets to her feet now. 'These guys have been on the road three years.' She smiles, stretches and shakes his hand. 'I'm Clare.'

She is as Alex described: strawberry-blond hair, slim. She

106

has a determined cleft to the chin.

'Jim.'

'If you can believe it they are Tom and Jerry,' she says. 'I only met them last night. They might be winding me up.'

'Those are our names, man! Believe.'

'Tom.' The man with the fringe points to the other, poker-faced.

'Be seated Jim,' Tom says. 'You're among friends.'

They sit in silence a while, the four of them, while from the forest a rhythmic pulsing comes, like summer cicadas multiplied a thousand-fold. Far beneath them swifts are circling the flow of water, wheeling in and out of the vast black cavern scooped out of the rock behind the falls. Even further below, an iridescent green is clawing its way up the sheer walls of the gorge, thirsty for the torrent.

From the Cessna it had all looked unreal – that tide of green beneath him; and rivers, gleaming circuitous pathways, like veins sunk deep beneath the trees. Now, on the ground, he is part of it – still dressed for London, but breathing the warm, thick air, streaming sweat, shirt clammy against his back, humid socks.

He gets to his feet. 'I need a change of clothes,' he says. 'I'm going to the plane.'

'Shake off those city shoes,' Tom says. 'Absolutely necessary, man. Agreed.'

Clare walks with him, her route taking them past a lodge; it is white, wooden, stilted, with hammocks slung from the beams beneath.

She had flown in to the falls for an overnight stop the day before, and is due to make tracks; but plans change. A radio call comes in from a mining community close to the border with Brazil; a fight, a man whose face has been cut up with a machete needing urgent airlifting.

They watch the Cessna bump along the runway. Thorpe asks how long it will be. She shrugs.

When he wakes it is evening. He twists himself up and out of the hammock – sees the three of them, silhouettes around a fire.

He joins them mid-conversation. 'Stop scratching!' Tom is pestering the bites on his legs. 'I can't.'

'Sit on your hands,' Clare says.

'You don't know me well enough to say things like that.'

'Sit on your hands,' she says again, laughing.

They eat rice and dried shrimp and plaintain that the three of them had rigged over the fire while Thorpe was asleep. They have bottles of manioc beer, cool from the shallows among the reeds above the falls. They toast the pilot, Bernard, who had thought to leave them supplies.

Jerry wants to hear about home.

Thorpe describes the odd, summer warmth of November and the sudden pitch then in early December, the temperature dropping fifteen degrees one day to the next, and finally, the wind, the sleet, the hail.

'Did you have snow?' Tom asks.

'No snow.'

'I remember one year when I was a kid we had so much snow we had to dig ourselves out of our own home.'

'You're exaggerating,' Jerry says. 'I was there.'

A storm is flickering on the horizon and they walk a way towards the falls where the view opens up and they can watch – sheet lightning – the wide sky and the forest cast with a silvery glow.

Back at the camp, Clare prods the fire alive and starts boiling water for tea. Tom brings over a carry mat and sleeping bag. 'Show them your ankle, bro,' Jerry says. The skin is swollen, red.

'It's infected. I have something.' Clare gets to her feet and walks towards the lodge.

Thorpe wonders what she carries with her – it's possible she'll have her field notebook; she must take precautions when she goes on excursions away from the body of her work. A sample is what he needs.

'So how did you guys get here? Did Bernard drop you off?' he asks.

'We came overland. You get to Linden. You take a boat upstream. Two days. Mining country. Insane.'

Thorpe imagines himself walking out of Customs, up his driveway, and on through the door of his home.

His wife's arms are around him. They phone their daughter. Together they tell her that they will keep the house, she will stay on at St John's. They laugh when she snaps at them for talking over each other, for talking all at once.

'So why Guyana, Jim?' Jerry asks.

'Oh. I wanted to go somewhere that didn't have its own shelf in Waterstone's, I guess,' he says.

'Good man.'

He will offer Clare £10,000, lump sum. Living in the field is cheap. It will cover the cost of any materials she needs for years. She can publish – a paper on this in *Nature* or *Cell* and she'll be tenured for life.

'So you guys travelled all about?' he says.

'Been all over. Started in Argentina, worked our way up.'

'Ushuaia to ayahuasca,' says Jerry, with a smile.

'When are you going home?' he asks.

'Not yet,' Jerry shakes his head.

'Not for Christmas?'

'No way.'

Thorpe imagines the demoralised, downsized office of his small biotech company. There he stands – the sample held aloft in one hand. It is glowing like an Olympic flame.

While Clare is busy with tweezers – 'There's something in here. How could you not notice that? Keep still' – Tom is talking.

'In London,' he says, 'most people... you live in your little flat. You walk to the shops. You go through a whole day without even speaking with anyone.'

'There's a disconnect,' Jerry nods.

'There's a disconnect, man,' Tom says. 'You don't know your neighbours. You don't even try. You get their post by mistake, you sit on it. They get yours, they do the same. You don't exchange cups of sugar. You don't share details with each other of your background, your family, your favourite kind of cheese.'

'Hold still,' Clare says.

Tom holds himself still, continues. 'We had a family lived close by? The father worked in Dubai, somewhere like that – there was this big family of kids, all chi-chi, in the latest clothes, never saw him, wife doing all her nail bars, salons and shit – they had home help or whatever when the kids were back from school, but otherwise they all did their own thing. One Christmas, the father, he comes back, and after giving them all their little goodie bags of the usual pointless shit, and they don't thank him, as usual, he lines them up in front of the stockings hung from the mantelpiece that no doubt he's expected to fill later on – and he blows their brains out, one by one. Merry fucking Christmas.'

They all look at him. Clare holds the tweezers mid-air.

'That's not even true,' Jerry says.

Tom sighs. 'No.' He scratches at his leg, looking dazed, into the fire. 'But we went back, for Christmas, the end of our first year away? God. I remember walking off the plane into Heathrow, and everything was grey, and all these pinched little faces, all these downturned faces, like nothing was right with the world. Total lack of soul. Total disconnect. That's what I remember.' He pauses. 'And it was cold.'

'It was brutally fucking cold,' Jerry says.

'The whole experience was brutal, man.' Tom shakes his head vigorously, as if trying to erase the memory. 'We didn't even make it back home. Just turned around. Got the first flight back to Peru.'

'You experience that, you just can't go back,' Jerry says, with feeling. He takes the water, now boiling, off the fire.

Thorpe becomes aware that Clare is looking at him. 'They're talking about yajé. Ayahuasca,' she says. 'They went to one of those psychotropic centres in Peru. You heard about these?'

He has. Of course.

The vine had been used forever by indigenous groups, but the tourism was recent – the centres that had sprung up over the Amazon, the spiritual workouts, personal quests. Not just gap-year kids and trust funders, but pilgrims seeking cures – to cancer, addiction. Too often these centres were run by mestizo shaman blowing cultural smoke, selling it as science.

But now is not the time. He gives a non-committal half-nod.

'Shall I be Mum?' Jerry pours the water into tin mugs.

'Ayahuasca's not like anything you'd get in London?' Thorpe asks. He allows himself this.

'I don't think you'd find yajé in London,' Tom says. 'But even if you could, you wouldn't take it there.'

'Right, right, right,' says Jerry. 'There's a process. It's part of this whole thing – the journey, the shaman, the ritual. It's not like popping a pill. I don't know how to tell you. It's like you're plugged back into the universe. You feel humble, but you feel connected to something so much larger than yourself.' He turns to his brother. 'Can you imagine taking yajé in London?'

111

Thorpe had written a paper as a PhD student debunking lazy offshoots of pharmacology; numb-headed cultural misappropriations. 'Herbal Voodoo,' he'd called it.

'Shit,' Tom says. 'Like, in Peru, you're channelling jaguars and anacondas and eagles. In London, it'd be like, Trafalgar Square pigeons. It'd be the most horrible nightmare. Evil pink eyes and skanky feathers. And you'd be channelling rodents, and earthworms. City earthworms. Dirty. Squashed.'

'Earthworms far from the earth,' Jerry says.

Clare holds up a splinter about an inch long. 'How could you not notice that?' She gives it to Tom. 'You could almost wear it around your neck. Like a shark's tooth.'

How many jobs are there where you can speculate, where you can dream of some drug just waiting to be found? Who wouldn't want that job?

You plug into something universal, work out the essential, the part that's transferable: that is the challenge, right there.

You get to change the future. You make people's lives immeasurably better.

What we have here – he tells his audience of investors, scientists, medics, psychiatrists – is unprecedented.

They are on their feet.

In the rush of water passing over the falls he hears the sound of wild applause.

*

He wakes in the night in a cold sweat, his hammock tight around him. His hands had been folded on his chest as he slept and the feeling has gone right out of them. Unholy sounds from the forest. 'Hello?' he says. 'Is anyone awake?'

He sits up, eyes open, looking out into the dark. Floating – just visible – drifting – vulnerable – a hammock slung mid-air.

112

Failure hovers in the night, black-beaked, suspended on the currents. It crawls in the skin on his back, up his neck. It makes its way deep into his chest.

He tries to focus on his breathing, slow it down, but hears a cry like pain, a howl, close by, high up.

A howl.

★

Early morning; Tom and Jerry are asleep.

Standing at the edge of the clearing, urinating, Thorpe sees mist hanging low over the forest and the falls. Down through the gorge, the succession of hills are semi-obscured. Some distance away, he sees a glimmer of water, a bend in the river.

She appears out of nowhere, picking her way beside the river, hair wet and hanging in long strands down her back. A small silver ring on one toe; flip-flops; a t-shirt and sarong.

Quickly, he zips himself up. He is staring, unprepared. Wrong-footed, he just starts talking.

'I know who you are,' he says. He is aware of a creepy smile playing on his lips, but finds it hard to stop.

There is a way this conversation is supposed to go. They would sit together, at ease – a bar in Georgetown would be best, a couple of beers, music playing, a bowl of nuts. This is what he was good at. They would talk quietly, confidentially, but they would be relaxed.

He could see it.

She's open, curious. He gives her his card. GaiaJen BioTech Limited.

Why GaiaJen? She's polite – she's nice. She asks the obvious question.

Those are the names of my girls – my wife and daughter – warmth in his eyes, pride.

That's just lovely, she says.

And things are off to a good start.

But this is not how it plays.

She speaks slowly; her voice is cool. 'What is it you're hoping to find here, Jim?'

The way she says his name, it is remade into a small, crude object and put down between them on the ground. He has the impression that it wouldn't take much for her to get to her feet and with one deft kick send him over the edge, into the ravine.

It is unfolding like a chilly dream.

'How did you find me?' she asks before he's even had a chance to respond. 'Who told you where I was?'

The clamminess. The unpleasant stickiness of his clothes.

'It was surprisingly easy. Everyone knows everyone, right?' He tries to project relaxation in his voice, to conjure the beers and the bowl of nuts.

'Did you go to the village?' she asks. 'Did you look for me there?'

Even with a flight to the nearest settlement, the village was a good way further off.

'No. No. No. You saved me the trek,' he says. 'For which I am eternally grateful.' He would have done it, but he'd have needed a guide, proper supplies. He'd had visions of himself lost in the forest.

She could smile, but she doesn't. Instead she repeats the question. 'Have you been to the village? I need you to be honest with me.'

'No,' Thorpe says. 'You're here. I found you here. I came straight from Georgetown.' He tries to maintain a level of bonhomie, imagines music in the background. 'I'm flattered that you see me as such a Jungle Joe – I'm really not.'

'You have to understand,' she says, 'my work in the village is a matter of trust.'

She has to be cautious. He tries to project a look of understanding: of course, of course.

'This is not a conversation I should even be having,' she says.

In the bar in Georgetown, the fans are slowly rotating overhead as he tells her he can help her with funding, as he tells her she will be acknowledged, down the line. We could even name it after you, he says. She's sipping her cool beer and smiling.

Instead though, they are talking about Alex. She is angry; it lights up her face.

'I don't know why he said what he said, but I have nothing to share. I wouldn't take your money. I don't deal with people like you.'

'A new brew of ayahuasca,' Thorpe says. 'Psychotropic. Serotonergic. Anti-viral. Bark – a new compound in bark.'

'How do you know he didn't make it up?'

'If you're in talks with someone else…' Thorpe says.

'About smuggling hallucinogens? Importing them? What?'

'You have this anti-viral – the Schedule One ban will be dropped for it. It will open things up. What is it you want?' he asks.

'Please.' She raises a hand now, gets to her feet.

'Just tell me what it is you want,' he says. 'I'm here to find a way to make this work.'

He follows close behind as she makes her way back towards the camp – can see the patch of sweat where the t-shirt clings to the small of her back; the fine hairs on her neck.

'You'll be having this conversation with someone soon enough,' he says. 'The Schedule One ban will be dropped.'

'There is no conversation. The knowledge isn't even mine to sell.'

Thorpe idles at the edge of the forest, looking on from a distance as Clare talks Tom and Jerry through their route – map held aloft and flat against the wall of the lodge. He walks over, finally, when it is clear they are about to make a move.

A sticky silence descends when, for a moment, they both watch the men picking their way towards the trail, and then Clare turns and walks away.

He is alone at the lodge, where their two hammocks hang side by side.

He unzips every pocket in her rucksack, pulls out every last thing – opens plastic bags of clothes, toiletries, and zip-lock bags with first aid, torch and batteries.

He is sitting, eating his way through an emergency packet of dried fruit and nuts when she returns.

'I was hungry,' he says – her belongings beside him, piled up.

He is surprised to see her smiling. 'Was it my underwear you wanted?' she asks. 'Or a small good thing to put in your pocket and take home?'

She props the emptied-out rucksack up against her legs and starts to sort through the mess. 'You think I'm going to carry samples?'

Thorpe sits quietly humiliated.

'Hand them out like gum?' she says. 'Sorry to disappoint you. But nothing leaves the village. It's a condition of my being there.'

'You make a find like this and you sit on it? Isn't the aim to get the drugs on the shelves?'

Clare is pushing her clothes back into their bags now. 'It doesn't belong anywhere in the world apart from in that settlement,' she says.

'Then I fail to understand the point of what you do.' Thorpe is starting to feel dizzy.

'The point is to protect the community.' She finishes repacking; props the rucksack against one of the stilts and straightens up. She holds out one hand. 'Shall I take that?' Thorpe's fingers tighten around the pack of fruit and nuts.

'It's really not that hard to comprehend,' she says. 'You let the outside in there's a change of perception, a degradation. The women leave, go to the city, marry outside the tribe – the community vanishes overnight, and everything is lost, all that knowledge. No one knows any more that this plant or this leaf is the right one. You can't let the world in, there, you just can't.'

'So smuggle it out.'

'You're incredible.' She is shaking her head in disbelief.

'You have a responsibility,' he says. There is a crawling in his skin, clawing in his chest.

Clare reaches into her hammock, retrieves the water-swollen, dog-eared book Tom has left.

'It's not like you can be here and not have an effect. You're the outside,' Thorpe says.

'I do my best. I show respect.'

It is a black-winged thing. Hovering.

'So that's it?' he says.

The hairs on his arms are up.

She picks up her bottle of water, and her sun block, and a bandana for her neck.

'People's lives could be different,' he says. 'What you're hiding here could make a difference.'

But she isn't listening.

I'm untouchable, her smooth brown calves sing. She is blithely swinging her legs – fearless; intact. As easy as that. She walks away from him.

As easy as that.

He imagines the moment of impact; rock on skull, her silly bandana blooming red.

Stop. He tells himself. Enough.

He follows the river upstream, watching the reflection. Land meets sky in a watery embrace, the wall of trees folds in.

He takes off his shoes and his socks, leaves them on a rock.

Closer to the bank the water is slow, but further out, he feels something like a tug, as if he's hitched his wagon to a freight train and is being pulled along. He swims a while, and then just lies flat, stretches his arms out to either side – up above him the empty sky – lets the current carry him, watches with detached amusement as his trouser legs inflate, looking like puffed up waterwings.

He isn't prepared for just how shallow the water will get before it reaches the lip. He feels the bottom against his back, tries to flip over to see where he is and what needs to be done but finds it too shallow even for that: dry season. He pushes himself onto his knees, and sits, surveying the scene.

He is still a few feet from the edge. The noise seems far away. Reeds nudged lazily in slow-flow currents, side to side.

Now he stands, takes it all in – the gorge dead ahead in its glory, emerald green rolled out like a carpet covering the land. A few steps and he is almost at the edge, on the brink, the slow waters at his ankles, the slick reeds beneath his feet.

From the bank – a commotion unrelated – no need to turn his head. Just focus on edging forward. Motion now, arms waved in the air. He doesn't really care but he turns to look. She is shouting at him, her mouth in odd distortions, looking like a crazy person. He cannot hear a word.

Afterword:

Ethnopharmacology

Dr Ian Vincent McGonigle
Department of Anthropology, University of Chicago

SOME OF THE Western world's most successful drugs have come from plant sources: quinine, taxol, ephedrine and digoxin to name a few; and more than a third of the world's top-selling drugs are either natural products or their derivatives. Amazonia is a particularly good 'hot-spot' for finding such bioactive material, as plants living in tropical forest habitats contain lots of chemicals, mostly to protect themselves from viral and fungal infection, as well as from animal and insect predators. One of the most famous drugs to come from Amazonia is 'curare', an arrowhead poison used by indigenous peoples for hunting. Due to its useful paralytic effects, curare became instrumental in the development of the general anaesthetic in Western medicine. Curare blocks the acetylcholine receptors that initiate muscle contraction and this discovery, and the pharmacology studies that followed, ultimately led to the development of the modern muscle relaxants that are now used by anaesthesiologists in medical surgery. In Amazonia however, 'medicine' is usually practised by shamans (local healers), and it is usually the shamans that hold the most knowledge of which plants have toxic/therapeutic value, how to find them, and how to use them most effectively.

The task of finding such drugs is the object of ethnopharmacology. Ethnopharmacology practice may thus be defined as 'the search for new drugs from traditional medicine', placing it at the nexus of natural product pharmacology and social anthropology – being concerned with 'social' and 'biological' issues conjunctively. And for ethnopharmacologists looking to find 'new' drugs in Amazonia, gaining privileged access to shamans' local knowledge is often essential. As the current laws protecting indigenous knowledge allow researchers and companies to claim intellectual property rights over biological resources and traditional knowledge once they have been 'slightly modified', 'illegitimate' plundering of such knowledge has led to the coining of the term 'bio-piracy', used to designate those adventurer scientists who go off-the-grid seeking to find 'wonder-drugs' in traditional societies, hoping to take a sample away with them back to their commercial or academic laboratories. Sufficient modification for legal proprietorship may be as little as a subtle alteration to the chemical structure of the active compound or the use of a semi-synthetic chemical analogue (a slightly modified version of the original compound). And so bio-pirates may only need a small sample in order to identify the chemical structure of a 'wonder drug' – if one were found...

In K. J. Orr's story, the mysterious 'wonder drug' is reputedly *like* Ayahuasca but with some bark extract additive. Ayahuasca is a particularly important Amazonian medicine. It is a hallucinogenic brew that has been utilised in rituals by indigenous and mestizo Amazonian people for over 300 years. Ayahuasca is usually composed of two plants: a vine (*Banisteriopsiscaapi*) and leaves of the *Psychotriaviridis* bush, which contain a psychoactive compound called DMT (a close analogue of the natural neurotransmitter serotonin). These leaves and vines are boiled in water for over ten hours and a dark, bitter viscous preparation is produced, ayahuasca, which is traditionally drunk during shaman-led rituals. The brew causes hallucinations or 'visions' during which participants may have a 'spiritual transformation' or undergo 'spiritual growth' or 'healing'. Visions may at times be extremely distressful as well as euphoric and insightful and the shaman plays a central role in guiding the participant throughout the ritual. Other plant or animal materials may be added to the ayahuasca brew during its preparation however, and these different ayahuasca brews may be used differentially to target specific illnesses.

In the story, there is an anti-viral compound addition that can be extracted from tree bark. This is perfectly scientifically possible: Tree bark, in particular, is known to contain bioactive compounds in order to stave off infection (for example, quinine[2]). Moreover, such additions to the ayahuasca brew are not without precedent: Mestizo Shamans in Amazonia are known to 'experiment' with different animal and plant material additions in their ayahuasca preparations. Furthermore, as referred to in the story, there is a growing body of mainstream scientific evidence that hallucinogens may be beneficial in the treatment of depression; and indeed, ayahuasca has also been used to treat addiction in several clinics in South America. The molecular basis that underlies any possible therapeutic effects from psychedelics such as ayahuasca has not yet been fully elucidated, but scientists agree that such psychedelic drugs mimic the natural serotonin molecules that are involved in mood, perception and reward signaling in the brain. By stimulating the same types of pathways – via serotonin receptor and transporter proteins – such 'serotonergic' drugs may hold potential for the treatment of related psychological disorders, such as depression and addiction, or indeed for the development of related therapeutics and practices. There thus remains great opportunity for Western science to find a truly transferrable medicine that could be globally used in medicine...

In light of these exciting possibilities, it is important to bring into question the ethical problems that inhere in the development of 'novel' medications through the utilisation of indigenous, traditional medical knowledge. In particular: does

2. Quinine originated from the bark of *Cinchona* trees. Originally used by the Quechua of Peru and Bolivia, quinine was first brought from South America to Europe by Jesuit missionaries. Quinine was widely used to treat malaria in the West, until its replacement by synthetic analogues in the 1940s. Quinine interferes with the reproductive cycle of *Plasmodium falciparum*, the causative agent of malaria. See also pp. 47–67.

anybody exclusively own such knowledge or is indigenous knowledge just 'local common sense' of no particular value? Should an indigenous medicine belong to the community forever, or should the drugs of tropical forests be considered the common heritage of all of mankind? Should indigenous people be rewarded for their role in drug development? Or could their very recruitment in the drug discovery process disrupt their communities irreversibly, as has been the case in past interventions by missionaries, forest loggers and colonial elites? These are big questions that should be tackled through interdisciplinary research spanning social, biological and philosophical schools; good bio-ethics necessitates such collaborative efforts.

Flesh and Blood

Simon Van Booy

I WAITED FOR David in the place we had agreed at twilight. November is a month of long nights. I leaned on the dark wall that runs the length of the Embankment. Pigeons pecked at the ground in small groups. The river was high because of heavy rain, and it swallowed the low stone steps from long ago, when currents of people had moved along the river's shoulders, working, eating, and washing their clothes. I imagined people stopping on the steps to talk, children sitting, watching boats, wondering what their lives would be like, worried about small things. David liked to speak of those times, long ago − when the only way to learn anything was by talking with others. To love someone then, he said, you didn't need to match them in any way, nor have any common interests − or even be attracted to them. The only qualification was that you simply couldn't be apart.

I attended university from home, and never actually met my fellow students and teachers. Now that I'm a few years out, I think I would have liked to walk around the park with other students after lectures, saying whatever came into my mind − even if I regretted it later. I told David when we first met a few weeks ago, that I yearn for a life of mistakes.

Waiting for him at the water's edge, it would have been easier for me to climb down onto one of the lion's heads, and then jump into the Thames − rather than confess the truth of how I had been deceiving him. I leaned over the wall and looked at the water. I saw my body in the air. He would arrive amidst the commotion. People shouting and pointing at the river. A woman has fallen in. A woman has been carried off. And the people who saw it, who watched until I was too far away to see, would then have to carry me for the rest of their lives.

David once said that to feel compassion for someone you dislike means you are truly free.

We've been together for three weeks – which doesn't seem like very long, but if you've ever had a love affair, try and remember those first days, when the measure was feeling rather than time.

We were supposed to meet last night, but I couldn't face him because I've been lying about who it is I am. I knew he'd be worried when I didn't show up. Before going to bed I sent him a message saying I'd got tied up at work, and was now *collapsing* into bed. I told him I hoped it was a good performance. He wrote back in the morning to say he was sorry we missed each other. He said he'd tried to contact me several times – that he didn't actually see the show because he was waiting outside the concert hall – worried, he said, in case I needed him or was stranded. I wrote and told him how nice it was of him to think of me like that. I wanted to keep it light until I could think of a way to confess. I imagined him walking around Covent Garden. Everything would have been closing. I thought of him in that long coat he wears, walking slowly in the midst of a defeat, wondering where I was – not yet ready to go home to his empty flat.

He called in the afternoon and I felt I had to talk to him. I tried to sound cheerful, and apologised again for not showing up at the opera.

He accused me of holding back.

I told him it was difficult to explain on the telephone.

'So there is something.'

I didn't reply. Then a lorry passed outside, rattling the windows.

'What was that?'

'It was a lorry,' I said with a smile, then: 'What do you mean I've been holding back?'

'Your text message last night was like we were colleagues or something – vague acquaintances.'

FLESH & BLOOD

It was one of the things I loved about him – how he was always *feeling* things. It was something I hadn't been raised to do. I explained how I'd always considered myself thoughtful, but David said that was different – even opposite, he said.

I was holding back for the same reason women had held back for centuries – because I had already gone too far. I was happy, but not yet ready to be vulnerable. After I met him, I called my mother and alluded to things, hoping she'd catch on and give me some advice. She claimed that it was impossible to be happy in a world of constant risk. Anyone who claimed to be happy was lying, as the feeling of happiness is accompanied by the unbearable fear that life ends, and so better to be safe, alone, and chronically disappointed, than happy, afraid, and unavoidably vulnerable.

I disagreed. Fear sharpened my sense of the world around me, which is why, even in school, I was attracted to boys with low numbers like 2:1 and 3:2.

I found out my own genetic score when I was 15, like everyone else.

I tried to keep it to myself, but my computer was hacked, and soon everyone knew my PF (probable fate). Some of the girls in the class teased me by leaving photographs of very old women on my desk. Perhaps as a reaction, I began living dangerously – running into the road, cycling like a mad person, without a helmet even – but it was all caught on CCTV, and I was suspended from school for a week, and then sent for SER (self-endangerment reassessment) at the local library, where all the books had been pulped, and in place of the shelves – hundreds of computers.

David was a 3:1. The first number meaning that sometime in his thirties, he will probably die from a disease caused by some mutant gene in his body. The second number in the score corresponding to the nature of the death. One is the worst you can get – which means excruciating pain, while 10 means peaceful, probably while asleep. The scale runs from 1 to 10. A 10:10 means you will live until you are 100 (or longer) and then die pleasantly. A 10:1 means you will live until you are 100, but die in excruciating pain.

125

A 1:1 is the worst score anybody can get and means a horrible, terrifying death within months. Most people die in this category before they get tested. 15 is the age when the required testing takes place — to be assessed before is considered inhumane, as children are too young to know how to cope with a PDD (probable death day). Many people are proud of their PDD, and some even get tattoos with the time and date.

The boys I was attracted to at school were twos, and threes. They attended special classes and learned about Buddhism, reincarnation, limbo, purgatory, spontaneous transmigration, and all the other historical theories of the human spirit that were supposed to improve quality of life until there was no more life. These kids had their own section of the cafeteria, but often spent lunchtimes in the woods behind the school, smoking cigarettes and listening to Chopin or The Smiths. The children who were doomed to die young grew their hair long and carried around poems by Keats — who scientists now say was an obvious 1:1, but who lived longer than expected.

My mother said that when she was my age, the testing was unregulated, and you could go out with someone, swipe their water glass or serviette, and then have them secretly tested. You could *even* get what was called, a Speculation Report (SR), which gave information about future health and personality traits based on lifestyle, diet, and environment.

When I got my results at 15, my parents admitted how they had once got their DNA sequenced in full for fun. Dad's said that if he ate too much red meat, he'd be prone to driving faster, and likely to die in a fiery ball in his fifties. My mother said her report claimed that if she didn't eat enough vitamin B12, she would develop an urge to smash eggs.

I met David on a dating website called, Threes-a-crowd. com.

The members of this website are all doomed in their thirties, but this was the best group in my opinion. Men in this category are known for not being afraid to make commitments or to follow through on ideas and desires.

My score came out as a 9:9. My parents were pleased, but admitted that people would see me as a timewaster – or not worth getting to know, because they'd be dead before me. There was also the question of money. I would need enough for at least another 75 years, which would mean a life in the suburbs of a city like Milton Keynes, or Gillingham.

You can imagine how depressed I was.

When I finished university, I was lonely, and so began to follow online dating communities. After observing the different groups for several months, I found the courage to actually join, and then a few months after that, actually got invited to a physical meeting for the people I felt most connected to in the 3:1 to 3:10 range.

I met David in the first hour of the meeting. He brought me a cup of water and asked if I knew any specifics. I told him that it would be a water related death and we both laughed.

He walked me home that night.

According to my fake DNA profile, I only had a few years left – maybe even months.

After accusing me of holding back over the telephone, David insisted that we meet. He wanted an explanation.

I suggested the Tate Neo-Modern – where talking about the art was forbidden. He laughed and said, 'Let's walk the Embankment.'

I spent the rest of the afternoon imagining us walking forever – like those great travelers of the deserts. David said there was a time when people knew nothing of their bodies, and didn't even have names for things that now dictate the quality of our lives. He said that anatomy first began on the ancient battlefields. Before then, he said, we were as spiritual as the animals, and our lives a blend of impulse and divine will. I told him that it must have been frightening – nobody knowing when they would die. He put his arm around me, and said, 'But darling we still don't know, really when it will happen – I could choke on an olive pit during an episode of *Big Brother: Moon Colony*.'

In his opinion, the luckiest people were those who'd been scored incorrectly, and so instead of dying within a few years, they lived for decades with the spirit that every day could be their last.

It was also easier to get a job if you had a low score, because employers knew that instead of having to fire people, they could simply wait for them to die.

As I waited for David, I had the sense that he would want to break up. He'd say that he couldn't bear the thought of me going through 50 years of grief for a few years of happiness for him.

Then he would just walk away, and I'd be alone.

He arrived early, out of breath. We held each other for a long time. I could feel the drivers watching us as they waited at a red light.

'Tell me everything,' he said.

At first I couldn't say anything. When there were no other people in the distance, I said:

'It's bad news.'

'Oh no,' he said. 'How long?'

'It's actually the opposite problem. I'm not a three.'

David stared at me in horror.

'I'm a nine,' I said. 'I've been lying to you and to myself.'

'Jesus, that's really great news – it means you're going to live a long time.'

But I could tell he was upset.

'It's awful,' I said. 'Longevity is ruining my life.'

For a moment he just stared. Then he looked away, and I saw the breath escape his body in a column of mist that quickly disappeared.

'It's cold isn't it?' he said.

'I just wanted to meet people who valued life more.'

David looked at the river. It was high and heavy. In the distance, the lights of a disused factory were held, flickering – on the surface of the water.

'You don't know what it's like...' I went on, '...you don't know how dull and lifeless people in good health are. They're like zombies, unable to make any decisions.'

Then just when I thought he would walk away – he reached his arm over my shoulders. It felt good to be touched.

'You're not the first person to have done this.'

'I'm not?'

I was surprised and I tried to picture from our group who I thought might be deceiving us.

'You'll have to leave,' he said. 'To make way for real young women with nothing to lose.'

We walked for most of the night.

Electric school buses hummed at red lights. Since the population increase, schools operated on a 24-hour basis. Children were given times to attend, but were also permitted to attend a certain amount of classes via their game consoles.

By midnight, we were still walking. It turned out that David had been given his score directly from the British Council of Social Justice, a government organization set up to advise people in the following categories:

(i) those people whose results have caused confusion, depression, and suicidal thoughts;

(ii) those citizens who have been living with *incorrect* scores;

(iii) those people whose environments have negated their scores (i.e. people who have contracted deadly diseases);

(iv) those strange cases where a person had outlived themselves by more than a decade or more.

David told me how he was born prematurely, and in his case the problems were serious. He was scored immediately, and the result was not good. A 0:0: horrible, violent death within the hour.

I cried when he told me this, and he looked guilty as if it were his fault. So we stopped talking for a while and went to a coffee shop. In the bright interior, David said it was actually the best thing that could have happened.

'But how can you be happy?' I insisted. 'How can you live not knowing the sort of life you'll probably have and how you'll probably die?'

David thought for a moment. 'But I'm happy, and I just hope every day that I keep going.'

'Haven't they tried to rescore you?'

'Who cares?' he said, his face flushed with anger.

'But you could die tomorrow? Why aren't you freaking out?'

'Why aren't you?'

'Because it's not supposed to happen to me – it wasn't on my report.'

'The reports are only a narrow corridor of possible certainties.'

'What does that mean?'

'I mean that the reports can't tell you how to be happy.'

'Then who can, David? Who can?'

The woman who served us took off her apron and helped herself to a piece of cake from a glass cabinet. Then she took a clean fork from one of the tables and sat at the counter.

'Just shout if you want something,' she said.

'So?' I said. 'Who can tell me how to be happy?'

We finished our coffee and went back to my flat, where we made love on the couch, with our clothes half-on.

I left the group a week later and saw David only twice again after that. The first time was for coffee near where the group met.

The second time was 25 years later.

I was with my husband in the car.

Our son had just left for university in America. We were stopped at a red light on the Embankment, and there he was, my David, doomed to die at any second, walking slowly with a woman just a bit younger than himself, in her early forties. They were holding hands, and looked happy.

When I told my husband the whole story, about the group I'd joined, and about David, he seemed interested, and said he had thought of doing it himself.

And then I confessed what a miracle it was that someone fated to die so young had lived so long. My husband burst out laughing.

Afterword:

Personal Genomics

Dr Ian Vincent McGonigle
Department of Anthropology, University of Chicago

VAN BOOY'S STORY depicts a world in which 'disease' is defined in terms of expected death, as something that is pre-scripted and pre-determined far in advance of any immediately *experienced* – or real world – suffering or 'illness'. And as we have seen with the story's characters, such predictions are not without real effects on how one lives and feels about one's life and health.

So as to paint a picture of where biomedicine presently stands, I will briefly trace the developments that have unfolded over the last sixty years, locating the current capabilities of molecular-genetic medicine in its correct scientific, cultural and epistemic genealogy. As a potentiality then, genetic medicine may be said to have begun with the elucidation of the structure of DNA, achieved by Watson and Crick in Cambridge in 1953. They revealed DNA's double-helical structure and with that intimated a hypothetical function for it as the self-replicating substance of which genes are made. Following on from their discovery, the 1970s saw rapid advances in the ways that DNA could be precisely manipulated, and the broader field of molecular biology gave birth to recombinant DNA technology, revolutionising the basic biosciences by allowing DNA to be routinely mutated and artificially engineered – rendering possible the cloning and recombination of genes in ways that had not previously been possible. DNA had thus become a malleable and fungible material, and scientists had developed the tools to work it with dexterity. With further extension of these manipulative capacities, 'biotechnology' became one of the fastest growing industries in the 1980s; and in the 1990s – in the lead-up to the sequencing of the human genome – there was much speculation about the implications of uncovering the human genetic code and what it could make possible. So much so that researchers in several countries made plans to create genomic databases or 'gene banks', built up from citizens' genetic material – provided by volunteers, patients and the general public. And in several countries (including Britain, Sweden and Iceland), researchers promised that these data would reveal the genetic basis of many diseases, and that this knowledge would eventually lead to new diagnostic and therapeutic products. In 2001 then, with the first publication of the sequence of the human genome, there was great hope (and hype) around this promise of developing cures for many of the diseases afflicting mankind...

Running in parallel to these basic scientific developments in molecular genetic technology, since the 1950s there has also been a transformation in the way that human health is both perceived and detected in the clinic. Pre-WWII, disease was something that generally presented itself as a disruption in experienced daily wellness, where patients typically went to their doctors complaining about an experienced problem – they *felt* unwell or sick, and could identify the ailment by its effects on how they felt. With the advent of biochemical analysis and molecular diagnostics, disease recognition underwent a tectonic shift. From once being a mostly qualitative system of symptom presentation and self-directed description – reported by the patients' own experience of illness – there was born a more quantitative regime of risk detection, where patients became classed as being *at risk*, possibly long before they felt unwell. Nowadays in the 'developed world', patients regularly attend medical check-ups, and are indeed commonly determined to be at risk from diseases that have yet to show any sign of existence. Consider for example the crucial bio-indicators of high blood pressure, blood plasma cholesterol or blood glucose metabolism; these are all commonly employed as biomarkers of being at risk for the potential development of heart disease, diabetes and similar diseases of the so-called Western lifestyle. Screening for these biomarkers, often far in advance of any experienced illness, now forms the basis of a standard medical exam. Being classed as having 'hypercholesterolemia' or 'high-blood pressure' – invisible and unfelt indications that may or may not lead to the development of a specific disease – one is thus classed as being 'at risk'. While these preemptive strategies have greatly reduced the incidence of premature deaths from what are now treatable and gratefully avoidable life-curtailing diseases, they also bring with that enhanced longevity a preventative medical logic, with the potential for an extension of the experience of 'illness' into the domain of what was once a 'healthy', if at risk, life. Indeed, symptomless biomarkers can now be experienced as a disease in itself or as its looming onset; and while the benefits of some preemptive treatments are not in doubt, such movements also result in global pharmaceutical and therapeutics corporations aiming to progressively lower the scientifically published thresholds for being 'at risk' so that more people can be medically classed as at risk, thereby increasing the pool of candidates available for medication, and with that, boosting their long-term prescription sales. Patients may therefore now experience illness as a risk category – and be medicated for that risk – far in advance of any symptomatic experience; and precisely because of this transformation in 'illness experience', many people now take precautionary medications in order to prevent illness that would actually only occur in a small percentage of the total drug-taking cohort. These patients are medicated precisely because they all fall into an identifiable, *quantitative* risk category that is generally and statistically defined, but subjectively indeterminable.

This *transformation* in illness experience is critical to the way we approach Van Booy's dystopia, which is the ultimate and grotesque extension of this type of preventative logic: a world where one's medical fate becomes an inescapable burden that one is expected to live in accordance with. A prognosis for medical diagnostics that marks people with a certain probability of being alive at a particular juncture in the future – presumably based on how long other people considered to be in similar demographic and genetic groups have lived for – configures a world where people live their lives by relating their lived experience of the world to the most probable arrival time of their death, defining 'life' then as a morbid temporal state of being that dialectically affirms its very essence from 'not dying'.

One problem militating against such a scenario is the fact that diseases are usually multifactorial and can rarely be identified as the consequence of a single gene in a perfectly predictable way. There are some exceptions to this, particularly with rare 'Mendelian' diseases such as Huntington's, for example. Huntington's is an inherited neurodegenerative disease that is already somewhat predictable (the child of a person with a copy of the mutated *huntingtin* gene has a 50% chance of developing the disease). Such diseases, with the possibility of their early detection and with their high probability of leading to the disease, do indeed raise ethical questions, particularly as to whether one should know early in life if one is likely to develop the disease. But these 'Mendelian' diseases are by far the exception, and most of the Western world's most common diseases cannot be causally linked to a single specific gene.

So, given the current capabilities of DNA- and genomic technologies, could a person really have their personal genome analysed and correlated with statistical probabilities for a whole population so as to come up with a reliable index of healthiness, projected longevity, or even an estimated time of death? Well, steps have already been taken to attempt to make whole population genome analysis a powerful predictor of health and disease. Indeed, 'personal genomics' is a growing industry, offering people the opportunity to have their own genome sequenced and have the results analysed in order to identify individual differences in 'normal' and 'disease-associated' regions and gene sequences. Such services are now commercially accessible to 'healthy' individuals, and the US-based company Illumina, for example, offers a personal genome sequencing service at a price of $19,500 (as of October 2011), with discounts offered to groups of five or more. Individuals identified to have variations in certain genes could possibly be associated with a higher 'risk' of developing certain diseases when compared to individuals without such variants, but these kinds of associations are unlikely to have any powerful or reliable predictive capacity on an individual basis alone. Indeed, since it is rarely a one-gene-per-disease relationship, personal genomics research aims in the future to map the interactions of many or possibly even all of the genes in the genome in order to map their complex, global interactions in the possible cause – or pre-disposition in the development – of diseases. Such efforts demand the coupling of genome analyses to long-term family medical records, making the task a long-term project. This strategy has yet to produce any conclusive evidence as to its effectiveness and reliability, but such a breakthrough would certainly mark an epistemic rupture and a tremendous overhaul of the capacities of genetic medicine. Having said that, it will likely remain that, more than genetics, individuals are far more susceptible to the varying and un-mappable influences of chance, changing environment, lifestyle, and possibly above all, individuals' own agency in the ultimate outcome of their personal health and illness.

The story's parodic future world, in which health and illness are categorically predetermined by one's genetic code is therefore both amusing and shocking. While no statistical prediction of longevity could ever stake a claim to a pre-destined fate that is absolutely 'true' for an individual, the story still manages to shock because it offers a glimpse of a world where certain freedoms are taken away: namely the freedom to determine and control one's own health; the perception of one's health; and how one 'feels' about one's own future. In this era of post-genomic mythology – despite the objective limits of genetic-medicine to predict real, lived experience – *claims* to genetic fate may well end up functioning as a mysterious but compelling imperative – an invisible threat one would only foolishly ignore.

Story Time

Sean O'Brien

June 1st

IT IS EARLY summer. There is a metalled single-lane road that turns into a track and tilts downhill into the woods. Once I am in the woods the water becomes visible, a great reach of it with a scatter of islands. I suspect – I have no map – that the large forested area a quarter of a mile away may itself be an island, which in turn provokes the possibility that where I stand might be an island too. But this cannot be so, surely. I seem to remember that I arrived overland.

At the foot of the track is a clearing set back a little way from the water's edge, and in the clearing stand a whitewashed farm cottage and one or two half-derelict looking sheds. A tabby cat slinks away at my approach and watches from behind a birch tree.

Although it is summer a curl of smoke rises from the cottage chimney. The door is open. I knock but no one answers. Hesitantly I put my head round the door. Beyond lies the dim kitchen – the heavy varnished table with its loaf and board and knife, a family Bible with a place marked deep in the Old Testament, the cavernous fireplace giving out slightly too much heat, the ugly dresser with its ugly carved flower-patterns. The whole apparatus of nameless provincial life, halfway between Balzac and Perrault. The clock, in pride of place on the dresser, ticks. It is just before noon. I look at the marked verse of scripture: *yea, also the heart of the sons of men is full of evil, and madness is in their heart while they live, and after that they go to the dead.*

On the far side of the kitchen a further door stands slightly open. It is clear what I must do, but this is as far I as I want or feel able to go. I turn to leave.

June 3rd

'Mixing memory and desire.' Who said that? I should remember. But I should not desire and, ergo, should not remember, either.

The library is wholly inadequate to my requirements. I complain but go unheard. It is I who must change and not the place. Or so they say.

June 5th

I have never liked cats. They look as if they have greater seniority. They cry, they mate at the back of places, they sleep all day as if full of accomplishment. I approach the cat on the edge of the clearing. It walks away but does not run. It will not scare. I think of picking up a stone. I think of shouting but my mouth remains clamped shut.

The birds are silent, I notice. Nothing moves on the vast reach whose water reflects the high clouds. Smoke still rises from the cottage chimney. I knock and no one answers. I enter and nothing is changed. I take a seat at the table. Since it would be rude to eat the loaf, I open the Bible at the page marked with a prayer card. *The wages of sin is death*.

That will do for today.

June 7th

I am fobbed off with entertainments, detective novels. Poetry is inadvisable, it seems. But I'm the sort of lad, the class of boyo, who can find the poetry in Dick Francis. I wonder if anyone else has actually read this filth. Is this what you want of me, Doctor? Surely not. Orange with tranquillity, most of my sad companions are not in a position to read or indeed do anything for themselves, while the administrators like to think they have better things with which to occupy themselves. Over-promoted poseurs.

Since I rarely sleep I am rapidly exhausting the library's stock. What will happen when I do? Go over it again? Aren't we supposed to be getting away from all that? Isn't that part of what we're 'trying to put behind us'? What if I fail? But if I fail, it will not be me who fails, will it, Doctor, not really? Another boy did it and ran away.

June 10th

A bad day. No stories.

June 12th

Through the woods, down the gentle hill into the clearing. The cat is nowhere to be seen, though it can probably see *me*. The door is ajar, the kitchen empty, the fire winking redly, the loaf white and stiff as a cork float, like evidence and not food. Across the room the inner door stands slightly open. In the passage behind it I can see a broom leaning against the whitewashed wall. Neutral, open. And the Bible too is open where I left it on the table. *The wages of sin is death.* So the mood today is still proverbial, and the accompanying reading is of an improving, not to say threatening kind. *The wages of sin is death*: the phrase reminds me. I have forgotten to bring something. Or I have come here to the cottage in the clearing by the water for some purpose I cannot recall. I would like to thrust my hand into the fire like Latimer — was it Latimer? Is this something I should remember or not? — when they burnt him at the stake. I turn the heavy pages. *And I was sore afraid.* But I am not afraid. A little anxious, perhaps. But not afraid. Fear is elsewhere. I look into the fire for some time. I warm my hands. But I do not burn them. Why would I?

June 14th

It is wearisome to be treated as a fool by fools. Let us

speak plainly. When I look under historical fiction I find *The Da Vinci Code*. Has anyone else read this, the 'work' of this 'Dan Brown', this obvious degenerate, this semi-literate petty criminal?

I ask again for poetry, but poetry is bad for me, and anyway, what poetry do I mean? You know, I say, that I do not remember. That is the point, is it not? How should I remember what I do not remember, O my doctor? The idea, surely, is that I should not. There follows the smile, the reassurance professionals give each other, their sense of strength in numbers, as if their white-coated kind stretched in a great queue down an endless corridor waiting their turn to be in here, doing as their colleagues do. *Rather strangle an infant in its cradle than nurse an unfulfilled desire* speaks itself unbidden through my mouth. A note is made. It is clear that they do not recognize the source; but neither do I.

June 15th

The rustic scene has lost its charm. Metalled road becoming track, running downhill, clearing, wide water, whitewashed cottage, ruinous sheds, cat nailed over the lintel of the door with its head under its arm. In fact I made that last part up. Is that allowed?

I feel like an estate agent showing myself round a property I wouldn't dream of buying. I never dream now, not since the intervention. Blank nights, the strange, deep blankness, as if everything were over or had never taken place. Perfection of a kind. Of my kind. Of my sort, knorramean?

Kitchen table, Bible, fire, dresser, proggy mat, hideous crockery, smoke-brown genre painting over the fireplace. Bags of potential, I'm sure I'll agree, for a young professional couple planning to set up as child murderers.

And the inner door. Yes, that. It hasn't gone away, still half-open with the broom behind it leaning on the whitewashed wall of the corridor. The scene itself is indifferent: act, don't act, it makes no odds to the scene, which is always here around this time, with the beautiful loaded neutrality of a detail in a picture by Chardin. Across the canvas the great silence of the woman writing a letter, or the servant sewing, goes on. But I know what is required of me. Go over. Stand by the doorway. I know that comes next. Don't spoil the party.

June 16th

You, Dr Murdoch, you, I see, are afraid. Oho. You are, I think, wise in this respect at least. You look at me slightly too long before you take your glasses off to tuck your long, red hair behind your ear. You and I might make a connection, but I would bet money that you will be absent from the next session. Afraid. Everybody would be wise to be afraid, under the circumstances in which we find ourselves, whatever role is given us to play in this medical panopticon. It is a scene of crime – crime actual, crime dreamed on the brink of waking, crime planned with patient passion through the long dim afternoons. It leaks from the walls, does crime. You find its residue under your fingernails, on the cuffs of your blouse and the toes of your tights when you undress for bed in the tidy flat I can imagine in every detail. Crime. You know it makes sense.

Imagine this great building underwater, sealed and secure for centuries on the bed of a great lake, and then one afternoon a doctor – you, Dr Murdoch, for example – finds a patch of damp in a cellar corridor, and feels a skin of water growing patiently beneath her touch. By then the state is already undone. The prisoners in the deepest oubliettes have drowned in crime. Those who survive the inundation will be crime-drinkers, breathers of crime, mutations built for their element, the criminal depths, deeper than the Atlantic, deeper even than the bottomless city of Paris. Who said this? I don't remember. Me, perhaps.

I ask you for poetry. You give me pills to help me adapt to the changed conditions. To adapt to the adaptations. When I object, you are stung. You point at the books on your shelves – books you will not lend me – and tell me tersely that I am a machine driven by desire. Not any more, I say, not according to you. Not if it's worked. All that's supposed to be over with. A silence falls, not of your making. You struggle to claim it for yourself. I add a little goad: *Who is as the wise man? And who knoweth the interpretation of a thing?* Stop it, you say, I am trying to think.

What about belief? I ask. You shake your head. What about the spirit? You snort and make another note. We're done, you say, for today. But, surely, I am undone, Doctor? I am not that strength which once I was. My right arm has lost its cunning and my liver is damaged by the drugs I am given to help me adapt to the changed conditions, and there is nothing to fucking read. You suggest I play table tennis.

June 19th

The sky is white but where it meets the trees it has a slaty, purplish note. It is much too hot but rain seems unlikely. The cat is in the rain barrel and the cottage smokes like a chimney. The door grates open, as if a piece of chalk has lodged under it. In the baking kitchen I sit at the table, feeling exhausted. A cauldron hangs from a hook, filled with a hearty stew, the sort added to for weeks on end, bubbling with steady complacency like a mud-pool near a geyser you can set your watch by. It is noon. It has never been anything else. Flick the bread with a finger. It sounds like a de-tuned snare-drum.

Somebody has moved the broom from its place leaning on the whitewashed wall beyond the opened doorway. Now it stands against the dresser, tensed as if about to multiply. This fills me with anger. I feel so full of anger it might start leaking from under my fingernails. Whose business is it to move the broom? I was getting round to it in my own time. One has to build up to these things, to prepare to make one's move. Now I think I see what you would have me believe. I take the broom and go to the doorway. You would have me suppose that there is nothing beyond, that the patch of white wall is all that is the case, and otherwise nothing obtains.

There is no corridor, there are no rooms leading off it, no beds and dressing-tables, and if it were possible to multiply an absence, even more certainly no*body* there. There never has been. Your will is to make me your creature, a wreckage of half-memories steering clear of the bad words until death intervenes to spare me further humiliation. All that was, is no more, shall be no more. I shall not think of it, shall not smell the smell of self at work in a further room.

It must be true, Dr Murdoch. You have squared the circle, seized the fire, found a cure for capitalism and brought cancer to its knees, downsized God and erased me from myself, leaving this tabula rasa, year zero, hollow man, to gibber harmlessly to himself and *not go back there or think of doing so.*

As you wish. All I do is place the broom back in its original position against the wall beyond the inner door. I do not look to either side. I feel no draught, smell no spoor, follow no line of association. I turn back to face the kitchen and go over to sit on a stool by the baking hearth. I take the lid from the cauldron, the heat stinging my palm, take up the iron ladle and stir. Your bald head surfaces, the eyes like bleary eggs, the skin slick with fat. I take a plastic spoon from my shirt pocket and begin to eat your brains with it. Are we done? Can I go now? You tell me. I can't remember.

Afterword:

Programmable Memory

Dr Simon Stott
Centre for Brain Repair, University of Cambridge

IN 2009, THE scientific journal *Cell* published a report in which scientists demonstrated the ability to program a specific memory into the brain. By artificially evoking activity in certain brain cells with pulses of light, the scientists were able to program behaviourally meaningful memories in fruit flies. They induced a negative association to a particular stimulus without any negative events having occurred in the presence of that stimulus[3]. Before this study was published, several laboratories around the world had already presented results showing the deletion of specific memories in mice[4]. Mice were taught to associate a particular sound or light with a negative feeling (e.g. discomfort). The scientists then gave the mice a specific drug that removed that learned association and the mice reacted as if naive. These and subsequent papers[5] have led many to speculate that one day soon we may have means to therapeutically remove traumatic memories. This line of research, however, has raised many ethical and moral questions concerning the use of such technology.

At present, memory manipulation techniques for humans exist only in fiction. Our understanding of the mammalian brain still remains extremely basic. The crude methods that are used at present in flies and mice face a long

3. Claridge-Chang A, Roorda RD, Vrontou E, Sjulson L, Li H, Hirsh J, & Miesenböck G (2009) 'Writing memories with light-addressable reinforcement circuitry.' *Cell*, 139(2), 405-15.
4. Cho MH, Cao X, Wang D, & Tsien JZ (2007) 'Dentate gyrus-specific manipulation of beta-Ca2+/calmodulin-dependent kinase II disrupts memory consolidation.' *Proceedings of the National Academy for Science USA*, 104(41), 16317-22.
5. Clem RL, Huganir RL (2010) 'Calcium-permeable AMPA receptor dynamics mediate fear memory erasure.' *Science*, 330 (6007), 1108-12.

evolution, before we get to the point where they can be scaled up to the level of the human brain or to the scenario that is suggested in Sean O'Brien's story.

In Sean's story the speaker is asked by a psychologist to engage with a specially selected image – one which may or may not have certain associations attached – for therapeutic purposes. This is an elaborated version of the kind of 'journey narrative' sometimes used in counselling. The visit to the cottage is a test of the narrator's ability to remain calm in the face of certain stimuli (the door, the passage) which might provoke memories, as a way of testing whether such memories have been successfully 'dealt with'. The doctor in the story is clearly a psychologist of some kind, but the 'treatment' referred to is very definitely neurological – my field.

For decades, scientists have been working on the molecular mechanics of the brain, in an effort to understand its mysteries. The screening of the genome at the start of this century brought to our attention thousands of unknown genes that appear to have a role in the brain, resulting in an increase in the work yet to be done. In addition, new roles for previously known biological components (such as microRNA) have demanded a revisiting of old dogmas and opened new fields of science, yet again increasing the realm of unknowns.

One of our current theories of memory maintenance holds that networks of neurons are responsible for different aspects of each memory. These networks are believed to overlap, with individual neurons being involved in multiple memory networks. We learn by associating one thing with another and we believe that these associations strengthen the connections between various networks of neurons in our brains. These networks are evident given that there is no single neuron that remembers your grandmother. If there was and it was lost through injury, would you remember who she is at Christmas dinner? Memories are far more complex than that. We remember multiple aspects of our grandmother, from the way she looked and dressed, to the sound of her voice and perhaps the way she held our hand. In addition we may remember those same aspects in various ways based on different occasions in the past. Future memory manipulation technology will need to perform the delicate trick of affecting certain networks of memories involved in the event to be deleted, without affecting overlapping memory networks about other things that are to remain. This will require an understanding of the brain that is far beyond anything we have at present.

If the human brain ever does one day transcend itself and develop a thorough understanding of its own inner workings, there is little reason not to believe that memory manipulation will be possible. The road to that end will most likely involve some very blunt instruments at first – resulting in the removal of large tracts of memory. With refinement, however, later tools will emerge and memory manipulation may take on a cosmetic dimension. The obvious candidates for memory removal are victims of traumatic events or perhaps the perpetrators of the events, as in the story presented here. For the victims, there can be a strong desire to forget. But the question must be asked: if we remove the memories of their time during the event, would they simply go back to who they were before it happened? We are making an enormous assumption that everyone will handle the procedure in the same way. And for the perpetrators of unforgivable actions, will the removal of a memory render the individual back to 'normal'? Or will the desire to perform such an act remain?

Post-traumatic stress disorder is currently treated with medication, such as serotonin re-uptake inhibitors, which help reduce the anxiety and depression associated with the memories. But there is nothing available at present to help people forget events completely. As a result, counselling makes up the foundation of any treatment, in an effort to desensitize the memory and allow the victim to live a reasonably normal life. This counselling can include keeping a personal dairy (as in the story presented here) or cognitive behavioural therapy, which seeks to change the way victims act and feel by changing their patterns of thinking and behaviour. These treatments are long journeys and demand much from the individuals involved. The appeal of a 'quick-fix' memory deletion approach will be hard to resist when such a thing is available.

With the relentless progression of technology and the 'desire to forget', there is a need to begin asking the moral and ethical questions that will arise with memory manipulation. For example, should we allow for the removal of small parts of our being that make up such a critical component of who we are? And who ultimately should decide if the memory is to be deleted or not? Is it a personal choice? If so, to what end? What are the consequences of memory removal on the individual psyche and sense of self? If the day ever comes that we can perform such wonders, answers to these questions will be required.

Shake Me and I Rattle

Sarah Schofield

THE TELEVISION IS loud in my grandmother's bedroom. A news bulletin features a couple nursing a framed photograph of a grinning boy. Their son. It is a photo selected in the peculiar way that tells you he must now be dead.

'Siobhan. What are they saying?' Gran says.

The man stares at his palms. 'We're warning other parents. Penti Berries are dangerous. They're saying there's no certain link, but we knew our son and we know it was them that killed him.'

It cuts to the reporter. 'Despite being withdrawn from sale last month there are concerns that Penti Berries, sometimes referred to as Penti Bears because of their recognisable teddy bear shape, are still available through illegal sources. Claims from the manufacturer, that they improve children's concentration and brain development, have turned bitter after 27 hospital admissions and eight fatalities have been circumstantially connected to the supplement. The Department of Health advises that remaining Penti Berries should be taken to a chemist to be destroyed and that anyone with concerns about their children's wellbeing should seek medical attention...'

Fear prickles again under my arms. 'It's nothing, Gran...' I switch the channel to a gardening programme and hand her the remote control.

She looks at me curiously. Her eyes are speckled cerulean like the rock pools not far from here on the sea front. Then she considers the remote control in her hand. I fuss over her dinner tray. The corned beef in her sandwich has darkened like a scab.

'You've not touched your tea.' I try to swallow back my note of desperation as I draw the curtains. Neither of us has been outside today.

She tucks the television remote into her sponge bag. 'It was port shore.' She pauses over the oddly threaded words. But the moment passes. I stroke her arm until she bats me away.

'Your tablets.' I hand her an assortment of prescription drugs. She cradles them into her mouth, sips her drink, swallows hard. The water in the glass has a pink taint like dentists' mouth rinse.

'Shake me and I rattle,' she says, while I mouth the same. Every day. Every single day. We smile at each other.

'Drink your water, Gran. Bed?' I lift the green plastic pearls from round her neck but she grips me, digs her nails into my wrist. Shakes her head and scowls.

'A few…' She tries her lips around some wispy word shapes then turns back to the television. My grandmother squints at the screen.

I bite my lip.

'What are they saying?'

Downstairs, I drop her tray on the table and put away her medication bottles and boxes, checking how much we have left in each and tightening lids. One box spills out little strawberry flavoured bears, with outstretched paws and half smiles etched onto their faces, containing 0.5 % Penti Berry extract.

These are what people believe have been killing their children.

I've been giving them to my grandmother for the last six months.

I go back upstairs to her.

'Yes?' She reaches up and strokes my hair.

'Yes,' I reply. She is calmer now. I am sure she is

wandering less. And lately I am finding fewer of those little unwanted surprises; the bath sponge in the bread machine, cheese crackers in the CD player.

In the morning I work on a client's website design, while my grandmother rearranges her strings of beads and necklaces in her jewellery box. I glance up from time to time. She handles them like rosaries. Their familiarity seems comforting to her as she recites where and when they came to her; bought or given. It was the first sign for me that something wasn't right, a while before she was properly diagnosed with dementia, that my grandmother was pairing her array of carefully selected beads with oddly matched outfits.

The phone rings. My grandmother reaches reflexively for it but I manage to get there first. She sulks and huffs and turns away from me.

'Siobhan? It's Phil.' My boss hardly pauses. 'How are you getting on with the Barrington site?'

I look at my computer. 'Phil, I'm going to need a bit longer. I'm sorry, but...'

'We've already made excuses to them once.' I can hear the faint click click click of him typing while he speaks to me. I imagine him, back in the office, at the desk that once was mine. Our colleagues sipping takeout coffees and talking about their weekend plans. I don't say anything.

Gran stands and wanders into the lounge. I follow her and watch as she picks up a comb.

'Look, I can get you a bit more time... but I did say, didn't I? Working from home would lose you immediacy. I can't keep making excuses for you.'

Gran kneels and sweeps the skirting boards with the comb.

'Yes. I appreciate that...' I brace the phone against my ear, take the comb from her and run it through her silver hair. She pulls underneath, batting me away.

'Right. A couple of days enough? And Siobhan, we're

planning a work night out. Next Friday. You really should come…'

I pull a stained underskirt from behind the radiator. Gran deftly slips a pair of knickers from the ironing pile up her sleeve, like preparation for a saucy magic trick. I hang up.

'Shall we get out in the fresh air for a bit, Gran? Have a walk to the hospice shop?'

She looks at me with focussed terror like I'm about to hit her. 'Those things, round the corner.'

I try to decipher her as we go upstairs. In the end I just ask which coat she'd like to wear.

She shoulders me aside and clatters back and forth along her overcrowded wardrobe rail. After watching her for a minute I wait downstairs and stare at the Barrington website. She emerges a while later in a silver flare skirt she used to go dancing in, over a pair of long brown culottes, a green tweed jacket with a yellow fleck and an oven mitt that I'd vaguely missed three months ago.

'Do you know, I don't think it's glove weather, Gran,' is all I risk. It's not a worthwhile fight. It's me, not her, who notices the people staring at her unconventional outfits. Sometimes the same people that she used to chat to, carefully filing away details about their families to politely ask after in the future. These details have not trickled away. They have just become irretrievably jumbled. They surface in our conversations, in irreverent chronology. Mrs. Graham's daughter's miscarriage, Gupta's sister's visit and the impossibility of sourcing asafoetida locally. Long ago events happen for her freshly every day. I am ashamed that I do not know how these fragments fit together. I was never as diligent a listener as her. We sit over them like two blind people trying to piece together a broken vase.

'I haven't been out in ages,' she mutters as we walk along.

'We went out for scones the day before yesterday,' I say.

'No. Not for a year.'

I leave it. And carry her handbag after she loops it onto a low-hanging tree branch. There are three freezer meals inside, slowly wicking up the lining.

We go into the charity shop. The shelves ache with crockery, clothes, ornaments and books. I stand with Moira by the till. Gran potters about lifting things and putting them down again like mysterious artefacts.

'How's she doing? She's looking well…' Moira asks, lips crinkled into concern.

'We're trying some new meds,' I say softly.

'I do miss having her in the shop. Even towards the end when she was turning poorly… we used to have a right natter.'

'You can pop over… whenever you want…'

My grandmother wanders to the till carrying a lilac porcelain cow with a chipped tail.

'Yes, I'll try. It's busy though, the shop and family things…' Moira wraps the cow abruptly in newspaper.

And I hold my grandmother's hand, and think about the pies and casseroles she baked for Moira after she'd had her hysterectomy.

Country vegetable soup, when thrown, goes a surprisingly long way. I'm showing Gran how to turn the spoon the other way up to scoop the soup into her mouth. And in a sudden jerking shriek, it has reached the furthest wall of the kitchen.

'Sandra! Why it is?' Gran cries, slamming a hand onto the table.

I breathe slowly, turn my face away and let her stomp off round the garden while I clear up. I wring the cloth into the sink with whitening knuckles.

Dr. Bold makes an unexpected house call while I'm sponging soup from her jewellery box. His comb over, more frazzled than usual, is a welcome humorous distraction.

'I can't stop long. I'm up to my eyeballs in worried parents. What happened there?' The doctor points at my blouse.

'…it was nothing. Sometimes when I try and help she..'

'It's not uncommon.' He stares at my blouse.

'Her necklaces got it too,' I rattle the jewellery box at him. I give a pathetic laugh.

'Coping?'

'Fine.' I click on the kettle. 'Coffee?' He looks at me with concern so I start talking fast over the kettle's crescendo. 'When she's confused… sometimes she thinks I'm my mother...'

Dr. Bold holds up his hand. 'I know you might feel like they're interferring… but social services really can do a lot to help.'

I close my eyes. Up until recently, I hadn't realised Dr. Bold knew about the battle my grandmother had had with the social workers to keep me.

'We're happy. She's really happy.' My cheeks flush.

His eyebrows crease, and I wonder exactly how much my grandmother has told her doctor about it all.

He glances at the clock on the wall. 'Don't take it personally. Dementia causes all sorts of behaviours.' He wrinkles his face. 'Are you sure you don't need some extra help?'

'No,' I say. 'I'm looking after her.'

'You're young. You should go out – enjoy yourself.' Dr Bold puts his case down on the table and I turn to the window. Tighten my jaw.

'Coffee?' I ask again.

'A quick one. I can't stop long. I've got to go into St Michael's. Do a special assembly for the parents and pupils.'

I watch Gran walk slowly round the garden, talking to the rhododendrons, waving her hands like a passionate Italian. I tap the glass.

'These bloody Penti Berries,' he says ominously and rolls his eyes. 'The school bought into a bulk deal, the manufacturer was flashing data from league tables... drug trial results. All run by themselves I might add. No independent clinical trial because it was categorised as a food product. Picture it – all the kids lined up at break for their milk and poisonous little bears.' He looks vitriolic. 'Do you know where it comes from? It's an Amazonian hallucinogen. What they were pushing to improve kids' concentration has been used for years by shamans to invoke visions...'

'Their research said it was safe, though?' My voice has an edge I try to soften. I tuck Gran's crusty porridge bowl, with its pink-dusted rim, into the dishwasher.

'No, but...'

'If the authorities allow the company to sell it... I mean we're not all experts.' I turn away, stir his coffee.

'You haven't got kids, have you? So we can have a sensible conversation about Penti.' He takes the mug from me. 'I'm dealing with hoards of anxious parents presenting children with vague unconnected symptoms. They bought into it like it was as normal as calcium-fortified yoghurt. Like herded sheep they started taking them, now they're all convinced their children are going to die and they're stampeding in the opposite direction. Do sheep stampede? Oh well... you see what I mean...' He shakes his head. 'It's ridiculous. It'll happen again, unless they change the legislation.'

'But do you think Penti's actually do anything?'

He frowns.

'I mean... despite the health risks?'

'Honestly?' He sips his coffee. 'I think it's placebo.'

I look up sharply. 'Some parents raved about it.'

'Perhaps because children were given them as a reward, they worked harder. It's no coincidence they're shaped like sweets... Parents and schools got into monitoring their children more closely and that eeked the stats up. Who knows,' he sighs. 'The clinical trials will tell us more. Although if Penti is found to be safe, I don't think many parents will give it to their children… Remember that MMR nonsense?' he rolls his eyes. 'And MMR was proven safe from the start…'

'Do you think they're dangerous?'

He looks at me oddly. 'I don't know. But at best they were a waste of money.'

'At worst…'

He raises his eyebrows.

Pressing my shaky hands together I go outside to get Gran. She lolls in a plastic chair on the patio. For one heart clenching moment, I think she is dead. But she opens an eye. Pushes her lips into a culpable grimace. The chipped porcelain cow, nestled in its newspaper, is in her lap. She looks down.

'Mish match.' She pulls away from me as I help her inside.

'Hello Betty, how are you?' Dr. Bold says.

I watch them together from the doorway. She's polite and sweet. Like her old self, again. Perhaps it's me. I'm letting her down. I pick up the cloth again, rinse it in scolding water and run soapy water over a length of beads.

I catch Dr. Bold on the way out. 'I want to review Gran's medication. See if there's anything else…'

He glances at his watch. 'I've got to…'

'And she needs a repeat prescription…'

'Come to the surgery tomorrow. First thing.' He pulls a bundle of leaflets from his case and presses them into my hand.

For dinner I serve lamb stew followed by ice cream and Penti sprinkles. Afterwards she is better; more lucid. I put Charlie Parker on and we dance mildly around the lounge. Gran hums and sways her arms like a flapper.

'You remember this one?' I say.

When I help Gran to bed that night she is smiling.

'Who's that boy?' she puts her arms up, lets me slip a nightie over her head.

'Dr. Bold, Gran.'

She presses her fingertips together. 'I once lived by the sea,' she says.

'You still do.'

'I went there for raspberry nipple.'

I restrain a smile. 'I know. You used to take me.'

The seaside. One of her favourite repeats. In her retelling it becomes glossy postcard simple.

I pass her a soapy flannel.

I've taken her to the sea front once as an adult. It was a late summer afternoon just over a year ago. After a visit to Dr. Bold where the decision was made that it was time I moved back in to care for her as she slowly eroded. The sea front visit was a rash, instinctive act; it was only as I knelt by the passenger door pulling her rhizome feet into a second pair of socks and her fur boots that I realized why we'd come here, like an unimaginatively returned present.

The sea was in. Wind slapped the hair across our cheeks. My throat tightened around the stupid intuition of my action. This was where we always used to come. We'd throw stones hard off the pier into the ocean. This was where we built sandcastles and then, in rumples of terrible laughter, stomped them flat, sand propelling anger out of us. This was where, when we lacked the words, we would do battle with the tide then salve ourselves with ice cream.

And that day we returned. I'd looked up at the woman who had nurtured me, picked up where her daughter had let go and, with flickering candidness, she'd reached down and stroked my face, her dry-skin knuckles skimming over my wet cheek.

Now she hands me back the flannel. I help her into bed. Pull the duvet up, tuck it in.

'We can always go back there, to the sea front.'

'I once lived by the sea.' She turns; a curling, breaking wave.

I open my laptop at the kitchen table.

In a parenting forum someone has anonymously written; 'I know you will judge me but I'm continuing to give my son Penti Bears. He's been taking them for six months. No side affects. He has exams next month. I've run out of Penti's. I need more. He says he can't concentrate. I'm at my wits' end. If anyone has spares... Please don't judge us...' I read a couple of the hateful messages following the post then close the screen.

I go to the drinks cabinet. I count what I have left, estimate how long the supply will last. I take one of the boxes. Flip it over. On the back is a Penti Bear puzzle. The cartoon bear on the back has speech bubbled suggestions. 'Try my puzzle.' 'Feeling crafty? – Make this box into a car – see inside for how!' 'Make music! – shake me; I rattle!'

I replace the box and turn the key.

I lie in bed trying to read one of the dementia care leaflets. The house is silently straining like a lungful of held breath. After a few minutes I get up and stand in her doorway.

Her nightdress is back to front now. She has an arm through the neck hole. She's pulled a Satsuma net over her hair, one ear popping out. It is nearly funny and I want to weep. I go downstairs, bring up her jewellery box and put it back on the dresser. I swallow back a cool, latent resentment.

I was a shy child when I first moved here. Uncertain how to be with other people. Over the first few weeks my grandmother asked every child in my class home for tea. There was always laughter. One time, aged maybe six or seven, we were eating baked potatoes. Whenever one of us hovered our forks near them they started speaking. 'Don't eat me. Please! No!' I spotted the Dictaphone from her work in her pocket and she winked at me and I smiled back.

I sit in the chair beside her bed. Her eyes flicker beneath

the lids. I smooth her sheets. Asleep like this, it's almost like my grandmother isn't slipping away.

In the GP surgery waiting room, there are no empty seats so I have to stand beside a poster for a new cholesterol lowering supplement. I pretend to study it while my cheeks flush. I have just given Gran her breakfast; a bowl of fruit and yoghurt with a smattering of delicate pink. I press my nails into my palms and avoid the eyes of the waiting parents and children.

'Miss Easton? Dr. Bold is ready for you.'

The parents watch me slip through the door to the surgery.

'Have a seat, Siobhan. Did you read those pamphlets?' Dr Bold leafs through papers on his desk wafting the weft of hair across his pate.

'I wanted to check... if there's anything else she can take at the moment...' My gaze slides away to the window.

'She's not declined significantly? When I saw her yesterday...'

'I just wanted to be sure there's nothing else that would help... With aggression...' The trees around the car park appear in slices between the venetian blinds. The crisp lines blur.

Dr. Bold looks at his monitor. 'I appreciate it must be difficult for you. But she seems fairly stable at the moment. Yesterday she was brighter than...'

'Yes, but... I can't leave her long, is there any...'

'It's a symptom of vascular dementia.' He pulls a face. 'Ups and downs... And don't underestimate the seasons. People generally decline through winter... I'll do you that repeat script. Have you had your carer assessment yet? Seen the CPN?' The printer whirs, spitting out a long prescription.

'I can manage,' I say. Dr. Bold rises, hands me the

prescription. Holds open the door to the hum of the waiting room. He looks suddenly fatigued.

'Back to it,' he says.

I wander around the pharmacy with a basket while I wait for my grandmother's prescription. I get my phone out to call her and say I'll be back soon, but put it away again. I pick up a box of evening primrose oil capsules and cod liver oil. The Echinacea, St. John's Wort and flower remedies have closed ranks. I scan the brightly packaged promises.

After that first dusting of powder did I sit with her more? Play longer games of beetle drive and snap. Was I looking and seeing things that were real, or selfishly, hopefully imagined?

I go back to the pharmacy counter. On it is a stand of colourful seed bead necklaces. A sign beside it says 'Aids in Africa. £3 donation suggested.' I push a fiver into the box and choose a string of green, black and white beads.

'Betty Easton?'

The chemist hands over the bag full of boxes and bottles. I slide the beads in too.

When I return, the house is disarmingly quiet. I haven't been away from her this long in ages.

'Gran?'

I hurry upstairs. She is slumped portside in her chair, half a glass of pink-tainted water in front of her. 'Gran?' I shake her urgently. She wakes with a start, fixes me with fear that twists to malevolent, trembling anger.

'Who does you… you…' she grips and pincers onto my arm. I grasp her hand, try to unfurl her stiff fingers.

'Gran, it's me. Siobhan. I just nipped to the chemist…'

'Get off. You…' She lets go, flails her arms at me. I try to catch her hands to stop her from striking them on something.

'Not even fit.' Her eyes are milky and darting. She pulls to free her hands. I let go.

'Gran…'

'Druggy slut.' She strikes me across the cheek. It makes an ugly sound. Like a stone smacking on water.

I raise a trembling hand to my cheek and stand there with my mouth open. I go to the bathroom, splash water on my face and listen to her sobbing like a baby.

I wait for my heart to slow. Her crying turns to a pitched whine. I hear the rustle of the paper bag. The scatter of boxes. I go back into the room. My grandmother rocks forward and back in her chair. Medicine boxes and bottles are strewn across the floor. The string of charity beads is round her neck, her fingers clutched around it. She tugs at it with each ebb and flow of her movement. It tenses and sags like a boat tether in a storm.

'Gran, please.' I rush forward. I try to lift her hands away, hold her stationary. She looks up at me terrified, desperate. She forms shapes with her mouth. But the words come out as hisses.

And then she wails loud and long. Drowns me out. Pulls. Pulls. Pulls.

The necklace string snaps.

Beads radiate away from us. They bounce across the carpet. Patter against the walls. Roll under the television stand. We cling together. Hot sobbing. Clawing.

We stay that way for a while.

Then I look at her. Gran rests her forehead against her outstretched palm.

I go to her wardrobe, pull out a thick jumper and her fur boots. I put her boots on her while she scoops together the beads that remain on her table. I wrestle the sweater over her head. Hoisting her onto her feet, we make a shaky passage down the hall. I lean her in the doorway while I open the drinks cabinet and sweep the boxes of Penti Berries into my handbag. I lead her silently to the car.

We drive wordlessly. She gazes out of the window; one finger taps a staccato rhythm on her seat.

When we arrive at the coast, I park the car facing the lashing sea and we sit for a while.

Then she turns to me. We don't say anything.

She reaches for my hand. I clutch hers tightly.

We make our way slowly down the pier. At the end we watch the water swinging in across the Irish Sea. It beats against the struts, but we hold onto each other; our arms laced together.

I get a fistful of Penti boxes out of my handbag, rattle them out into my Gran's white outstretched palm. My grandmother doesn't ask questions. She laughs as we skim them into the waves. Her throws are strong and jagged, mine hard and determined. One after another, the pink bears sink, waving their paws into the sludgy water. We hoot and cheer as boxful after boxful disappears.

We cling together. Shivering.

Later we sit in a café licking ice creams. Gran has raspberry ripple. I have double chocolate. I wipe the run of pink milk trickling down her chin. I realise with a chill that she is out in the daytime with no necklace or jewellery on, probably for the first time I have ever known. But she neither notices nor cares.

The sun is setting and we watch the seagulls spiralling the currents across the orange-streaked horizon.

Afterword:

Over-the-Counter Medicine

Dr Angharad Watson

Cardiff University

WHAT IS 'GOOD for you' and who decides? And if something really can improve your health or cure an ailment, does that make it medicine? Where is the line drawn between 'supplement' and 'drug'? These are the questions that we should be asking as we reach for the latest alternative or complementary cure-all in our quest to feel better than healthy. At the same time, however, there exists a growing mistrust of the conventional medicine that gave us the wellness we now take for granted.

Although this feels like a modern phenomenon, we are not so different from our predecessors: fortunes were made in the 19th century by companies selling tonics, pills and cure-alls to people eager to feel 'better'. These companies have now evolved into pharmaceutical giants (Pfizer, Wellcome), and many of their original products have been relegated to chemistry labs and history books. But, importantly, at the time, consumers had great faith in the powers of these lotions and potions. Some of them were later found to be based on genuine pharmaceutical properties, such as salicylic acid (of which aspirin is a well-known derivative) and digitalin (now purified into the drugs digitoxin and digoxin to treat heart conditions). Some were useless, but harmless. Others were simply downright poisonous, such as calomel, which is mercury (I) chloride, and, because of its effective antibacterial properties, was widely used in Europe for over 150 years to treat diseases such as syphilis. Up until the mid 1950s, calomel was a component of teething powders in the UK, which resulted in 'pink disease' or potentially fatal mercury poisoning in infants. Imagine yourself as the mother of a teething baby in 1956, with your mother on the one hand advising calomel, and your doctor telling you it's poison. Who do you believe? Which argument is more persuasive, 'My mother swore by it...' or 'New research shows...'?

The word 'vitamin' was coined in the early 20th century by the fantastically named Polish scientist Casimir Funk, and was originally 'vitamine', an amalgamation of the words 'vital' and 'amine', referring to the amine group found in thiamine (vitamin B), which was discovered through investigation into the cause of the disease beriberi in the late 19th century in Japan. Therefore, while elixirs and tonics have been commonplace since the Georgians, it was the 20th century that saw the first widespread understanding of the daily need for compounds additional to the proteins, carbohydrates and fats that give us energy. Within a generation of the invention of the word vitamin, cheap multivitamin tablets were available in shops, and now dietary supplements form part of many people's daily routine. As a child I can remember being given small, bear-shaped multivitamins with my breakfast, just like the children in the story. Even as an adult, at the slightest hint of a sniffle, or even just tiredness, my mother asks, 'Have you been taking your vitamins?' The honest answer is generally 'no', and the admission makes me feel guilty, like admitting that I haven't been to the gym lately. I feel that I am admitting that I haven't been looking after myself properly. But is that really true?

As mentioned in the story, the ranks of dietary supplements are now legion, with the usual vitamins joined by comforting, olde-worlde-style plant extracts, exotic herbs, and complex, futuristic-sounding antioxidants, probiotics, phytonutrients, and coenzymes. These creep into our beauty products and into our foods, becoming so common and familiar that we all now feel comfortable with the idea that these abstract words represent things that are indubitably good for us. We have been taught by smiling young women in glossily-produced TV commercials that antioxidants are absolutely good for us, fighting off molecular assault by nasty, subversive 'free radicals'. These free radicals are out to get us, to give us wrinkles on the outside and cancers on the inside. But is it really that simple?

A free radical is any atom or molecule that has an unpaired electron in its outer shell. Electrons are sociable things, and like to go around in pairs, so, upon finding themselves alone, they seek out any passing electrons, to urgently try to pair up, like a drunk singleton at the end of a Christmas party. Other electrons, happily paired, are stable, and so uninterested in ditching their partners to form new pairs. Therefore, the free radical must be super-reactive in order to attack a stable pair, causing electrons to be displaced, chemical reactions to happen and new compounds to be formed. In biology, the atom carrying this offending electron is usually oxygen, and so radicals are generally referred to as 'reactive oxygen species'. These molecules are generated in our cells as a normal part of respiration, and we have evolved a range of enzymes that contain them safely until they can be put to use, or convert them into harmless by-products. However, if too many are produced this is called 'oxidative stress' and has been linked to a range of diseases, including cancer. Antioxidants are able to safely mop up these reactive oxygen species. The observation that a diet rich in fruit and vegetables, which contain antioxidants such as vitamin A and vitamin E, leads to reduced incidence of diseases like cancer and heart disease, led to the conclusion that dietary antioxidants would protect us from radical-based maladies. For decades, this rationale was sound, and generally borne out by data. Recently, however, studies involving giving antioxidants to lung cancer patients as a therapeutic measure not only failed to improve their conditions, but the antioxidant group actually had a higher incidence of death than the non-treated controls. This surprising outcome led to a re-evaluation of the roles of reactive oxygen species in the body, and in fact they have important roles in immunity, amongst other things; in cancer patients it is possible that the antioxidants might be affecting these immune functions. The latest systematic review recommends that nobody should take vitamin A or E supplements, as the possibility that they are harmful cannot be ruled out. That's quite a sobering thought. So much for the idea that 'it's not doing me any harm.'

At the same time, we know that other vitamins and supplements are vital, such as folic acid during the early stages of pregnancy. The importance of vitamin D for healthy bones has been known for generations, but in recent years it is being implicated in other diseases, such as multiple sclerosis and Alzheimer's, indicating a more varied role for this vitamin than previously thought. The grey area really arises when we consider alternative remedies, which market themselves as alternatives to, and, in some people's minds, replacements for conventional drugs and medicines. If something is claiming to do what a drug does, why isn't it a drug?

So who do we trust? As the news reports new scientific studies that contradict older studies, it can be very tempting to revert to alternative medicines, to ancient knowledge that has been passed down through generations. Continuity is comforting. But saying something over and over again doesn't make it correct. There was a time when it was normal to own another human, as you might own a chair or table. In cultures across the globe, for centuries, this was viewed as normal, natural, right. The only reason we now find slavery abhorrent is because someone stood up and questioned the received wisdom. This is what science does. It questions the received wisdom. It checks, checks again, re-analyses and re-evaluates. A conclusion is the very best that can be drawn with the data available. As time goes on, more data become available, so the conclusions can change. The honesty comes in admitting the errors of the past, and surely that is more trustworthy than blindly sticking to your guns, however wrong you may be?

And here is the key: in science and in medicine, hypotheses are *tested*. You say your drug does this? Prove it. Carry out properly controlled trials, and submit your methods and findings to peer review. Food supplements and alternative or complementary medicines are not subject to such stringent testing. Because of this, there is a reluctance to move from 'supplement' to 'drug', as this could lead to the removal of your product from the shelves as lengthy and expensive clinical trials take place. For a small company with a single product, this could lead to ruin. This situation is, I believe, slowly changing. Advertising standards legislation has led to more accountability for product claims, and papers are slowly emerging examining the efficacy of complementary therapies, and many commonplace supplements and over-the-counter medicines are being re-examined in the context of serious diseases using state-of-the-art techniques. At the other end of the scale, more accountability is also being demanded of pharmaceutical companies, with increased pressure on them to make their data more freely available, and calls for an end to shady practices such as paying doctors and academics to promote 'off-label' (and thus untrialled) uses of existing drugs.

To illustrate how important this is, I would like you to consider a scenario of two patients, both newly diagnosed with cancer. One goes straight to his consultant oncologist, takes the newest drugs, undergoes several rounds of chemotherapy. The other goes straight to a herbalist, consults an expert in Chinese medicine, and embarks upon a full lifestyle change to rid himself of the toxins and bad energies that he believes have caused his cancer. They both die. What can you conclude from this? The ordinary person on the street might say it shows that cancer is untreatable, inexorable, and that no intervention can help. What if they both live? Does that mean that the alternative path was as effective as conventional medicine? A scientist would want more information: what kind of cancer, how severe was it, how long did both patients live after diagnosis? Then they would want more patients, and this is the basis of clinical trials. Almost anything can happen once, but can it happen twice, five times, a hundred, a thousand times? If, instead of one patient in each group we have 1,000, matched for age and type of cancer, then we can start asking, and, more importantly, *answering* questions. What proportion survive to six months, to a year, to five years? Which treatment is best? This is the difference between data and anecdote.

The situation presented in 'Shake Me and I Rattle' is all too plausible, and should give us pause for thought. What is good for us? How do we find out? Who do we trust? What is the difference between a drug and a supplement? Speaking for myself, I prefer to see claims backed up by real, peer-reviewed, openly available data. Mystical-sounding knowledge passed down through generations is not data, it's anecdote, and I wouldn't like to stake my health on an anecdote.

The Wrestler

Simon Ings

I WAS DEEP into something, some rant, driving everybody crazy as usual, even the insect life had had enough of me, and as I lifted it to my lips a bumblebee embedded itself in the mustard of my hotdog. I saw it too late to stop it, dropped the hotdog, felt the stinger sew its gobbet of hot lead through my lip. I wailed and danced, appalled at myself, stomping bread and processed meat into the lawn. Clarita's brother's kids were laughing at me. Only a bee, for goodness' sake. I got myself calmed down, took myself off to the bathroom, between the 4-by-4's parked on the front lawn. The beat from Carlito's pick-up was bass-heavy enough to set the lead in my lip hammering in sympathy.

Sunday, all the Cubans in Miami set light to stuff, grill stuff, fry stuff, vehicles on the front lawn, grease, smoke, guts swelling from under exhausted T-shirts or spilling over the top of white stretch jeans. I passed my wife, Clarita, stick-thin Clarita, the Bump a small and telling curve among these rolling balls of indulged plenty. All afternoon it had been exciting hugs and kisses, promises of outgrown clothing, shoes, toys, basins, bouncers, old sterilising kits.

She saw me passing, hand clamped to my face, asked what's wrong? I waved her off, meaning never mind, but impatience overworked the gesture, the way it does these days, and she sat back down, hurt. Lost in her lawnchair. A thing her brother's wife must have chosen, big enough to fit a family of four.

In the bathroom cabinets (many on each wall), Carlito's wife's big dead herb collection. Ginkgo Gotu Kola Supreme. Phyto-proz for Healthy Mood. Intense Eyezone Cream. Extra Rich Bust Lift (is she fucking kidding?). No spray-on ibuprofen, no numbing unguent.

I looked at myself in the mirror. Well.

Back outside to find Clarita with Carlito (her brother: what got into their parents with their cutesy name game?), them standing hand in hand, wreathed in barbecue smoke, Rhett and Scarlett watching Atlanta burn. I was on my way over to them, hangdog and smiling, apologies for this break in transmission, when he put his arm around her shoulders and I knew, even before they turned around, even before I read it in her eyes that she'd told him. Waited till I was out the way. And told him.

Blood over water every time with this bunch. Every time.

Spina bifida. The backbones fail to close all round, leaving the nerves a knotted ball in the small of your back. At worst, paralysis. At best, leg braces. According to the scan the Bump was looking at a lifetime in a wheelchair. The internet (what else?) told us she had one chance: an operation while she was still inside the womb. It's certified, only our insurance company was working off old information and refused to pay. They said that it's experimental, that it's too much risk.

And since there didn't seem to be a way to make this happen, I'd said to Clarita, let's save poor Bump from this and try again. Bump 2. She looked at me like I was suggesting we trade in our car. 'But she's our little Bump,' she said.

The party done, I drove us over to the university. Charcoal and meat smoke still clung to our clothes.

She had work; not me. The laboratory I work in is better organised than her moot board. No Sunday emergencies for me. And our patent application's off, so my workplace isn't exactly a hive of industry right now.

I drove in silence, nursing my lip with the tip of my tongue. My jaw was heavy with the effort of holding my mouth still for so long. It hurt to speak. And in that silence, all the choices we were making that day were copying and dividing inside me, over and over, cramming me into a corner of myself, squeezing me out of my own head.

I wanted to ask her why she'd had to wait until I was gone in the house to drop the bombshell on her brother and his family. What had he said? I wanted to know what the look he'd given me signified. The looks they'd all given me. No Hispanic wants a man of colour in the family, that's a given, but this was something else. Like they had already passed judgement on me.

My kid's disability being my fault, of course. I should never have wound up their kids. It's not like half the things I'd told them really happen any more. Aerosols aimed at the back of a dog's throat. Bunny eyes red and bleeding. All the hard work, the meat and potatoes of toxicology, was done a generation ago. Now, with their data safely tucked away in our back pockets, we can pretend that this sort of thing never happened. Or that if it did happen, it wasn't anything to do with people like us. It being a universal given that, oh, we're so much kinder now.

I don't know what it was got under my skin on that visit, maybe his wife's dead herb collection, or some magazine article around the place, some Wisdom of the Ancients, or maybe none of that, maybe just my own dumb pride – anyway, a couple of visits back, I figured that Carlito's kids should know just what labs like mine had gotten up to, back in the Jim Crow days. Figuring the lethal dose on higher mammals. On primates. Pioneering days. And this is important: unavoidable. 'You don't like it, don't use Flit.'

The Hispanic nightmare: a black man of no faith, brandishing a pipette.

'What do you do, Uncle Jack?'

I make insecticides.

Carlito's wife, with her Gingko Biloba this and her St John's Wort that, is sure to conclude that the Bump's disorder is down to me. Disaster clinging to my smock. Poisons spraying from my red-rimmed eyes after a hard day's vivisection of *Drosophila*. I doubt anyone else in the family will credit this much, except me.

That's the catch, you see. I do blame myself. Against all knowledge, against all reason. Because, when push comes to shove, these things do not get decided by knowledge or reason. They depend on what you tell yourself about what is happening to you. Any story, even a story that has you crippling your own child, is better than no story at all.

Now: a true story. The first green pesticide was green. I mean, it was green in colour. It was crap for the environment, being an arsenical poison. But it was very green. Emerald. Why do you think little farmgirl Dorothy dreams of an Emerald city? That colour stands between her and her family's ruination. Cupric acetoarsenite held back the Colorado potato beetle for around seventy-five years. Saved the US cotton crop from chewing pests. Controlled mosquito larvae too, saving who knows how many from malaria? It and its cousins. Paris Green wasn't the only product out there. In them thar days you could pick your poison. Arsenic, copper, lead, mercury, sulphur, fluorine. Botanicals, too. Nicotine. Pyrethrum. Rotenone.

Synthetics came next. DDT, accumulating faster than credit-card debt, thinning eggshells, killing bees. But Paul Müller deserved his Nobel. How many children did he save from insect-vectored disease? The *good* DDT has done is incalculable.

Little by little – and this process is painfully slow – we learn how to narrow and focus our destructive power. Year on year, we cause a little less collateral damage. The grail, for us, is to be able to treat the disease without kicking the patient to death. We're not there yet, but we've come a hell of a long way from Paris Green.

Miami's law campus wasn't one I know that well, though Clarita had been teaching there three years. She guided me round the narrow lanes – bike lanes, really – to her door. Late prep for her moot competition.

'Pull in here.'

Still nothing really said.

I parked up in the shade of a low, dilapidated red-brick block, its frontage disfigured by a low, laborious disabled ramp painted acid yellow, I guess on the assumption that if you'd lost the use of your legs you were probably half-blind as well.

Through clenched teeth: 'You'll be okay?'

She kissed me carefully on the cheek. 'I'll be late.'

'You'll be exhausted.'

'Yeah.' She got out, and waved, and left all the unsaid things in the car with me.

Miami's law faculty and much of the rest of South Campus used to house the CIA's JMWAVE operation against Fidel Castro. I wonder if Clarita ever told her grandmother.

Vera Kozlovskaya. Born 1928, Moscow, the year Stalin repealed Lenin's New Economic Policy. Whenever some weasel TV commentator says of a politician that, 'he at least stands up for what he believes in,' I think of Vera, I think of what she did, what she was a part of, and I reach for the remote.

Comrade Kozlovskaya: star pupil in that class of regimented children to whom Stalin handed the country's science base, once all proud nails were hammered down. Geneticists. Eugenicists. Botanists and engineers. Ruined or dead, the lot of them. And in their place, the Veras. Apparatchiks of the prison state. Shockworkers on collective farms. Toadies and sneaks, all rant and cant and rage. Down with formalist Mendelist-Morganism! Down with the anti-grasslanders! Each and every one stabbing their neighbour in the back in the struggle for tenure, denouncing each other, staging honour courts, every month writing their passive-aggressive letters of resignation, pleas to patrons for assistance against the forces of bourgeois idealism, anonymous accusations of toadying to the West. Children of the Great Terror, they drank in its methods with their milk, played them for stakes, talked up every move as though it were a military operation: 'Action on the Agronomic Front.' And what's a purge, after all? A little terror, to keep Joe sweet. Small sacrifices – a career here, a livelihood there – to the politburo Gods.

Vera was part of this. Chanted along. Penned modest hymns to the inheritance of acquired characteristics. Led catechisms denouncing intra-specific competition. From this distance, an unwinning combination of the absurd and the obscure.

I wonder: over the span of her career, in Moscow, in Havana, through her words, her publications, her breathless hagiography of Michurinists like Wilyams and Prezent, Lysenko and Kol: how many did she make go hungry? How many did she kill?

When her name came up on Google I didn't know whether to laugh or spit.

The Vera Kozlovskaya Pediatric Teaching Hospital in San Miguel del Padrón. And, inevitably, it took Vera's personal intervention to arrange Clarita's operation. Bump's operation, I mean, in Clarita's womb.

All I had to do was arrange the trip to Havana. And what a bunfight that was. There is still no ferry to Cuba. US citizens, waving the right papers, can get to Cuba by plane. But Clarita, twenty-three weeks in, refused to fly.

'They'll carry you,' I said.

'I'm not risking Bump on a plane!' There were tears. I couldn't for the life of me understand why I should be getting it in the neck for pointing out to her that an airline would fly her up to twenty-seven weeks in.

'I'm not risking her life on a plane!'

I could see what this was. This was story-telling. Even as I was beating myself up, thinking my nice, safe laboratory job had crippled my child, Clarita was weaving her own self-myth: how no-one wanted Bump but her.

I can't remember exactly what we said to each other, and there would anyway not be much point setting it down. It wasn't pretty.

A lesson from our couples' guidance sessions: it's best not to treat the people you love as though they were machines in need of repair. 'You are always trying to fix things,' being Clarita's major refrain. And from me: 'You are always asking me to fix things and then halfway in to my fixing them you are telling me not to bother after all.'

Anyway, I fixed this. There's a ninety-nine-dollar one-day cruise leaves Fort Lauderdale for Grand Bahama at 10am. From Grand Bahama you can catch a ferry to Havana and hope to Christ the authorities don't take it into their heads to stamp your passport, or it's a ten thousand dollar fine. (If we'd had that kind of money to throw around we could have just paid for the operation in the US.)

This is not the kind of surgery Havana is famous for. Not an inter-uterine impregnation, or dentistry, or a nip-and-tuck. It's a whole other level of serious. There's only a handful of doctors in the world with any kind of track record in this procedure and happily for us one of them was a Ukrainian professor living with relatives in Havana. Oh, the happy coincidence. Oh, the incredible good fortune, global geopolitics conspiring to give our child the chance to walk. Well: hobble.

Clarita shrugged. She actually shrugged. 'I suppose.'

'Jesus!' I laughed. 'What are we waiting for? Babe? I'll

call emigration. I'll call the airline. Jesus!'

People are much more than machines in need of repair. But when the repair is there for the taking, why would you not grab at the chance? Why would you not give in to hope?

To Joseph Stalin's way of thinking, the whole of nature was a machine in need of repair. His dachas had large greenhouses, so that he could walk straight from his bedroom into a collection of exotic plants. He was fascinated by the idea that it might be possible to alter the nature of plants. It was his only hobby. His only exercise. He had ambitious plans for lemons.

At a jubilee to celebrate the fiftieth birthday of Trofim Lysenko, the charlatan who destroyed Soviet genetics, Stalin handed that appalling fraud the Order of Lenin and the keys to the 'Great Stalin Plan for the Transformation of Nature'. He wanted to plant forest belts to save the Black Earth Belt from erosion. He wanted to reverse the course of five Siberian rivers. He wanted heaven on earth.

He wanted – and got – a movie. A fairytale called *Life in Bloom*.

It goes something like this:

One day Michurin, an old gardener, decides to invent new varieties of apple. Apples to feed the world. Apples that will flourish just about anywhere you care to stick them.

He buys a riverbank plot where the soil is gravel and silt and doesn't grow shit. He digs up his orchard and carries his trees down to the river and his neighbours reckon the man's gone out of his mind.

Jump cut.

A professor explains to Michurin about genes, chromosomes and mutations. Michurin replies: 'It is time for biology to get off the pedestal! It should speak the language of the people, and not get lost in the fog!' (For some reason, everyone has started shouting).

Two spivs from the US Department of Agriculture turn up to move his research to the United States. But Michurin wants to give his work to the people of his country – to the simple folk from the Ural Mountains and Siberia who understand and appreciate what he's trying to achieve.

Jump cut.

A priest wags a finger, shouts: 'Do not turn God's garden into a brothel!' Michurin ignores him.

Jump cut.

The Bolshevik revolution. The simple folk come to power. They understand Michurin. They comprehend everything. They come up with brilliant suggestions for further work and Michurin makes several important discoveries.

By now, strange plants are crowding Michurin's garden. The apple and pear trees strain under the weight of their fruits. The winding stems of Far Eastern Actinidia bear large, heavy, sweet, amber-coloured berries that smell and taste like pineapple. Peaches flourish beside apricots. Almond trees throw out shoots seven-feet long. What look like grapes hang from the branches of a strange tree – a blend of the sweet and sour cherry. Vines weave their tendrils in a light breeze.

Believe in your dream, and the material world will yield. This is the moral. Disney couldn't have put it better. The difference being, Walt didn't attempt to seize the science base of his country. All he ever did was freeze his head. (And why would he not give in to hope?)

Outside, the cicadas were singing. The VCR snapped to a stop and began to rewind. From her corner – tiny, shapeless, a bundle of grey sticks – Vera clapped.

Vera's generator. The ceiling fan in her bedroom. Her untunable television. Getting the VCR running so we could see *Life in Bloom* pretty much made me Vera's friend for life – or what was left of it, she was well into her eighties by then. There was no soundtrack. She insisted on talking us through

Alexander Dovchenko's entire masterpiece in her broken Spanish. She talked herself raw. Entire speeches. Whole strings of dialogue. Now and again Clarita wrestled the Spanish into English for me but her heart wasn't in it.

To hear Vera tell it, the film script was all her own work. At least, the bits that mattered had come off her typewriter. She meant the shouting. The parades. She spent a good year rewriting, revising, adding new scenes, interpreting the latest political instructions. (From Dovzchenko's diary: 'I am exhausted as if I had been dragging heavy rocks around all day long.')

Work in the censors' office, giving Dovzchenko's original screenplay what-for, provided Vera's career with its glamour. Otherwise she spent her time revising Soviet textbooks for the new, Michurinist age. Speeches for Trofim Lysenko. For Olga Lepeshinskaya. ('What happiness! At last, the dialectical materialists have triumphed, the idealists are paralysed and are being liquidated as the kulaks were once liquidated. And yet, among the sincere repentants, there are some wolves in sheep's clothing trying to save themselves from liquidation!')

And when Stalin died, Krushchev swallowed the same bullshit, proved an even bigger supporter of Michurinism than Stalin had ever been. It's why they deposed him in the end. In propping up Lysenko's career, he was threatening to dissolve the entire Academy.

Vera could see where this was heading. Like all her generation, she had antennae tuned to political change. The age of ideologues was drawing to a close. She would have to get herself a proper job.

Which is how she ended up here, managing hospitals in Havana. Rural clinics. Mobile dispensaries. Handing out antibiotics and vaccines to the rural poor. Doing her bit to build one of the most cash-efficient health services on earth.

Vera married a paediatric consultant – a quiet, worried man, discreetly devout. (I've seen photographs of him,

Clarita's looks come from him: his extraordinary, troubled eyes). My mother-in-law, Verita, was born in 1960. The apple of her father's eye, she inherited her father's religion but none of his spirit. She lived with him after the divorce, but in 1980, without a word of warning, she got the hell out of the country through Mariel with never a backward glance.

Verita's mother was a national treasure but her father was no-one, an easy target. Communist stooges stood outside his house, screaming obscenities, pelting his house with eggs and garbage for hours.

Within a year of settling in Miami Verita was married. Carlito was born in 84, Clarita in 86.

When Verita's father died in 2006 she didn't even visit for the funeral. 'Mum can be really *cold*, you know?' That, anyway, was what Clarita said to me, the night we met. She'd just that day returned from her granddad's funeral. Her skin was spiced from the Caribbean sun. She smelled delicious. Strange.

She couldn't get over the way we looked in bed. Honey and liquorice, she said.

The wedding came soon after. The pair of us, just look at us. Both giving in to hope.

Our own apartment.

Bump.

You don't own the Mona Lisa just because you went to the Louvre and studied it. By the same logic, you cannot patent folk knowledge. So the project that had gotten me a decent salary and launched us on a life of married comfort stuttered eventually to a stop.

Gingko biloba. Hill apricot. Silverfruit. The tree that famously survived the Hiroshima atom bomb. A living fossil: more than a quarter of a billion years old.

Gingko leads a pest-free life. 270,000,000 years have given it time to evolve the perfect chemical defence. No insect nibbles its leaves and lives. The neurotoxin it manufactures is so powerful, at first glance it's a mystery why it doesn't kill Carlito's wife stone dead of a morning; why their bathroom cabinets aren't crime-scene taped or monitored by Homeland Security.

Gingko blocks an insect's RDL receptors. RDLs are ion channels: the building blocks of the invertebrate nervous system, repressing or transmitting nerve signals depending on their chemical state.

An ideal insecticidal target site.

What makes the whole business slightly creepy is that a bug's RDL receptors are virtually identical to the equivalent receptors in vertebrates. Which means that bust-lifting, eye-refreshing, skin-cleansing, dementia-shifting Gingko, every hippy's favourite home remedy, is not much more than a single protein fold away from being a mankiller.

Why Gingko extract blocks the invertebrate receptor and leaves the vertebrate one alone is a study in protein architectonics we've been labouring at for years now. The trouble is, in unpicking the puzzle, we've found ourselves unable to improve upon it. The living fossil has us beat. It's just about perfect.

Which means, of course, that no-one's going to invest in it. Somewhere inside Ginko is a world-beating narrow-spectrum insecticide, but it'll never reach market. There's no patent here, you see. Instead, beauty companies and snake-oil merchants will continue to make money dropping weak Ginko extract into eye cream and bust enhancer and gelatine capsules meant to arrest senility.

Another true story: Stalin-Prize-winning biologist Olga Lepeshinskaya once announced to the Academic Council of the Institute of Morphology that soda baths could rejuvinate the old and preserve the youth of the young. A doctor in the audience asked her whether mineral water would work instead. Lepeshinskaya, oblivious to his sarcasm, told him no. A couple of weeks later Moscow completely sold out of baking soda.

The trouble with Lepeshinskaya, with Vera Kozlovskaya and her sugar-daddy Trofim Lysenko, with his sponsor Joseph Stalin and with the whole lot of them, from Marx all the way up to Krushchev – is that they were *fans*. They loved science. They worshipped it. Glamorised it. Aspired to it. They even understood it, some of them, pretty well. But like fans everywhere, they had no patience. Deep down they resented what they thought they revered. And deeper still in their most secret places, they longed to wield a rod of iron over their adopted gods.

Genetics is largely a Soviet invention. Soviet geneticists, the cream of the world's crop, and internationally renowned, spent the whole of the 1930s explaining to the leadership that crops change slowly. That it takes more than a dozen years to establish a new strain of wheat. That anything cooked up in a lab has to be trialed in the earth, year after year, a dozen years at least, and even then there is no way of knowing whether the desired variation will hold or not. That the world is rich and complex and unpredictable and change is full of risks. That living things shrink from such risks: they don't *want* to change.

But with the blood of millions already on his hands from collectivisation – not to mention the wholesale disappearance of countless varieties of domesticated plant – Uncle Joe heard none of it. He wanted food. He wanted it now. Enter Lysenko, peddling an idea of evolution already two centuries out of date. Trofim Denisovich Lysenko, who became Stalin's unlovely poster-boy. Lysenko said things change their form in response to the environment, and pass any changes directly to their offspring. No element of chance. No randomness in selection. No genetic code to learn. Giraffes have long necks because their parents *stretch*.

And there's no brake on this process, neither, according to Trofim and his kind. No natural conservatism. Things want to change. They just need some kindly direction. So spin your wheel and stick in your thumbs: the living world is clay. Oats will turn to wild oats, pines to firs, sunflowers to zinnias.

Animal cells will turn into plant cells. Plants into animals! Cells from soup! 'How can there be hereditary diseases in a socialist society?' From the nonliving will come the living.

Vera, who met the great Lysenko at the premier of *Life in Bloom*, became, they say, his darling and his squeeze. His protogée, for sure: the year before Krushchev was deposed she published her first scientific paper in his *Byulleten'Yarovizatsii*: how a chiffchaff laid an egg with a cuckoo.

In Havana, she continued her experiments, though by then they were more of a hobby than anything else. Beetroot seeds here. A little pilfered blood there. The older Vera got, the more she fell under the sway of the mystical concept of the blastema, the source of 'vital substance'. It was an open secret, tolerated, and while she delivered on the day job, no one was going to stop her making her films of spontaneous generation.

She was a terrible scientist but a brilliant bureaucrat. There is a street named after her in Havana. A children's hospital.

She only had one child, the unlovely, suck-lemon, rosary-clicking Verita, my mother-in-law. But she and her husband adopted four others. Street kids. Tearaways. They all made something of themselves, I've been told. She had that kind of unsentimental practicality. 'You need to get some rest,' she said to me, at the hospital.

'I'm fine.'

'Clarita is in no danger. The worst it could be is the child dies.'

I stared at her. She smiled an open smile. Her teeth belonged to someone forty years younger. I'd thought when I'd first met her that she was wearing dentures.

She genuinely meant her words to comfort me. This woman who took in mongrel children, and lived through famines, and helped cause a couple. She was immune to tragedy.

'I'll stay.'

She shrugged and walked away, letting me be with all my visions of the little knives and scissors playing about in my wife's belly.

My daddy went to Bethune-Cookman in Daytona Beach. He studied to be a doctor. Halfway through he cut loose for Baltimore, to Eden Street, turned Panther to avoid the draft for 'Nam.

Not every door was closed to him in his life. Just enough of them. Today I get to wear the white coat he did not. From the home, from his chair, through his oxygen mask, he says he's proud of me. Of what I've done. I showed him a department brochure once and he fair bust a lung: 'Goddamn,' he said, 'y'all like the Goddamn Klan.'

Yes: we are a priesthood when we want. Rubber boots and respirators. Plastic wear-and-burn. But that sort of CDC garb is more to jazz up the undergrad prospectus than for use. Most often we slop up to work in jeans, to hunch in front of monitors, spinning models of this protein, that receptor, seeing what can be made to fit. Tetris for the biochemically inclined.

RDL receptors. GABA-A. 'We conclude that the insecticidal activity of *G. biloba* extracts can be attributed to their effects at insect receptors, and the presence of a Val at the 2′ position in vertebrate GABA-A receptors explains why these compounds are not similarly toxic to humans.'

GABA-As: a vertebrate's ion channels. The parts of the nervous system benzodiazepines were made for. Inhibit her GABA-A receptors, and you reduce a person's anxiety. Inhibit them further, and you send her to sleep. Sometimes for days. Rarely, for years. Sleeping Beauty starts here. Unless the overdose is truly monstrous. In which case – what else? – you'll kill her.

Alprazolam was Verita's ticket out, drawing out her death as passive-aggressively as she had drawn out her life. She didn't leave a note, assuming everyone knew by then that she was too good for this world. A hell of an exit: poor Clarita sat there by her bedside, watching and waiting, week after week. The suck-thump of the respirator.

Clarita and I buried her mother around the time we brought an end to our couples' counselling and started trying for a child. People think it was trying for Bump that stuck our fracturing relationship back together. I think it was Verita's death.

There was, after all, no fixing it. No hope for me to pull us into. Nothing for Clarita to drag me out of, halfway through. It was something over which we could agree.

Clarita began attending church soon after. And though I take every public opportunity to polish up the badge of my unbelief, I have to admit that it put me out of sorts that she never said: Jack, come along with me.

Why this unbelief? Why not give in to hope?

Because hope is without rigour. Because hope is blind, and blinding. Hope is like Paris Green: a broad-spectrum application that destroys as much as it saves. Too much hope, too much faith in the world, too much following your dream wherever it may lead, and you end up like Vera. I mean, just look at this shit. She's done with practical work now, her arthritic hands can do no more mischief, and the lab she built in her garden (Uncle Joe had his lemons, Vera her beetroot) resembles nothing so much now as a potting shed gone to seed. It's only when you're inside, and your eyes have had a chance to adjust to the gloom, that you get a measure of her work. Its enormity. Schlenk flasks and mortars, conical and volumetric flasks and pigeon droppings.

Is that monstrous pig-iron apostrophe, propped on bricks in the corner, an actual *alembic vessel*?

It is.

Vera recruited her entire extended family to her scientific enterprise. An adopted child of eight can pound beetroot seeds in a pestle as well as any grown-up. But it takes a woman of genius to demonstrate that, with the Vital

Substance present, any section of a plant ovule can germinate.

In the house, in the living room where we sit and entertain the old crow, waiting for Clarita's stitches to heal enough that she can brave the journey back, the walls are lined with books from the darkest days of Soviet biology. School textbooks carrying Vera's name describe the 'achievements' of Michurinism.

Vera is, perhaps, the last surviving member of that generation who wanted to repair nature but didn't have the patience. Like useless workmen, they blamed their tools. (The botanists. The geneticists. The histologists. Pretty much anyone they came across who actually knew how to use a microscope.) And in their place and over their graves they built their myth. Everything is malleable! And anything that is not malleable is ineffable! They were like children, only without a child's charm, its innocence. They were appalling.

Vera's all over me, of course. Embracing the dark. Son of a militant leftist! She imagines she is the least racist person I have ever met. Raised as I was in Jim Crow's nest. Keeps asking me how people *react to me* at home. It's touching, in a queasy sort of way. Papery fingers on my arm. Her little heat against me as I propel her round her ruin of a garden. 'Of course,' she says, all-knowing – how righteous her life has been here, and how dull – 'it was Lysenko taught us that factors other than genes had an effect on living things.'

Vera and I have been drinking coffee on her verandah. She wants to know all about *genetic modification*. She wants to know all about *horizontal transmission*. She thinks the richer, the more complex genetics gets, the more ambiguous, the more difficult to explain, the more it resembles the doggerel of her youth.

What she and her generation forgot, or chose to ignore, is that the world is madly rich, wildly ambiguous. So it's natural, it's inevitable, that the better your science is, the more confusing and complex it gets. At the unimaginably far-off end of your quest, your science *is* the world; the world *is* your theory. You want a last chapter? A conclusion? A *simple* conclusion? What are you, a child? In the end, this is not a straight story. In the end, I did not disfigure my child, and neither did anyone else. And how frightening is it, that life should turn out to be so desperately unlike television?

There is nothing Vera would like better, in her lonely old age, than to descend with me into the mechanics of her cant. To counter this, I have instead been telling her about the bees. These being my next allotted task, now that the Gingko business is dead.

I tell her: 'Pesticides do not stay still. They change.'

The environment changes them. Light alone can turn a promising crop spray into gunk, or turn a harmless laboratory dud into a broad-spectrum killer.

'But it's the subtle changes that you worry about the most,' I tell her. 'The slow effect. A killer accumulating over seasons, over generations.'

She sits forward in her chair, eager as a child. This, to her ears, is a story pitched against the excesses of contemporary western agriculture. How good pesticides spare the lives of bees. But that bee colonies continue to collapse. And how, once Clarita and I get home, I will be spending most of my time in the field — a rarity for me and, for once, literally true: *in a field* — attaching tiny, three-milligram RFID tags to bee thoraxes. I am going to be tracking bees across a square of agricultural land to see whether certain insecticides are getting them ever so slightly stoned. Because if something's getting the bees stoned, then it might be they cannot forage well. Or even if they do forage well, perhaps they cannot waggle-dance the location of their finds when they get back to the colony. And even if they can waggle-dance their discoveries, maybe the problem is their audience is too stoned to watch them properly. The possibilities are dizzying. The *world* is dizzying.

But fixable. Here and there. With time and, above all, patience, fixable. Like it or not. And there are never any guarantees.

Clarita says that when we return to the US, she will move in for a while with her brother Carlito and his wife. Because she needs time to think. Because she needs time to pray. Because Bump died inside her, on the operating table.

I think about this in the taxi, and reach for my wife's hand. But she does not notice, or at any rate does not respond, and all I can see, in the dusty glare out the window, is Vera's white smile, there in the cafeteria of a hospital named Kozlovskaya, as we were waiting out the operation. The open, blameless smile of a child.

Just now, in the garden, Vera said to me: 'I'm glad you brought her here.' We stood watching as the taxi climbed, whining, towards the house. 'Even so,' she said, 'I'm glad you made her take the chance.'

Vera's on my side in this, you see. Me being someone, so she thinks, so very like her younger self. A child of revolution. Knows how to raise his fist. A new kind of shockworker, on a new biological front. Wrestles nature. Spurns religion.

A materialist, seeking ways to right the world.

Afterword:

Articulating the Laboratory

Dr Ian Vincent McGonigle

Department of Anthropology, University of Chicago

INGS' AMBITIOUS STORY points the spotlight on a research pharmacologist and his foiled attempt to 'wrestle' with the perils of hope, promise, and risk – in both his family life as well as in his scientific career. One cannot, of course, ever achieve complete separation of these two spheres, as the boundaries of work and home life blur under close examination, just as the research output of a laboratory eventually spills out into the wider world, be that in the form of a new drug, a novel insecticide, or a scarcely available maternity treatment. Negotiating these two hypothetical domains is where the anthropologically interesting stuff happens, where scientific discoveries become household factoids, and where 'expert knowledge' becomes 'common sense', or the knowledge of 'the masses'.

We might well ask the question then: what is a laboratory space, and what makes it a unique or special place anyway? I shall give a simplified account of the way that sociologists and anthropologists of science have attempted to understand how scientists work in a laboratory, socially 'constructing' scientific facts. A laboratory can be thought of as a segregated physical space that demands a certain category of practice: people (scientists) wear lab coats, speak in a specialised scientific language, and through experiments, ritually utilize instruments and techniques to observe and record 'nature'. Scientists arrange their objectifying apparatuses in configurations that yield measurements, 'traces' from materials: measurements that are used to represent the objective natural world. These traces purport to constitute evidence that edify the linguistic statements about the natural world that hold true outside of the laboratory's walls. A laboratory might therefore also be considered to include those physical spaces outside of the laboratory floor where the same regimes of language and knowledge prevail. Eventually, the discovered facts emerge as public knowledge through mediated dissemination and cultural assimilation. This is a simple 'constructivist' description of how scientific knowledge is stabilised, emphasizing the role of human actors in the genesis of expert knowledge and showing that the ways in which scientists represent nature are sociologically informed.

Though the laboratory's practices aim to provide the conditions that mimic – or orchestrate a microcosm of – nature, these conditions can only ever *approximate* the 'natural' world 'out there', and the apparatuses that are put into force can therefore only make truth statements that asymptotically approximate absolute truth. This is all to say that whatever the abilities of scientists to dazzle with inventions, promises, and public spectacles, there remains an epistemic rift between observations made in a laboratory and the applications of these principals outside in the larger 'natural world', be that in a whole organism, a particular ecological niche, or a human body being treated under medical anaesthesia. Though conceivably small, this rift is the space where theory and practice contest, and where the uncertainty of truth is sequestered. I consider it important to think about the possibility of this epistemic rift going unrecognized, and to anticipate the potential for the whole scientific knowledge-producing machinery to make grindingly destructive assumptions.

Let me elucidate my point. Ings' story gives us a glimpse of Lysenko's heritage: how Stalin tried to master nature, 'reverse the flow of rivers,' and make genetics into a socialist dogma that would ultimately be a manifest justification of the political ideology of the day. Such histories reveal how efforts to articulate human capabilities in dominating and marshalling nature can bite back with unforeseeable disaster. After all, Soviet totalitarianism, in all of its violent top-down brutality did not succeed as was hoped, despite the best intentions and the sincerest commitments to truth made by the scientists working under the regime. History tells us that what is repressed often returns with reinvigored force, though in this instance we can see with facility that the cultural and historical backdrop of scientific knowledge production – totalitarianism at its zenith – determines what kind of science is done, what kind of knowledge and power are produced, and possibly most importantly, what is thinkable or speakable in a particular historical period.

The kind of research questions that get asked by scientists is one thing, but what questions and research projects get multi-million pound grants, state backing, and positive peer support is another. Society, ideology, politics and economic imperatives coalesce to determine scientific practice, to be sure, historically, and still to this day. Currently in the UK, basic scientific research complements a 'biocapitalist' mode of production that manufactures and markets molecular diagnostics and therapeutics, and at the same time, basic research moves more progressively to determine how human bodies work and how they can be accurately modulated to improve health outcomes. It is commonly assumed that state-backed research should rightly be directed to improve overall human health, but demystifying the state's veiled interests in this process reveals their crucial role in informing the mode of basic scientific knowledge production.

Nonetheless, I have tried thus far to show that scientific facts, as they are shaped and cultivated by the wider institutions of society, are at the most basic level, socially constructed and historically overdetermined. Though what does this tell us about the laboratory and its relationship to the natural world? It says that the way 'facts' get semiotically constructed as representing the 'natural world', through technical apparatuses and concomitant discursive practices, is prefigured by the economic mode of production at a given historical juncture, making the kinds of researches that are being done a litmus test for the type of economic and political climate incubating them. To balk at Soviet science as ludicrous and misguided ambition is a tempting and satisfying luxury, but taking such a smug stance would be to firmly embed one's feet in the 'here and now', directing one's gaze backwards through history with the privilege of 20-20 retrospective vision. It would be far more interesting, I claim, to shift one's subject position, de-centre one's gaze, and attempt to historicise 'the now', asking the provocative question of what our scientific culture can tell us about what we think '21st century Western nature' is today?

I was recently part of the study that showed that the extracts from *Ginkgo biloba* – an ancient Asian tree with bizarre pest resistance – are highly toxic to insects while harmless, or possibly even beneficial, to humans.[6] We made tiny measurements of insect and human neurotransmitter receptors (the molecular switches that are responsible for brain signaling), showing that a subtle difference in our human receptors makes us resistant to the toxic effects, making *Ginkgo* a perfect 'green insecticide' candidate. Well, maybe. The next step in the process would be to determine how *Ginkgo* extracts would function *en masse*, across a whole countryside, and through many years of use. We cannot know for sure what would happen, but we can take a guess and make a leap of 'faith' (or is it modern reason?), and hope that we land on firm ground on the other side. We make such hopeful jumps in daily life similarly as we do in scientific research: Fly to Cuba for specialist medical treatment; put investment capital behind a risky research project; or change the nation's landscape to improve agricultural output… However, various factors can make these jumps possible or impossible right out of the blocks: Can a US citizen obtain a

6. Thompson, A.J., McGonigle, I., Duke, R., Johnston, G.A., Lummis, S.C. (2012) A single amino acid determines the toxicity of *Ginkgo biloba* extracts. *FASEB J.* 26(5):1884–1891.

visa to Cuba, for instance? What kind of research is being funded by the state-backed funding agencies in the UK? What are the subsidies for growing corn or soya in Illinois, and what are the citizens' real nutritional needs? Such political realities come to the fore in human social life, the point where the rarefied contents of the laboratory wield little authority, and where wider histories come to bear heavily.

In the story, Clarita's 'bump' had a fetal abnormality, and her husband asked himself 'Why?' What was the cause of this terrible and unforeseeable problem? The mode of reasoning was scientific, yet no clear answer could be provided. The gap between science and nature could not be bridged, opening up a dangerous space for 'unreason' and potentially mythological irrationality to erupt. This dangerous space leaves scant room for comprehending, least of all accepting, such inexplicable tragedies. In days gone by, God, spirits and bad luck may have been the prime scapegoats for blame. In our rational scientific culture today, the unexpected is often kept under control, regulation, and putatively, rendered predictable – no room is left for the unknown, or even worse perhaps, the silent threat of the unknown. Though all of us remain subject to the betrayal of faith, it would seem.

Perhaps the only way to move forward and create anything worthwhile and meaningful is to make the leap, to take the risk and to put a certain degree of confidence in that which comes before reason and knowledge. To take a chance and fly to Cuba, to reverse a river, to make a new insecticide – what is possible and what is not can only be determined after the fact sometimes. Ings' story highlights beautifully the human component behind such brave moves and teasingly tells us that the space between nature and science is the realm of uncertainty, the dominion of politics, the space where risk thrives and hope secretes itself. Life, much like good science, demands a brave wrestler.

Madswitch

Justina Robson

MY MOTHER TRIED to kill me again this morning. She laid in wait for me behind the kitchen door with the iron raised. In a departure from her usual MO it was plugged in. The puff of steam from the jet holes puffed out in a bit of a giveaway as I trudged down the hall in slippers and dressing gown, tea-tray held at the ready. She always used to be ironing first thing when we were little; school shirts, then trousers, after pressing Dad's shirt to perfection.

Now she forgets what she's doing halfway through getting it out and stands there, usually without even the board, iron raised in her hand. She looks quizzical, like someone pondering where they left their keys. This morning she was pressing the steam jet. I held up the tray as I walked in and the iron thunked against it as if by clockwork. It wasn't clockwork however, it was partly alarm – she was always defocused – and partly a desire to do harm. Her malice was crafty and casual these days. My brother called her Gollumina, because like Gollum she had two sides now, one nice and pathetically sweet because she knew we were looking after her, one filled with a primal rage that had lain a long time in hidden caves where Dad had buried it under a landslide of little put-downs. These caves had been newly opened by the excavations of age and dementia and an ancient reptilian malevolence had emerged, triggered by sudden movements or any unexpected incident, such as someone walking into a room when she was standing behind the door, pondering.

'You're losing your touch,' I said, putting the tray down and removing the iron from her very carefully before switching it off at the wall and putting it to cool in the pantry.

She pouts, her fun spoiled. 'Where's your dad?'

'He died, Mum.'

'Oh. Where's the dog?'

'In the hall.'

'You have to feed him last or he'll think he's king of the house.'

'Yes, Mum.' I get her sat down and give her breakfast. My brother waits to come down until later when this pantomime is over. He has autism, of a form that makes it too hard for him to get a job dealing with other people in any way, particularly strangers. Between the two of them they could burn the house down by eleven in the morning should they get into a fatal clash of viewpoints so they must be managed separately.

Once Andy is safely occupied with his computer games and Mum has gone to the daycare centre for the morning I manage a hasty bit of cleanup and the emptying of the commode. Then I rush to the shed.

The shed is an old hut, some relic from WWII that my grandfather built with the notion there may be a need for something halfway between a bomb shelter and a refuge from Grandma's wrath. The latter was always more of a threat in this valley. It's his workbench that holds my equipment, sheltered from mice and spiders by a large opaque Perspex box under a tarp behind the gardening things. Opposite stands a woodworking bench and an old easel and some paints from two abandoned notions of artistic retreat.

When he'd had a few, my dad would come in here and rant and mutter that Mum and Andy should be left out for the wolves. They were millstones round his neck preventing us from being like everyone else. Andy because he wouldn't talk right and would never come to anything, Mum because she loved Andy. 'You, Carol,' he'd say, regretting himself. 'You'll do all right, won't you? You won't be like me. You won't be like him.' Coming here always makes me remember him trying to escape, but he wasn't an inward person so he'd sit and wait a while, then get out the lawnmower. When he was finished and

I'd done the edges and brushed out the bottom of the mower we'd sit together. He painted a little. The only thing he finished was a picture of a green dog, on a hill, under a blue sky with a blue bird in it. It was more abandoned than finished. There weren't any more.

There are no wolves in Todmorden and no green dogs either. If you want to get rid of something you leave it on the kerb on bin collection day and hope the council takes it away. My mum left the dog picture out not long after he'd died. I went out to get it back but the man who stepped off the huge truck and helped me to search our bin in the November mist found it in two pieces and soaked through with tea-stains. He shoved it in the truck and patted me on the shoulder. 'Never mind, eh? Yer can always paint another one, eh?' he said, nodding at me. He smiled and waved.

Under the Perspex box are the beautiful canisters, dishes and containers of my laboratory with their corporate logos stamped in clear, precise shapes. Beside them in a sealed crate are my books and papers and my iPad plugged into the ancient sockets on the extension cord.

As I get out what I need I'm reminded of Sunday School, watching the vicar remove his sacred bits and pieces from the mouldy-smelling damp of the vestry and laying them on the altar. I was never sure if they had real power or not. I always felt worried about them: in case they did and they were being disrespectfully kept in a poor place, and in case they didn't and we were all wasting our time on a few knick-knacks.

Centrifuge, beakers, tubes, Petri dishes, oh you beautiful objects! Let us see what you have grown today. A beard of mould it seems. That's disappointing. My cultures have died and been taken over by more robust contaminants from the shed itself. I clean them out and try not to feel despondent. Science is a marathon, not a sprint. Failures are information. And this has told me that I need better hygiene during my culture preparations. Anyway, it results in me spending the first minutes of my precious time back at the sink washing up. I doubt there's anything viable in the culture gel that can't be washed down a regular drain.

Near the paints all gone solid in their tubes is Grandad's original glass home brew gear which I've put to new use. I had to get new hoses and add a few items but it seems that although I might not be good at culturing germline, precision-engineered bacteria, I am good at manufacturing Ecstasy. My MDMA, as Grandad might put it, is turning out 'right nice'. It's at a stage where I can leave it and I don't have time to progress it now, so after admiring it and recalculating the final likely output I cover it all up again with mousy sacking and turn to the email.

Inside my lab newsgroups some people have answered my questions about *E Coli* re-engineering with a view to creating precursors to serotonin. They have also responded to my general call for information about oxytocin production. I read them avidly, in the way that I used to read the back of cornflakes' packets and the advertisements in women's magazines offering the latest suggestions for a happier life through the ingestion of different foods and supplements. Oxytocin binds us harmoniously together and reduces inflammation, literal and emotional. Serotonin, at the right levels, gives a sense of wellbeing and, notoriously, when it is lacking causes low mood, irritation and depression. I am far from the first person to consider engineering the unhappy family cell with chemistry. The MDMA is just my backup plan. I have two primary plans.

The first is to use tweaked gut bacteria to treat Mum's dementia with oxytocin boosting.

'Hi Local_Alchemist! Yes, I think, in answer to your question – greater oxytocin presence *could* help in the elevation of mood and a general sense of calm and wellbeing within patients suffering from dementia, even in advanced forms. I'm not aware of it being able to halt deterioration however, and the effects may be mild but there are some studies going on in relation to this. See links.'

I follow every one dutifully, and think it through. So, it won't bring back her memories but at least we might be able to traverse the house without being prey to a homicidal relative.

The first plan is also useful because Andy's autism, again not curable exactly, is partly exacerbated by low blood oxytocin.

'Dear Local_Alchemist, please find enclosed confirmation of oxytocin production and uptake in autistic people. Note that not all autism is the same and every individual would need to be profiled separately in order to establish whether or not the metabolic situation was, in fact, abnormal with regard to oxytocin processes. However, yes, it does seem a promising route for further research....'

If I could up his ability to receive the beneficial effects of oxytocin, he would feel better and be more receptive to ordinary social contact. But I can't just fill him with it. Part of the issue is that his receptors aren't sufficient or functional. I can't figure out how to get over that. I have queried the possibility of genetic therapy for him but what is required seems in advance of my abilities and officially he is not bad enough to warrant the effort via the NHS. I would have to take his cells, extract the genome and replace it with a copy in which the proteins causing the trouble have been 'corrected'. That would require that I know how their expression worked in the entire organism. I don't. This is why I thought of re-engineering gut bacteria to produce oxytocin or at least its precursors but...

'Dear Local_Alchemist, thanks for your queries. You should note that oxytocin cannot survive the environment of the human gut and would almost certainly all be destroyed there even if it were able to cross the gut wall into the bloodstream – a secondary obstacle of at least equal magnitude to the primary issue. I don't think such a plan would fly. However, you might have some mileage in serotonin precursors.'

But serotonin is an already abandoned plan: DIY neurotransmitter boosting was the first thing I thought of. Its precursors are pretty easy to come by after all. Eat tons of turkey! Precursors aplenty in there. Our freezer is stuffed full of turkey nuggets. But they've not been significant as far as I can see. Plus my mother doesn't like turkey and will only nibble the coating off. I was also unclear as to exactly how much turkey would be enough and what else was required. Lots of vitamin C for one thing. So I attempted to administer fruits, juices and tablets. Andy does not like orange, the colour *or* the flavour. But at least Andy understands and likes the idea that there is a simple chemical formulation somewhere that would be useful to him. Mum thinks nature intended everything to be as it is and is best left alone. I would say that turkey, oranges and hugs are all present in nature, but that would require we actually have the conversation in the first place. Since the last one of those ended up with her throwing me down the stairs I think the time is better spent my way.

So, my great first plan has some serious holes kicked in it now. My other plan has a tiny bit of good news however and I am just about to read it in the hope of finding something to cheer me – 'Dear Local_Alchemist, Yes, precedent aplenty! See this attached student study where cultured bacteria have been made to produce an entire range of colours by inserting the codes for pigment production (taken from other colourful creatures) into their genomes...' – when a sound of feet on the garden gravel path makes me slam the iPad cover down. Nobody can find out about this. I race to cover it all up, then dash out and forestall my mother tipping herself over into the pond as she looks at the sullen face of the one goldfish that the herons have not eaten this summer.

'Fish and chips!' she says, pointing at it. Raffles stands next to her in his own doggy world, wagging his tail and looking pleased with how things have gone. 'Your dad likes that. Where is he? This grass needs a cut. What will the neighbours think?'

'They're fine about it,' I say, glancing at the nail-scissors finish on the Marstons' lawn, their oddly flamboyant cement Victorian Lady standing in eternal *qu'elle surprise!* atop their ornamental rockery. *Surprise!* You're in Todmorden, not on Mr Darcy's Estate. No wonder you look so *surprise!*

Then I remember she's back early from daycare. How? An ominous feeling ticks through my bones as I ask her.

'Oh Mary brought me back,' she says with great confidence. 'We walked it. Not far is it? Just off the main street with that nice café thing and all their fancy hoohaa herbs, then another couple of turns, a wander and a shuffle and here we are!'

Mary was Mum's best friend when they were girls. She is still alive, in Liversedge, in an old folks' home. The Mary Mum is referring to now is strictly imaginary, and still only nine years old. I hope that when I get senile I remember my friends this way. On the other hand, this means Mum has walked out of the centre and all the way back alone, through 21st century traffic, equipped only with her 1940s mind. But she's here. My anger and fear and longing and strange frustration that such an adventure didn't provide me an easy way out must all die in the face of simple facts. I look at the fish. I don't know if he is Bert, Ernie, Scooter or Animal. He's one of them. The only Muppet left.

Raffles barks at him and lolls his tongue out of his mouth. If I could just make Mum into a dog… they seem to have such simple requirements. I pat Raffles and rub behind his ears and he growls and groans in total delight. Want oxytocin? Get a dog.

'Why don't you give Raffles a brush?' I suggest, going to the shed to fetch the Furminator™, a fierce looking device with metal teeth like shark jaws that is perfect for long-haired retrievers. I find it silly that even a dog brush has to have a name to make it sound cool and deadly, but it does make it more fun to use. Naming things changes them. I want to think more about that but I have to watch Mum instead in case she presses too hard with it and I soon forget.

We spend half an hour grooming the dog. I get out enough hair to stuff a cushion and Mum seems pleased that effort has been made, time not wasted. I sit her outside with tea, wrapped against the English summer, and haul out our mower and do the rounds with it, hoping to buy myself a quiet evening. Andy comes out to see what's what at that point and I go inside to discover he has emptied the fridge looking for cheese slices and left everything out and the door open. We have lunch at two. I'm done by three. I can't go back to the shed now, it's too late. I have to get through the evening and the night and then another morning before I can return.

But the next day's emails bring the final nails in the coffin of my plan to fix Mum and Andy without their, or anyone else, noticing.

'Hi Local_Alchemist. Re: extra blood oxytocin. Still not good. The final breakdown of the involved proteins to create oxytocin in the bloodstream is triggered only by the same faulty nerve cells you're trying to compensate for in the first place. You'd be better off investing money into ready-made oxytocin nasal sprays.'

In fact, that's the best idea I have heard all year and would have saved an infinite amount of time and effort. Screw science, just buy the crap, fill up a batch of Anti-Cold sprayers and then start work promoting terror of the 'flu among my family to ensure they snort the stuff up like socialites on coke. With any luck they'd form some addictive connection to the spray, in the way that you can form an addictive connection to anything that gives a rewarding jolt. We'll be living in a soft-focus world of bleary affection, blundering through life high as kites on feel-good chemicals administered by electronic cigarettes. *Brave New World* eat your heart out. The joy of ignorant bliss will do me nicely, thank you.

And what is it we are ignorant of, Carol? This thought creeps in as I make myself look up the prices; grab that notion and make it more real, haul it closer, closer... what must we not notice? We must not notice... but at this point it always peters out, either my willingness or my sense that there is an answer to the question. My fingers stop on the keyboard just two strokes short of buying all the love and trust I need in one easy-to-use bottle. I know there is something. I know it is here. It follows me around like a silent, planet-sized emptiness, watching my every effort with hollow eyes. It longs for me to put it out of its misery and silence. I see it from the corner of my eye. When I am crying I always see it there, on the edge, behind me, over my shoulder, everywhere that I am not exactly looking in any particular moment.

I page away from oxytocin sprays and electronic cigarettes. Then I bring up my dad's photo and I look at that. Around me the remains of my precursor-generating bacterial factories sit silent, all their ferocious activity microscopic and utterly invisible to me, watched over by the unnoticed Creature. It has no hope, no interest. It merely observes. I throw the sacks over it and go out for a walk.

My father's buried in the worst graveyard I have ever been in. I'd pay everything I have never to go there again. The place fills me with a dread I cannot express and it is the place I first noticed the Creature.

The church is in his home village, a half hour's walk away from where we live. It is inexplicably sited in a low hollow only a few feet above the height of both the river and the canal, nearly hidden in a clutch of woodland down a cobbled lane. The yard lies across the running water, as if the church jumped onto an islet in fear, having remembered that ancient protection against the undead. It has an empty, abandoned feeling in spite of the fresh flowers, the gardened edges, the tidied path. Like the mills that paid for it, the church building feels like it is just one more factory, the final one, through which to process families in their final rendering – it's impersonal, too stony, too big, devoid of anything but the power to host the Creature when it retreats there to brood and ponder.

Superficially the graveyard is pretty and well maintained; I suppose because there are an odd number of children's graves there, it seems to me. Babies, with mouldering toys and blankets tied to their fresh headstones. Children, plots covered in action figures going through a final inexplicable war; in Barbies trying to be cheerful and fashionable and pink under the festering lilacs. Plastic that won't rot, only pale in the sun.

Many graves are fenced in with gilded, low palisades which only serve to make them look more pathetically vulnerable. *The things we love: we bring them here,* I think. *We leave you here. Down in the dark with the water and the Creature. How could anybody leave you here? How do we?*

I talk to Dad. I don't believe he is in that yard of course. I don't believe he is in his image on the headstone. He has gone and we are alone. I look at him, a bit like me. Stubborn seems to be the trait we have most in common, that and pragmatism and a kind of Yorkshire expectation of, if not the worst, then not the best. Mustn't grumble. They don't have enough to eat in Africa. It's just a bit o' rain.

I must view these things only as setbacks. Just a bit o' rain. Serotonin precursors look more hopeful. I could still conceivably create bacteria which will produce L–Tryptophan. Or MDMA, but legal, in yoghurt.

The Creature looks at me sadly. It expands, lugubrious, to fill every unfilled space in the universe. And I think *What about Serotonin Syndrome? Even if you create a flood of serotonin there will come a reckoning. Body uses up things, gets low on supplies, then mood falls, inevitable, you don't know the dose, you don't know the threshold, you just don't know, Carol. You don't know.*

Monkey, Dad says, smiling, ruffling my hair. *You little Monkey.*

Monkey is sad. Monkey likes green dogs. Monkey does not like the Creature. Why does the Creature stare? What does it want? Under the bed and out from under. Takes things and ponders them in its big, ugly fingers. Mum's memory. Andy's ability to feel things like others do. My kindness. Dad. What's it doing with them all?

Don't cry, Carol. Think about Tryptophan. Crying is pointless but Tryptophan exists and is real and it could be helpful, even if only a little bit. But don't cry, Carol. Someone has to keep it together.

It's funny that I have to talk to myself in the third person because nobody else is here.

The problem is that everything is a finite resource and

the body is a finely tuned system for dealing with that. Tolerance rises and sensitivity falls. More stimulants are required to produce the effect. Eventually there cannot be enough stimulant and the effect catastrophically fails. Falling, we are plunged into the abyss.

I don't think I can fix it and I don't know what I will do if I can't.

Don't cry, Carol. Crying doesn't help. We have to get on with things. Can't sit around all day feeling sorry for yourself.

But I'm out of ideas. I ask the Creature, purely because it's there and won't leave me alone. It can't, I think. Now I've seen it once, it can't pretend it doesn't exist any more and neither can I. Even looking at it makes my whole body shake in mortal dread. It is worse than death.

'My name today,' says the Creature, gameshow-special, 'is *T. gondii.*'

Leaving aside my obvious sinking into madness the name does ring a bell. Toxoplasmosis, a parasitical infection primarily passed by cats, but infesting many or most human adults, is known to occupy many parts of the human body. In its active form it produces high levels of dopamine such that it is suspected to play a significant role in schizophrenia and other neurotransmitting malfunction situations.

I could plausibly re-engineer the genome of *T. gondii* to create oxytocin instead of dopamine. If it goes too far, yes, it will run into the MDMA issue: too much Ecstasy uses up too many resources and ends up leaving you on a worse low until levels resume. In bacteria, even those functioning with a madswitch that toggles their activity on and off in response to the surroundings, I could easily get the proportions completely wrong. Overbreeding could be catastrophic. Eat a Mars bar, chill out, and a day later jump into the canal to end it all. Tempting in some respects... But *T. gondii*, whatever else it does, exists only at minor influence levels and excretes in such a way that it clearly leaves most people perfectly functional, if somewhat over-attracted to cats. If I change that output to oxytocin it will leave them in a better mood, cat or no cat.

With the emergence of a new plan the Creature shrinks. I know it is an illusion that human beings are a problem that can be solved by the fixings of logic and science. The Creature itself will not be banished. Every day he finds another name. But he can be warded off here and there. Although I fear to push too hard. He has a way of creeping back through the cracks. Tomorrow his name will be Malaria. Tomorrow he will mutate into another form and burrow deeper and become entrenched in an unassailable compound.

But today I just have time to read some papers and make some orders. It will be a budget-blower.

*

It takes more than eighteen months, even with the help of every resource I can muster, to transform the local cat *T.gondii* into *T. Carolii*. I spend another six months practising and fine-tuning until they are robust and viable. I know it's not ethical really, but I test them on next door's cat. It has spent its adult life leaving richly disgusting piles of crap on our grass that must be picked, bagged and disposed of, so I find it hard to feel bad. Flushing cat soil down the toilet already leads to widespread *T. gondii* infection in the general population, where treatment isn't capable of accounting for it all. Useful to know. Meanwhile Tinkerbell the calico longhair has a taste for tinned salmon I'm only too happy to exploit. I'm not sure what oxytocin does to cats.

*

By the following spring Tinkerbell has grown fatter and more docile, shows less inclination to hunt and more to lying in the sun under the greenhouse glass. However, since I wasn't a great observer of her before it's hard to say if this is due to the *T. Carolii* or some other situation. But, analysis of Tinkerbell's deposits reveals a constant presence of *T. Carolii* cysts in addition to far fewer *T.gondii*. So my population, whatever else it does, lives on in one fat and idle cat.

At the sink in the shed I finish tidying up the old experimental works with a sense of satisfaction. I feel sure that if my parasite works as intended it could have far reaching beneficial uses for humanity. Oxytocin helps those in despair deal with their version of the Creature and what torment it brings and in the less neurotic it delivers all the benefits of love, or at least of warm contact and good intent. So what if it's a counterfeit love? Does it really matter if it's not my hands that touch, not my voice that speaks the words of acceptance? If you feel better in the end, then it's better.

I chuck away a load of old packaging and then, in a mood to spring clean a bit, decide to make some more room by getting rid of the paints and the old easel. They all fit in one binbag – there weren't many of them after all. Some of the paints have popped their tops, others have leaked odd coloured chemicals, oil and such. As I'm wiping this up and scrubbing at the table underneath them I come across some letters dug into the wood and suddenly I remember them, remember forming them with the point of my first compasses.

It was in the summer holidays and I was so bored. There was no TV worth watching in the daytime then, no games, no phones. It was dead quiet. The other children in the street weren't around for some reason and I'd spent ages in the garden already. I found myself in the shed just for somewhere new to look at. Our new mower had pride of place in the centre front, its flashy, orange electric cable wound up with the finesse and efficiency of a lifeboat's rope. Neighbours had come over on the day we got it to marvel that it didn't have any wheels. In the bib pocket of my dungarees I had my pencil set. I looked for something to draw on or measure, inspired by the quiet afternoon light and the dusty smell of dried grass and motor oil to do something important.

I already knew that compass points dug good marks into desktops at school. Everyone had at least one drawing or name scrawled to their discredit there, filled in with leisurely biro during RE or crafted over many weeks of algebraic incomprehension. I'd only carved the first letter of 'Carol' on my chosen free bit of a relatively new desk when Mr Briggs had caught me at it and sent me to my one and only ever detention. The shame makes my cheeks heat even now, alone in the shed, staring at my name on the old tabletop. I was rubbish at lettering. It was all in short straight lines, like runes. When I'd done it I fancied myself an ancient druid, discovering writing for the first time... When Dad found my handiwork he went ballistic and took away my paints and burned all the paintings I'd done that summer, all the ones from the kitchen wall, to show me not to damage other people's property wantonly. Later he bought me a book of Leonardo's drawings and said I should look at something worth seeing.

I rub my finger on the gouges. They're good and deep. They've lasted well under there. Karol. I don't remember why K. Maybe I messed up the C. The K gives me vertigo. I grab the table but it's too late, my balance is shot and my ankle gives way. I sit down hard on the floor, in shock.

In giving *T. Carolii* to Tinkerbell, I have already released it into the world in an uncontrollable way, without ever having understood the greater function and community within which the original *T. gondii* operated and without consulting a single other being who may be affected by its survival, spread or dominion.

I would like to be saved from all I have done, and undone. But these acts, like my father and his inexplicable motivation to be so kind and also so cruel at the same time, stretch ever further away in time, untouchable. I see them clearly only in hindsight, amazed at my overweening arrogance, and regrets or not they can't be changed. The Creature nods at me from its everywhere bed; it knows I've seen truly, and it knows I can't do a thing about it, because that's its nature. And I say to it, 'It's not so much folly as what you can do. The *why* – that's the thing you eat in the hours of the morning, three and five, awake in the dark with only yourself to abide it.'

The Creature hovers in the background expectantly. It enjoys the knowledge that in my efforts not to move or decide I have moved, and decided. When I read back over my journal entries I realise I have taken too much upon myself. But nonetheless, it is done.

I won't try to spread it. I will leave it and work on my secondary plan.

*

My mother tried to kill me again today, but in a more half-hearted way than usual. She didn't bother to hold up the iron at all, instead she attempted to make porridge and set a tea-towel on fire by leaving it wrapped around the pot handle and lighting the wrong burner. The alarm went off like a screeching metal rooster and Andy came down screeching in counterpoint to it, hands over his ears, barefoot and wild with terror. He set Mum off into a secondary howling of her own, bewildered, as I struggled to flick the towel off the grip and into the sink using the wooden porridge spoon. Finally it went out on its own, in spite of me, and I was able to get up on the stool and use the spoon end to prod the alarm button.

Andy continued to yodel, having discovered he rather liked the resonance of what he was doing and the impressive noise level, finding it comforting because he could listen to it for its own sake, removed from any sense of things being wrong. Mum wittered at the table crossly, knowing it was her fault and trying to explain that the pots should have handles, not be cast iron monstrosities, and can't we have something modern for once, those non-stickers with the wood.

I got down from the stool and said, 'It's all right. Just a false alarm. Go get dressed, Andy, and I'll make your sandwiches.'

For a moment he stopped making his sound. Then he seemed to decide it was OK to stop. 'Yer all mad,' Andy said, but quietly. He hugged me back briefly as if not realising what he was doing.

'Definitely,' I said with a smile, making light of what can't be got rid of.

Mum started eating her porridge, murmuring about the three bears, and within minutes you'd never know there was a thing wrong with any of us.

I took my own medicine in the end. I thought maybe it wasn't them. Maybe it was me. So I ate a tin of salmon, laced with my namesakes, and since then I've slowly begun to feel better.

I opened a tin of dog food and forked it out into Raffles' bowl. He came tick-a-tick across the kitchen tiles like a walking fern and waved the plume of his brilliant green tail.

'Did something happen to the dog?' Mum asked, looking at him, as if she really couldn't see it.

Andy grinned at me. 'Green dog is green! Carol made him.'

'It's just a spray from the pet store,' I said, lying calmly, smug with satisfaction about the total success of Plan B. 'They're all the rage.' One day they may be.

Today when Mum has gone to daycare and Andy is on the computer I take Raffles for a walk to the graveyard. We get a few looks on the way but the place itself is deserted. Raffles does as he's always done, sniffs the corners, cocks his leg against the gatepost. I ignore the things that used to upset me, and I don't see the Creature much, only now and again, smaller and less important than it used to be in the shadows of the new leaves.

I stand by the porcelain photograph of Dad and toss down the fabric pink roses I brought with me. The sun shines on them and their plastic raindrops and makes them bright and beautiful. From a short distance you really wouldn't know them from the real thing.

Afterword:

Homegrown Bio

Prof Martyn Amos &
Dr Jane Calvert
Manchester Metropolitan University and University
of Edinburgh.

CERTAIN TYPES OF bacteria live quite happily inside the gut of the nematode worm (that ubiquitous creature that often, in turn, inhabits the gut of other animals). The genes that allow the bacteria to cling to their host are referred to as 'mad' (short for 'maternal adhesion', as in 'stick close to your mother!'), and these genes are turned on or off by a section of DNA known as the 'madswitch'. When the madswitch is on, the bacteria are tiny and docile, but when the madswitch is flipped off, terrible things happen. For example... after invading moth larvae, a 'switched' worm will vomit up their bacterial partners, which have been transformed by the madswitch into a living bio-weapon – seven times larger than the dormant version, glowing red, and spewing deadly toxins. The bacteria and the worm then feed on the corpse of the larva, and the deadly cycle continues.

The idea that a switch can somehow change an individual from docile to deadly is at least as old as Jekyll and Hyde. *Transformation* – of a mother, a brother; even, with dark humour, a dog – are central to Justina Robson's near-future vision of an existence in which 'better living through chemistry' is a necessity rather than a recreation.

Carol, the narrator, plans to 'fix' her dysfunctional family, but her homebrew Ecstacy – chemical creator of 'peace, love, unity and respect' – is, she hopes, nothing more than a fallback position. Her real plan is to engineer bacteria to 'persuade' them to produce oxytocin – the so-called 'trust hormone' – and to then somehow spike her family with the modified cells.

The notion of bacteria serving as miniature drug factories is nothing new; human insulin produced by *E. coli* came into use thirty years ago. Genetic engineering is now combining with rapid advances in computer power and mathematical modelling to create a whole new field of research – *synthetic biology*. Across the world, teams of scientists and engineers are stripping down and rebuilding biology – not yet from scratch, but often with surprising, playful or profound results. Some want to make cheap bio-fuels, others cheap anti-malarial drugs. Teams of students show off their creations at an annual jamboree known as the International Genetically Engineered Machine Competition.

Until very recently, 'hacking' biology in this way has been open only to the professionals – trained researchers with access to the necessary, kit, chemicals, and expertise. However, a growing movement – so-called 'DIY (do-it-yourself) bio' seeks to bring to a much wider audience the power to tinker with life. Although, for now, these 'amateur' operations often include at least one professional scientist with transferable skills, DIYbio is opening up the possibility of non-trivial genetic modification of living organisms happening in a garage, kitchen or bedroom near you. The surprising thing is how *unsurprised* by all of this we have become. Genes and DNA are now part of everyday conversation. The artist Tuur van Balen recently discussed how engineered bacteria might – in the future – produce Prozac-laced yoghurt, with the aim of encouraging debate about how synthetic biology might be used in the future. The fact that his proposal was picked up and reported as happening *right now* is testament to the surface credibility of such ideas; as Christina Agapakis observes, our jaded imaginations now think nothing of 'mixing bacteria with the 'gene for Prozac' to create antidepressant yoghurt.'[7]

So, perhaps engineering bacteria to produce trust chemicals is not so far away. But if 'good' applications like that

7. http://blogs.discovermagazine.com/crux/2012/03/06/the-prozac-yogurt-effect-how-hype-can-affect-the-future-of-science/

are possible, then questions often follow about the likelihood of equally 'bad' uses. 'Why try to build your own nuclear device when you can procure anthrax relatively easily and cheaply?' the argument goes. In reality, the dangers of determined misuse are perhaps vastly outweighed by the risks from casual sloppiness and poor lab hygiene; from accidents than agitators. Carol's care-free disposal of experimental detritus down the drain (thus releasing it into the wild) is a much more plausible (and perhaps common) scenario than a bunch of bio-terrorists cooking up a deadly new superbug. We should worry about bio-error more than bio-terror.

Perhaps the most interesting issues raised by 'Madswitch', however, do not centre on possible intentional or accidental dangers of DIYbio (the focus of most ethical discussion around the topic). Instead, the story explores the personalized, *domesticated* use of biotechnology, in a way that is credible and thought-provoking. Carol may be doing science, but her reasons are different from those of many professional scientists – they are emotion-driven and deeply personal (although many scientists, of course, also have intense feelings about their work). The dog's green tail is a kind of memorial to her problematic father, and she wants to produce 'feel good' chemicals to calm her relatives and make her domestic environment more bearable. Perhaps one of the most interesting aspects of DIYbio is that amateurs like Carol might think about using the technology in ways that would never occur to professional scientists and engineers.

What Carol does have in common with some synthetic biologists, however, is the desire for *control*. In the quiet of the shed, and in the company of her 'beautiful' beakers, Petri dishes and containers, she has temporary dominion in a world that is otherwise hard to manage. There are clear similarities here to one of the main aims of synthetic biology practitioners; to make 'messy', complicated living things behave rationally and predictably.

That said, such control may not always offer the best solution in the domain of human relationships. Carol immediately thinks technically when she looks for solutions to her troubles. Rather than trying to hormonally placate her demented mother and autistic brother, perhaps she should consider joining a social-support network for full-time carers?

Sadly, Carol concludes that maybe the problem lies not with her relatives, but with herself. Her solution is to self-medicate. The fake roses on her father's grave look real from a distance, and so does her happiness... Or does the story actually have a happy ending? Does Carol master biological engineering, and is her family moving towards a better life, thanks to her technological skills?

Much discussion of DIYbio (and synthetic biology more generally) is either optimistically utopic or terrifyingly dystopic. 'Madswitch' offers a refreshing, alternative view that is neither – it refuses to give us a simple message.

Anaka's Factors

Sara Maitland

'HEY, SHINY,' SHE called from the kitchen, 'what have you been up to?'

'Hang on a moment.' There was a short pause and then Anaka appeared in the doorway. 'What is it?'

Sally noticed suddenly how much she had grown recently, from charming chubby child into something wilder, more colt-like, all legs and eyes and eagerness.

'I have here,' she said, picking up the sheet of paper, 'recovered from the depths of your lunch box, a note from Mr. MacLean asking Fumiko and me to make an appointment to see him. Urgently.'

There was another short pause. Sally tried to look stern, although Anaka was, to be honest, pretty good at school and such a summons was unusual.

'So I asked you what you had been up to.'

Sally looked up and realised immediately that Anaka was genuinely baffled. 'I haven't any idea,' she said. 'Perhaps he wants to tell you how brilliant I am.'

'He did that at parents' evening last month.' Sally smiled, 'OK, Shiny, I'd better make the appointment and find out. Pity Fumiko's away for another fortnight. He does say it's urgent.'

'Well you're always better at that stuff than Fumiko — she never pays attention to school things.'

There was no umbrage in her voice, which was lucky because in many ways what she said was true.

So three days later she sat down in Mr. MacLean's tidy office and tried to look like an attentive, concerned and serious-minded parent.

'What seems to be the problem, headmaster?'

He said, 'I'm sorry Dr. Kobayashi couldn't be here.'

'She's in the States, at a conference. She doesn't go away more than she needs to, you know. And you did say "urgent".'

'Yes, I know. I apologise.' He shifted a pen from one side of the desk to the other.

Abruptly she realised the man was embarrassed. She was surprised; he had always seemed tolerant, unperturbed, more than capable. It was one reason why they had wanted Anaka in his primary school. There was never any point looking for trouble. She waited.

'Yes, I know,' he repeated. 'We're not really used to internationally distinguished parents. I tend to forget how eminent she is.'

She went on waiting.

'Look,' he sounded aggressive, but she realised it was more that he felt awkward and forbade herself to respond in kind. 'Look... obviously it is your own business, but Anaka and her whole class are getting bigger now, and I can't... I mean, I'm not sure it's a good idea to... perhaps you will only confuse her... she's so bright... and I... Well, you know what I mean.'

'To be frank, Mr. MacLean I haven't a clue what you mean. When I got your note I asked Anaka what she had been doing and she hadn't a clue either.'

'No. Good. Well. Ms. Favell was very careful, of course; she thought it better to bring it straight to me. Which I agree with.'

It sounded odd. She was confused now, but smiled calmly. Her friends would have been amazed and impressed by her patience. She was amazed and impressed herself. Perhaps it was mother-love or something. She copied her daughter's management technique and let the pause go on.

Eventually he drew a deep breath.

'When you first came to see me, before Anaka started here, you explained, I was pleased at your openness; it makes things so much easier, doesn't it? I mean you explained about you and Dr. Kobayashi...' He really did not want to have to say the word 'lesbian' which was making things difficult for him, poor thing '... that you and Dr. Kobayashi were... were a couple, in a partnership, and really, as I well know, that is quite common nowadays and has never been a problem for us at St. James's and... There's a tendency to assume with Church Schools that we'll be judgemental, prejudiced, but...Well, I don't think so... I hope not. But anyway, on Monday Anaka's class were talking about parents and how everyone, and every mammal indeed, had a mother and a father and Anaka suddenly announced that you were her father, her − Ms. Favell said she actually used the expression − that you were her 'biological father'. And I felt we needed to sort this out. I can't feel she should be allowed to believe that, or to confuse the other children.'

'Thank you. But you see, the thing is, I am.'

What followed was not a pause. It was definitely a silence. He looked at her, almost squinting. She guessed what he was thinking.

'No, I am not a post-operative transsexual. I am not a transvestite either. We − Fumiko and I − we conceived Anaka *in vitro* by making one of my stem-cells... perhaps 'persuading' is a better word... by persuading one of my stem cells into becoming a spermatozoon. My cells, therefore my genes and therefore I, me, am, in point of fact and for what it's worth, Anaka's biological father. I'm delighted to be sure that she understands that.'

She felt some sympathy for him. When Fumiko had first raised the idea with her she had been a bit dumbstruck herself. And it was always worse for men; she could understand that, though frequently in a somewhat smirking sort of way which she tried valiantly but not always successfully to suppress.

'You can't, surely, expect us to lie to her, or ask her to lie to other people?'

'No. No, of course not.' He moved his pen again. It rolled over as he released it and his hand shot out and banged down on it hard. 'No. But...'

'Do you think,' she had to be careful, she had to be clear, 'do you think it might help if I explained it to you, I mean the science?'

'I am not very good at science.' He sounded almost sulky, like one of his Year Four boys. She tried not to smile.

'Nor am I unfortunately, but it is quite a lovely story – and I know people can find it helpful.'

He looked more nervous than ever. He picked up the pen and this time, rolled it between his fingers and appeared to inspect it extremely carefully. She ignored this.

'You are a bit younger than me, Mr. MacLean, and perhaps you grew up in a very different environment, but I was born in the late 1960s and so I was quite a small girl when my mother got heavily involved in the early Women's Liberation Movement. Looking back it was quite strange for a child because it made her terribly happy and excited and fun – but at the same time she lost her full focus on me. My father picked up a lot of the slack – and I adored him. You must understand that he was deeply sympathetic, not just to me but to her too. Until he died a couple of years ago, I would say they had one of the strongest relationships I have ever known. My mother still finds things terribly difficult without him. But – and this is hard to describe in these more PC days – he was a terrible tease and extremely funny. And one of his jokes was... there was this slogan in the early women's movement: Biology is not Destiny. And whenever it, or anything related to it, came up he would turn his toes out and waddle round the house, flapping his arms and saying 'quack-quack'. When anyone asked him what he was up to, he'd say he was a duck and if challenged in any way he'd announce, 'If I choose to be a duck, I am a duck: biology is not destiny.' And when I told him and my mother about

Anaka, there was a long silence and then he said, 'Oh dear, I really am a duck.' And we all laughed a lot.

So you see the idea that biology is somehow 'natural' and everything else is 'fake' never had much root in me. Fumiko is rather the same, though for different reasons: like a lot of Japanese people, she really does not have that Frankenstein horror thing. For Japanese children most forms of technology, like say robots, are positive, playful and helpful. So perhaps it was easier for the two of us than for other people.

So although of course we know Daddy's-seed-in-Mummy's-tummy is a pretty good story, a true and useful story, it is not the only story. You know that. There are rubbish stories, like the storks and cabbage patches ones, which really we would both agree children should not be told any more. But here are more stories which are true and useful but differently from the common biological one: Adam and Eve, Leda and the Swan, cosmic eggs, saintly miracles... so you can see ours like that. We think it is a deeply true story and one that will become more popular because it is completely child-centred; it sort of is not about Mummies and Daddies at all, but about the child herself.

In our story something beautiful and unique happens at the moment of conception; the sperm and the egg each bring their 23 genomes into a moment of fusion, where the two become one, a mystical marriage if you like. This is the moment that Augustine saw as the source of Original Sin, because of the parents' sexual pleasure, but we see it quite differently – as the moment of Original Grace, solidarity, community, what I would shamelessly call love. Suddenly, miraculously and delightfully, there is a new life form – a brand new organism. I see that moment as the source of the desire that drives us through life, the desire for unitive love, and it is good for even very small children to know it.

That glory is very brief. Just a day or so, that's all, and then – and this is what I think of as Original Sin if you need that concept – there is a terrible wrenching, a splitting. That lovely unitary cell pulls apart, becomes two. I think this is the first, the core binary. Our desire to divide everything into twos – female, male; good, bad; black, white; dark, light; whatever – they're all secondary to and imaginatively grow out of that first division.

And once it has started it goes on and on – 2, 4, 8, 16, 32. But – and this is the bit that matters – these new cells are totipotent. That means they have the power and the capacity to become anything, any kind of human cell at all; after about five days they move on from being totipotent, and after a week they decide what sort of cells they will be. First they choose one of three (not two, three – it is very theological, Trinitarian, you see, almost a proof of God) different kinds of cells to be, which will go on to make guts and lungs, the nervous system and skin, and thirdly muscle, bone and blood. And then these go on to produce ever more specialised cells and clump together into organs. They give up unity in exchange for complexity and diversity. And within the groups there are always stem cells which are pluripotent – they can't become *anything* but they can become lots of things, for doing repairs and so on.

OK so far? Then, in what I am told is one of the most elegant pieces of research, a doctor called Shinya Yamanaka - after whom Anaka is named of course, though most people think it is after Fumiko's anarchist youth - discovered exactly which genes get switched on in order to make these changes: there are about four key genes – all with rather silly names like Sox2 – which can seduce, say, a skin cell into reverting, and then lure it into being something else. Once you know exactly what is going on you can replicate in the lab what happens in the body. If you see what I mean. You bathe these cells in precision quantities of the necessary ingredients. It is extremely delicate and tricky and no one is very good at it yet. You have to treat the cells very tenderly; you lay them on a bed of human proteins, wash them in a bath of hormones and so on – just like caring for a tiny baby really. But it can be done and we did it: we took some of my cells and lured them back into pluripotency and then redirected them and after about a fortnight they became mature spermatozoa and Fumiko got pregnant and that is Anaka's story. She has two parents who both have XX chromosomes, but one of them is her father. Biology is not destiny – except of course that we always knew she was going to be a girl.'

It has to be said that Mr. MacLean did not look reassured. He looked appalled. He put the pen down, picked it up again, focussed his attention on it and said, 'It sounds terribly risky. How do you know she will be all right?'

'We don't. There are risks – cancer perhaps. In the early laboratory stages too many of the mice got cancer, though they say they've sorted that out. And Dolly the Sheep aged too fast – her chromosomes were too short for her real age, and she got arthritis and stuff - so possibly, perhaps, these cells have some sort of memory of their own past, know they are not freshly minted, that they were something else before they were sperm. We don't know. But we do know that everyone said this sort of 'risky', 'dangerous', 'unnatural' stuff when Louise Brown was born in 1978 and now you yourself have just told me that IVF babies are perfectly ordinary nowadays, even for Lesbians. And we – Fumiko and I – had the opportunity for proper informed consent, at least we believe so, which is more than Lesley, Louise's mother, did. I'm not going to say it isn't risky, or that I don't care that it is risky. I am going to say that she is ten now and there have been no problems so far – and we watch her like hawks, seeking our grey hairs and wrinkles – so the sense of risk diminishes year by year. I am going to say that someone has to be first: Fanny Longfellow, Louise Brown, Anaka Kobayashi-Morton. I am going to say that from the day she was born, from the day she was conceived, I have never thought the risk too great. I have never regretted it for a single moment.

You know, it is all so risky, every pregnancy is risky, every life is terribly, terribly risky. You just have to catch the joy as it flies. Anaka is a very pure joy to us, Mr. MacLean. Our sunrise. The risk is part of the joy.'

The two of them sat there for a moment. She could see that though he understood he was not consoled. He did not like it. She did not know him well him enough to guess whether his distress was moral or the terrified reaction of too many men who saw terminal redundancy on their horizon whenever she or Fumiko tried to explain. She could understand, sort of, but there was nothing she could offer them. It was his problem.

He transferred his pen to his other hand and then back again. And again. It looked like fidgeting to Sally. Finally he said, 'What are we going to do about this?'

'Sorry,' she said startled.

'Well, we can't have her muddling up the other children, upsetting them. Babbling on about it.' He sounded cross.

'She hardly babbles on about it. She's been here for five years. She's known about it all that time. And this is the first time it has come up.'

'You know perfectly well what I mean. I don't need to remind you this is a school with a strong Christian ethos; that is why parents choose it.'

'No you don't; that is why we chose it. Tolerance, love, truthfulness, high standards. You said at the start of this that you appreciated our "openness". And we appreciated yours. What's changed?'

He dithered a little. Then muttered that it must be against the law, criminal.

She laughed. 'Actually it isn't. Not like cloning. It probably would be but no one has caught up with us yet. You only make laws against things you know people are doing. Like Cannabis in 1928. You don't have to worry about that. Though to be honest it's why it was never announced. Anaka was first, but she's not the only one – we did not want to rob other couples of that. It was pretty generous of Fumiko's colleagues really. I mean they published on 'viable sperm', but never actually said 'live birth from': so the media never really picked it up. Soon they'll go public, which is an extra reason why Anaka needs to know.'

He mumbled some more. She wanted to say, 'Oh, get a grip,' but she also did not want Anaka to have to change school. He started on something about the Church and traditional morality. She began to feel exasperated.

'For heaven's sake, headmaster! Every year this school lays on a charming little play, in which Anaka along with all your other pupils participate with delight and the parents love it. It's called the Nativity and it celebrates a God who does Virgin Births. I very much doubt, theologically speaking, that he is going to have much of a problem with Anaka.'

She got up and left. She was determined neither to laugh nor to cry.

Over tea, Anaka asked, 'What did Mr. MacLean want you for?'

She was caught out. Tolerance, truthfulness, high standards. Love. She told her daughter, 'He wanted me to tell him about the Yamanaka factors and how Fumiko and I came by you.'

'I thought Miss Favell didn't believe me. I did try to explain.'

'You shouldn't have to now. I think Mr. MacLean will explain it to her. He and I had an interesting chat about whether or not biology was destiny.'

'Did he go "quack" like Granddad?'

'No.' But she laughed suddenly and happily.

'Fumiko gets home tomorrow, doesn't she? It's lucky she was away. She never enjoys those things like you do.'

'Oh Shiny, I did not enjoy it.'

'Bet you did really.'

221

Afterword:

Yamanaka: Factors to Consider

Dr Melissa Baxter
University of Manchester

WE ALL START life as the ultimate stem cell. The fertilised egg;
a single stem cell that goes on to form all the different,
specialised cells of a body. This single stem cell divides into
two stem cells, both identical to the first. These two both
divide into more stem cells which keep dividing and dividing.
Each has the potential to become any type of cell in the body,
only hasn't decided which one yet. They have all the potential,
but remain unspecialised. After four days decisions start to be
made in the tiny embryo (which is now about as big as this
dot: ·). Stem cells sense where they are, what environment
they are in and how many other cells they are next to. All
these different clues form instructions that change the cell's
identity from a stem cell into a cell destined to become fully
specialised like a liver cell, a bone cell or a skin cell. Once a
stem cell receives instructions that 'program' it to form a
particular type of cell the decision is final and won't be
reversed. That's why the different instructions that program
these decisions must be so neat and precise.

In 1998 scientists discovered a way of growing the stem
cells from four-day-old human embryos in the lab. Human
embryonic stem cells are grown in very specific conditions:
submerged in a liquid medium – a sugary soup of nutrients
and proteins. These precise conditions keep the stem cells in
an artificial state of limbo. Where normally they would start
deciding what they will become, in the lab the cells continue
to divide but remain identical. In fact their ability to divide
but remain identical – to self-renew – is unlimited. Each one,
like cells of the early four-day-old embryo, still has the
potential to become any cell of the human body. This is why

we describe them as 'pluripotent' stem cells meaning 'many powers'.

The difficulty scientists face is to recreate the complexity of the developing embryo that instructs the stem cells to change into a specialised type of cell. While this may take months in the body, in the lab-based medium it only takes weeks, so conditions must be very precise. It is even more difficult to create the correct series of instructions to direct a stem cell only into a particular type of cell that you might be interested in. And there are lots to choose from. So far scientists, including myself, have managed to turn stem cells into liver cells, nerve cells, retina cells, cartilage cells, pancreas cells, bone cells and blood cells to name a few. The potential application in medicine is vast and should not be underestimated.

One of the most promising advances scientists have recently made has been to turn human embryonic stem cells into retina cells. There is good evidence that transplantation of these cells might improve vision in patients suffering macular degeneration – the leading cause of blindness in the developed world. Already these cells are being used to treat human patients and early results are promising. Similar advances have been made in instructing stem cells to become nerve cells that have the potential to repair spinal injuries; pancreas cells that can make insulin and when transplanted could cure diabetes, cartilage cells that could be used to repair damaged joints. Or liver cells that can be used to safety-test newly developed drugs and reduce animal testing.

Let us pause now for a moment, because you can not write about embryonic stem cells without referring to the ethical issues involved. I want to be completely transparent here; Human embryonic stem cells are isolated only from embryos from IVF clinics that would otherwise be incinerated. Not any embryos that would be used for implantation and pregnancy. Also embryos are only used for stem cells after fully informed consent from the human donors. However with the derivation of embryonic stem cells the embryo itself is destroyed. This is why some people find embryonic stem cell research hard to accept.

But what if pluripotent stem cells could be made from specialised adult cells like skin cells instead of embryos? This is exactly what was achieved by Shinya Yamanaka and colleagues at the Institute for Frontier Medical Sciences, Kyoto University in 2007. Any cell in our body (including skin cells) contains the same DNA that the original stem cells did in the developing embryo. But the difference between a skin cell and a pluripotent stem cell is that they have different genes switched on and off. So skin cells still contain stem cell genes, only they are switched off. Yamanaka and co. discovered that if you switch on four 'stemness' genes in a skin cell, it can be 'reprogrammed' in a week or so into a pluripotent stem cell. These four particular genes (SOX2, OCT4, cMYC and KLF4) are now known as 'Yamanaka factors'. It has since been shown that these Yamanaka factors can reprogram not only skin cells, but other cells including liver cells, blood cells and nerve cells into pluripotent stem cells. Like embryonic stem cells these reprogrammed stem cells can remain in limbo, dividing indefinitely until they are instructed to turn into any specialised cell of the body. It has already been shown that these reprogrammed stem cells, like the embryonic ones can make specialised cells including pancreas cells, liver cells, nerve cells and retinal cells. Experiments have shown that reprogrammed stem cells have the potential to treat Sickle Cell Anaemia. They have also been made from skin biopsies of patients with diseases such as Parkinson's and diabetes and been used to generate cells that display the symptoms of the disease. This technology is already being used to model diseases in-a-dish and help develop new therapies.

Last month it was even reported that stem cells made from skin cells can turn into immature sperm cells. So patients that have been made infertile as a side effect of cancer therapy might one day be able to have sperm cells made from their own skin. The fact that they are only primitive sperm cells highlights one of the main hurdles; how to make stem cells turn into cells that are mature. Most often the liver cells, pancreas cells and nerve cells that are made from pluripotent stem cells are immature, like they are in the foetus. The myriad signals and instructions that occur during normal development are very complex. So complex that reflecting the right conditions to generate a mature type of cell is (and believe me I know this!) ...very difficult, to put it mildly.

Since 1998, when scientists first isolated human embryonic stem cells, the field has expanded enormously. It is still early days and to make stem cell therapies ready for the clinic will take time, but advances have been rapid. In just fourteen years we have learnt how to grow stem cells, turn normal cells into stem cells, keep them dividing and instruct them to become useful cells for therapy. Anaka's Factors is an extremely specific example of a wide range of possible applications of stem cell research. However for me this intriguing and surprising story emphasises how equally exciting the next fourteen years of stem cell research could be.

Call it 'The Bug', Because I have No Time to Think of a Better Title

Toby Litt

IF MY MOTHER weren't dying of ovarian cancer, and I hadn't come home to be around my father, I might have written a story something like part of the following (Choose Your Own Adventure, please): A young woman, Ela, travels by great glass elevator to one of the geostationary spaceports encircling the toxic Earth. Ela has made contact through some minimal, slangy future form of the internet (retina-based) with Clar, an old woman. Clar's implant – which I was thinking of calling an 'imp' or an 'iBug' but am now simply and exhaustedly going to call a 'bug' – Clar's bug is still fully-functioning. For years, Clar's bug has protected her (a read-out here, an alarm there) from ninety-five percent of humanly-occurring infections, viruses, cancers (that flesh is heir to) (our species-wish to disinherit ourselves). Clar's bug, note, was an early-ish model, and she could never afford (after the divorce) (basketball player) to upgrade – newer models, assuming we are in 2055, cover ninety-nine point eight percent of humanly-occurring viruses, etc; and the mean average human lifespan can no longer be calculated because, at the top end of the economic scale (Berlin or Mumbai or Yerevan), so few people are dying. It is (the mean average) probably somewhere between two-hundred-and-twenty and two-hundred-and-fifty years. Deaths do still happen – the longer people spend alive together, the more annoying they become to one another. There are therefore murders, suicides, domestic accidents, overdoses. But Clar herself is dying in her poor woman's cell of an untreated because undetected – by her bug – because hyper-rare, degenerative disease. It affects the ability to swallow; it causes constant involuntary tears; it coats the body in lesions. Clar is dying slowly, gently – and Clar, because of who she is, and because that person is a person very like others – Clar does not want to be alone when she dies; and Clar cannot afford off-world nursing; and Clar would rather die than suffer the social humiliation of a return to Earth. Her only asset, apart from her undesirable cell, is her bug – which has a working life of up to three-hundred years. It was designed to be self-installing, and self-uninstalling, so as to be available to the maximum number of consumers, including those in the world's least sanitary countries (Australia and Haiti and Austria). For bug installation, no surgery is necessary – the new host simply swallows the bug, which is about the size of my mother's little fingertip and which disassembles in the stomach; for uninstallation, no surgery is necessary – when the bug detects that brain activity has (legitimately) ceased in its host, it reassembles in the liver and makes its way down through their lower intestine, using needle-like pinions, quickly emerging from the rectum. At this point, the bug is ready to assimilate itself to the first health-host that comes along and swallows it. As a precaution against murder, the designers made sure the bugs could not simply be ripped from the living flesh (they embed around the liver) – this would cause signature brain distress, the detection of which causes bugs to become inoperative (unhackably dormant) (anti-vulture defenses) until rebooted by a licensed reseller. All this story-information would have to have been conveyed without laborious exposition (see above; mother; apologies). We would have seen Ela meeting Clar – a buzz at the cell door, a slow-sad admittance – white unimagined furnishings, or black; and Clar and Ela would *hate one another on sight*, without me having to use that phrase. But because Clar has no time to find another watcher-wiper-warder, and because this is Ela's only chance at a working-order bug, they go ahead. Ela's bag hits the floor – and she is in Clar's life, and death. There are scenes, proper scenes with proper dialogue – an early conversation going wrong. 'I never asked for this,' one of them would say that. 'Neither did I,' the other would shout back – although 'Neither' seems a very unfuture word. 'I didn't ask for this!' 'You think I did!' (A bit better). The story, I should have said (incompetent with tiredness) would most likely have been third-person but with exclusive access to the contents of Ela's head. She would (we'd overhear) resent Clar, and think of the cancers she (Ela) might – defenceless, unbugged – even at that minute – be incubating. Why couldn't fucking Clar just fucking hurry up and die? Her cell contained no hint of human connection; this would be a griefless death – no nieces waving, no nephews trying to be cool and warm. Then, slowly, (and isn't this a bit schlocky?) (isn't this where the story would have started to go wrong, to disappoint you?) Ela comes to see (more scenes, more head-details) some value in Clar. At night, Clar tries to cough as little as possible; she doesn't ask – once, more than once – for something she really needs; she describes for Ela a nostalgic-foodstuff they both turn out to adore. And so Ela doesn't come (gradually, subtly) to love or like Clar, but she begins almost to respect her. Ela can't wait for Clar to die, yet Ela begins to feel guilty about her own impatience. Clar has nothing to live for but – still – her life is not nothing. Ela, who has brown hair, also begins (convincingly, gradually) to despise the makers of the bugs, who would probably have been Apple Inc. (I was going to call them 'bugs', I should have said earlier, because they are like the listening devices once used by spies to catch out enemy infiltrators). (Bugs, I was going to call them, because I have a memory of *The Gold-Bug* – wasn't it an SF film?) I don't have much time to do this, copied longhand into a notebook; I have to go (from my father's house) to collect my partner from the station and drive her to see my mother. My mother would hate to be described, in her current state, so you will have to imagine the state of a person who would hate to be described. Everyone talks of *comfortable*, in the hospice, but what we all really want is to be secure – secure in health. If implant technology had been available to my mother (here is not my point), if she had been able to swallow a bug (in 2000) – even one designed by Microsoft – software and hardware meeting wetware – she might be alive and coming to our house (in London) this weekend for a weekend that wouldn't stand out, that in five year's time (readout, alarm) she would probably not even remember. By contrast, the cell in which Clar is still dying as an annoyed Ela lifts a plastic cup to her lips seems unbelievably devoid of culture. I haven't got time to imagine the language they might speak (to one another) (space station jargon and Earth-dialect meeting-point). I would like to have put some other future-developments-from-present-developments into the story, along with the minimum that is the bugs, the space station. I would like to have gone into further detail about my imagined money-replacing currency, virtù (social credit, non-transferable or tradeable). No time before the hospice visit. Ela looks at a screen on the cell-wall, showing what a porthole in exactly that position would show. Ela looks at Africa and then the Indian Ocean and then, on the horizon, unmoving for weeks, Goa, where (it seems) she lives – so perhaps Ela wouldn't have been her name. Ela, as she looks at Goa while Clar, increasingly sleepy, dozes – Ela wonders my thoughts: Do the dying really turn their faces to the wall? Is there a death-rattle you know is just that? At least Ela knows she will know when Clar is dead – because the bug will emerge from Clar's anus, and sit there glowing with a pulse radiating *ready* – like the glow of an Apple computer dot (sleep indicator light), though surely Apple or Microsoft will have come up with something different (by 2055) to signify technology's cute eagerness-to-serve (by the time Clar is affluent enough, on the eve of her marriage, to swallow the bug, with a glass of champagne).

Pulse, pulse – the bug will show it is maybe not *as good as new* but still *as ready as ever*. At this point, because I haven't had time, because my mother has no time, the story breaks into possibilities. If I had been able to, I might (earlier) have introduced the threat – vulture-like figures who hover around the dying, in the hope of being the first to grab the still faeces-covered bug and shove it down their own craven throats. This would have involved some scene-setting of a slum-like space-station, which is a little unbelievable. To be in orbit will surely mean to be rich, or a high servant of the state (not just the ex-wife of a basketball player), for many decades to come. So perhaps Ela and Clar should be relocated from the start, although that means losing the description of the light glinting off the sunward edge of the geostationery space-station – a description I had been looking forward to opening the story with. In the ugly fight version of the ending, Ela stands over Clar's dying body, pointing some kind of non-laser gun at the vulture-figures. One variant has her fighting them off and chucking the shit-tasting bug into her mouth, and then swallowing it down in compromised triumph. (She will live longer, this Ela, but what kind of psychically damaged life?) Another variant has her successfully swallowing the bug only for it to stick in her throat and choke her to death. (This I call the *Tharg's Future Shock* variant of the story, after the cartoon strip in *2000 AD* magazine – and there's nothing wrong with the Thargesque: I got to him long before I did Asimov, Clarke, Lem; long before I knew of *The Twilight Zone*). In yet another variant, Ela struggles to snatch the excreted bug away from the vultures and a mass fight develops, from which Ela takes a mental and then a physical step back – No, we watch her think, this is worse than dying. I will take my biological chances rather than sink to this immoral level. I am prepared to wait for someone to die. (I am even prepared to marry a basketball player). But I am not prepared to scrabble in a dead woman's crap with half-a-dozen vultures for the chance of twenty or thirty years of compromised life. (Of course, if I had more time Ela would be far *less* articulate). But then, at this point, this Ela might or might not change her mind. Fuck ethics, she might think, anything for those extra years – anything to avoid a death like Clar's, like my mother's. But Ela can't get near the bug now, too many vultures have invaded the cell, and finally one of them triumphantly pink-necks it. (Although if Tharg has his way, they would then twistily choke to death (Zarjaz!)). I have no more time, although there are more variants – and I should say that for each of these endings to be credible, Ela would have to have behaved subtly differently earlier in the story. I have no more time – it's time to drive to the station and collect my partner, to drive to the hospice to see my poor mother. I can't describe my bugless mother, as my partner will soon be seeing her, but I could take license to describe Clar as Ela sees her, a few hours before her death. But I won't – Clar wouldn't want to be described any more than my mother would. Fictional characters, even underdeveloped ones, should be accorded their human dignity. (Of course, this isn't my usual reasoned view – but at the moment I can't, I just can't). I have to go, the car, the hospice, the time. Clar dies, calmly (I assert) and with dignity, and with no vultures, please – thank you for Choosing Your Own Adventure. Ela washes the glow-pulsing bug carefully, reverently, having learned (from her experience) profound human unschlocky lessons. Ela lays out Clar's tiny body. Ela looks towards the screen – Goa, her maybe-longer future. Ela drinks down the bug with the champagne she has been secretly (even from me) saving. She drinks – to Clar, and (without being aware of it) to my mother.

Afterword:

Implant Technologies

Dr Nihal Engin Vrana
Division of Health Sciences and Technology, Harvard MIT.

AS THIS IS such a personal story, I thought that maybe I should offer a personal afterword, and explain why I got into tissue engineering and implant technologies in the first place. My father died of Multiple Sclerosis, which is an auto-immune disease, in my first year in college after years of suffering. While his disease progressed and every medical option failed, I, as a high school student, decided to find out the potential cures available for it. I was checking the possible solutions for his illness in all sources I had access to (which was quite limited in those days). After wading through all the commercially motivated hype and hard-to-understand medical jargon for a while, I finally alighted on the subject of tissue engineering as a method of replacing damaged nerves. Another option was directing nerve movement by artificial conduits. Suddenly I was fascinated and full of hope. It struck a chord in me and after fifteen years, here I am, doing tissue engineering research as a profession. But...

Nerve tissue engineering hasn't worked very well, yet. MS is maybe more manageable now, but it is still a debilitating disease. Moreover, for each successful artificial tissue our field has come up with, we failed with ten others, and people keep dying due to replacement organ shortage. So I completely understand the sense of disappointment that pervades Toby's story. The frustration one feels about the existence of a treatment out there somewhere, but inaccessible to one's loved ones is not unfamiliar to me. After all, we are constantly bombarded by news of 'exciting developments' in medicine, which makes us feel that immortality is just around the corner.

There were many 'miracle drugs' back then, there still are today, and there are still millions of people suffering. I think that most of the technology developers do not really understand how the expectations they create affect the general population and I think that they should be cognisant of that. The promises and opportunities I told Toby about during our talk and how it can sting when those solutions are not actually available, and might never be, make for a good lesson for anybody involved in this process. What I had read as a lay person was not what I saw when I actually got into the field of implants, and I think that the onus is on us, as scientists, to match public expectations with reality.

But, on the other hand, the reality in many ways is genuinely exciting. Is personalised medicine around the corner? Yes. Right now genome-wide association studies are coming up with all the genes related to all possible inherited diseases and at some point in the future everybody will be able to know which diseases they are prone to.[8] This will bring in an even more proactive approach to our health, as we will be even more conscious of all the time-bombs ticking inside us. Moreover, the medical tests that need significant amounts of blood now can soon become common household items, the way glucose sensors for diabetes patients are already. With their further miniaturization, implantable, real-time blood glucose sensors (and, of course, myriad other biomarkers) will soon be feasible.

The question is: will this create even more segregation between the lives of the rich and the poor? Most probably, every new technology brought up has a bigger price tag and we are actually paying for all the other failures that cost the companies money. So maybe there is not much of a leap from whole artificial bodies – as depicted in, say, Richard Morgan's novel *Altered Carbon* – to the life-extending implants in Toby's

---

8. See 'Flesh & Blood' pp. 127–136.

story. If the availability of these implants will define your life expectancy, then what kind of segregation would that produce? I think that such segregation might be untenable, as knowing that someone will definitely live *longer* than you, let alone *better* than you, is a very strong stimuli to reject the established order. A different kind of equilibrium needs to be established in such a world.

But it doesn't need to be that way, of course. We should learn some lessons from the development of the computer sciences and how, in the end, computers became affordable. Indeed, there are some good developments in implant technology that will enable very cheap diagnostic tools to be applied quite soon. A big part of current biosensor research is about coming up with ingenious, cheap solutions to diagnosis or detection problems where the technology won't need high-end facilities. There are already paper-based biosensors or portable microscope based assays to be used in challenging environments. We have very precise detection methods and also antibacterial and antiviral agents which we can deliver with high precision and the production of which we might even be able to incorporate into the human body. The 'bug' that can make us invulnerable instead of sick is a hard-to-attain but nevertheless theoretically possible dream and who knows, in the end, it might be available to everybody. You won't need to marry Lionel Messi to get one.

In vivo biosensors with wireless connections, more sophisticated multifunctional, implantable devices with inbuilt bioreactors for self-sustenance, complex delivery and detection systems, lab-on-a-chip devices that can become implantable to direct the movement of the bioactive agents inside the body... and one day maybe fully artificial organs with novel functions. All these may come to pass, given parallel developments in computing and miniaturization technologies.

But people will continue to die, and it will still be difficult to cope with that reality.

Our race with death is rigged and, no matter how clever we get, it always finds a more clever way to get us. We have always been vain about our capabilities. From our earliest, simplistic attempts, such as using glass to replace the cornea or just putting up a wooden stick to replace an amputated or severed leg, to the latest designer hip implants and cochlear replacements, we have always believed that, if needs be, we can replace our missing parts. But the reality is there will always be situations where we can't.

I think that it is our responsibility to think about the social changes we will induce with such devices. Maybe we should restrain the hype we create around new technologies and their possibilities. All these exciting possibilities might be interesting, but the loved ones we lose along the way won't come back, so it is in our hands to keep a leash on the hype and be honest with people about what we can really offer. There is nothing worse than false hope.

About the Authors

Simon Van Booy was born in Great Britain and grew up in rural Wales. He is the author of *The Secret Lives of People in Love, Love Begins in Winter* (winner of the Frank O'Connor International Short Story Award) and the novel, *Everything Beautiful Began After*. His first play, *HINDSIGHT*, was recently staged in New York City. He teaches at the School of Visual Arts in Manhattan, and was a finalist for the Vilcek Prize for Creative Promise. His work has been translated into thirteen languages. His latest novel, *The Illusion of Separateness* will be released in the autumn of 2012.

Jane Feaver was born in Durham in 1964. After reading English at university she worked at the Pitt Rivers Museum and then in the Poetry Department at Faber and Faber. In 2001 she moved to Devon with her daughter. *According to Ruth* (2007) was shortlisted for the Author's Club First novel award and the Dimplex Prize; *Love Me Tender* (2009) was shortlisted for the Edge Hill Short Story Prize. A second novel, *An Inventory of Heaven*, is out this year from Corsair.

Simon Ings was born in 1965 in Horndean and educated at Churcher's College, Petersfield and at King's College London and Birkbeck College, London. His six novels include *Hotwire, Headlong, Painkillers* and *The Weight of Numbers*. He is editor of the *New Scientist*'s new publication, *Arc*. His short story 'Zoology' was specially commissioned for *When It Changed* (Comma, 2009).

Annie Kirby was born and grew up in Dorset, and has been writing stories since she was five years old. Her short stories have been published in various anthologies, including *Bracket* (Comma, 2004), and adapted for broadcast on national and local radio, and for audio download. Her story, 'The Wing' won the 2005 Asham Award. She lives in Portsmouth.

Toby Litt is the author of eight novels – *Beatniks: An English Road Movie, Corpsing, Deadkidsongs, Finding Myself, Ghost Story, Hospital, Journey into Space* and *King Death* – as well as three collections of short stories: *Adventures in Capitalism, Exhibitionism* and *I Play the Drums in a Band Called Okay*. In 2003 Toby Litt was nominated by Granta magazine as one of the 20 'Best of Young British Novelists'. He lives in London and is a member of English PEN. He has previously contributed to Comma's *Lemistry: A Celebration of the Work of Stanislaw Lem*.

Sara Maitland grew up in Galloway and studied at Oxford University. Her first novel, *Daughters of Jerusalem*, was published in 1978 and won the Somerset Maugham Award. Novels since have included *Three Times Table* (1990), *Home Truths* (1993) and *Brittle Joys* (1999), and one co-written with *Michelene Wandor* – *Arky Types* (1987). Her short story collections include *Telling Tales* (1983), *A Book of Spells* (1987) and most recently, *On Becoming a Fairy Godmother* (2003). She has also contributed stories to *The New Uncanny, When It Changed,* and *Litmus* (all Comma) and is currently writing an entire collection of stories for Comma, in collaboration with scientists.

Adam Marek is an award-winning short story writer. He won the 2011 Arts Foundation Short Story Fellowship, and was shortlisted for the inaugural Sunday Times EFG Short Story Award. His first story collection *Instruction Manual for Swallowing* (Comma, 2007) was nominated for the Frank O'Connor Prize. His stories have appeared in many magazines, including: *Prospect* and *The Sunday Times Magazine*, and in many anthologies including *Lemistry*, *Litmus* and *The New Uncanny* from Comma Press, *The New Hero* from Stoneskin Press, and *The Best British Short Stories 2011*. His second collection, *The Stone Thrower*, was published earlier this year. To subscribe to Adam's blog, Twitter and Facebook updates, visit www.adammarek.co.uk

Sean O'Brien's latest collection of poems is *November* (Picador, 2011), a Poetry Book Society Choice. Its predecessor, *The Drowned Book* (Picador, 2007) won the T.S. Eliot and Forward Prizes. Previous poetry collections include *The Indoor Park* (Bloodaxe, 1983), *The Frighteners* (Bloodaxe, 1987), *HMS Glasshouse* (OUP, 1991), *Ghost Train* (OUP, 1995) and *Downriver* (Picador, 2001). His essays have been collected in *The Deregulated Muse* and his translations include Dante's *Inferno*, Aristophanes' *The Birds* and Zamyatin's *We* (for radio). His collection of short stories, *The Silence Room*, was published by Comma in 2008 and his novel *Afterlife* by Picador in 2009. He is Professor of Creative Writing at Newcastle University.

K.J. Orr was born in London. As an undergraduate, she won the Dan Hemingway Prize at the University of St Andrews for a short story later published in the anthology *Doris Lumsden's Heart-Shaped Bed & Other Stories* (2004). Her work has also appeared in *Cheque Enclosed* (2007) and the Bridport Prize collection 2010, and her story 'The Human Circadian Pacemaker' was shortlisted for the 2011 BBC National Short Story Prize. She has won awards for both short fiction and plays, and been shortlisted for the London Writers' Prize, the Asham Award and the Bridport Prize. She is a graduate of the MA in Creative Writing at the University of East Anglia and in 2010 won Arts and Humanities Research Council funding for a collection of short stories, as part of a PhD on the form at the University of Chichester.

Justina Robson attended the Clarion West Writing Workshop and was first published in 1994 in the British small press magazine *The Third Alternative*, but is best known as a novelist. Her debut novel *Silver Screen* was shortlisted for both the Arthur C Clarke Award and the BSFA Award in 2000. Her second novel, *Mappa Mundi*, was also shortlisted for the Arthur C Clarke Award in 2001. It won the 2000 Amazon. co.uk Writer's Bursary. In 2004, *Natural History*, Robson's third novel, was shortlisted for the BSFA Award, and came second in the John W Campbell Award. Novels since have included *Living Next-Door to the God of Love* and *Keeping It Real*. Her short story 'Carbon' was specially commissioned for *When It Changed* (Comma, 2009).

Jane Rogers was born in London in 1952 and lived in Birmingham, New York State (Grand Island) and Oxford, before doing an English degree at Cambridge University. She taught English for six years before the publication of her first novel, *Separate Tracks*. Since then she has written eight novels including *Mr Wroe's Virgins*, *Island*, *The Voyage Home* and most recently *The Testament of Jessie Lamb* (Sandstone Press), which was longlisted for the 2011 Man Booker Prize, as well as original and adapted work for television and radio drama. In 1994 she was made a Fellow of the Royal Society of Literature, and is currently Professor of Writing on the MA course at Sheffield Hallam University. In 2009 her story 'Hitting Trees With Sticks' was shortlisted for the BBC National Short Story Prize. Her first collection of short stories was published by Comma this autumn.

Dilys Rose lives in Edinburgh and teaches on the Masters in Creative Writing at the University of Edinburgh. She writes mainly poetry and fiction but has also written some drama and, more recently, text for music. Awards she has received include: The Macallan/Scotland on Sunday Short Story Award (1991), Society of Authors' Travel Award (1998), two Scottish Arts Council Book Awards (1993, 1999), Canongate Prize (2000), UNESCO/City of Literature fellowship (2006), and the McCash prize (2006).

Sarah Schofield is a new writer whose recent prizes include the Writers Inc Short Story Competition and the Calderdale Short Story Competition. She was shortlisted for the Bridport Prize in 2010 and was runner up in The Guardian Travel Writing Competition. Her story 'Traces Remain' appeared in *Lemistry: A Celebration of the Life of Stanislaw Lem*, and 'All About You' is to appear in a new Comma showcase, of the same name, in late 2012.

About the Scientists and Ethicists

Martyn Amos is a Professor of Novel Computation at Manchester Metropolitan University, and the author of *Genesis Machines: The New Science of Biocomputing* (Atlantic, 2007). His research interests include complexity theory, artificial life, synthetic biology and natural computing.

Dr Melissa Baxter is a stem cell research scientist at Manchester University. She is currently developing ways to turn stem cells into liver cells for drug testing and safer medicine. Her recent publications include the development of a new, efficient way to grow stem cells. During her PhD (2001 to 2005) she published research showing how adult stem cells age, and was the first to genetically correct diseased stem cells from bone marrow stroma.

Dr Jane Calvert is a sociologist of science at the University of Edinburgh. She has a background in human sciences (Sussex), philosophy of science (London School of Economics), and science policy (Sussex). She is particularly interested in the social dimensions of synthetic biology, including interdisciplinary interactions in the field, intellectual property and open source, and design and aesthetics.

Sarah Gilbert is Professor of Vaccinology, Jenner Institute, University of Oxford. She studied at the University of East Anglia and University of Hull, and worked for a biotechnology company prior to moving to Oxford University in 1994. She leads the Jenner Institute Influenza vaccine programme and also works on the development of new vaccines to prevent malaria. This entails organising clinical trials with volunteers to test both malaria and influenza vaccines.

Dr Jane Haley is the Scientific Coordinator for Edinburgh Neuroscience, University of Edinburgh. She has a BSc and a PhD in Pharmacology from UCL and spent 20 years recording the electrical activity of nerve cells trying to understand how chronic pain and memories are formed. Her role is now to bring together researchers to create a vibrant neuroscience community in Edinburgh. As part of these activities, in 2010 she coordinated a series of debates looking at the use of brain imaging technology (and fMRI in particular) outside the medical and research arenas.

Dr Nick Love is a researcher at the University of Manchester studying the biology of Xenopus tadpole tail regeneration. He is winner of the 2012 Westminster Medal and was shortlisted for the 2011 Guardian/Wellcome Trust Science Writing Prize.

Dr Ian Vincent McGonigle holds a BA in 'Biochemistry with Cell Biology' (Dublin) and a PhD in 'Molecular Pharmacology' (Cantab) and has been published in the *Journal of Neuroscience*, *FASEB Journal* and *Biochemistry*. He is currently studying Socio-Cultural Anthropology at the University of

Chicago, with research interests in bioethics, epistemology, ethno-pharmacology and medical anthropology.

Dr Ainsley Newson is Senior Lecturer in Biomedical Ethics at the University of Bristol. Previously (2003-6) she was a Research Fellow in Ethics and Clinical Genetics at Imperial College London. Ainsley works on the ethical aspects of genetics and emerging biotechnologies and has published and lectured widely on these topics. Ainsley has a PhD in Medical Ethics from the University of Melbourne as well as Bachelor degrees in Science and Law. From January 2013 she will be Sesqui Senior Lecturer in Bioethics at the University of Sydney.

Dr Simon Stott is a research scientist working at the Cambridge Centre for Brain Repair at Cambridge University. His specific area of interest is the molecular mechanisms behind neurodegenerative diseases such as Parkinson's disease. He has a PhD in Neurobiology (Lund University, Sweden) and is also an associate lecturer for the Open University.

Dr Nihal Engin Vrana is a postdoctoral researcher at Harvard–MIT's Division of Health Sciences and Technology. He has previously been a postdoctoral researcher at INSERM U977, Strasbourg, France. He has a PhD in Engineering from DCU, Dublin, and an MSc in Biotechnology, and a BSc in Biology from METU, Ankara, Turkey. His research interests include tissue engineering, biomaterials and cell-material interactions. He has published 16 peer reviewed articles in international journals, one book chapter and one patent.

Dr Angharad Watson read Biochemistry at Oxford. Her studies led to a PhD position at the University of Manchester, where she worked as a postdoctoral research associate, researching complex sugars in the disease Mucopolysaccharidosis. She is now based at Cardiff University, investigating tumour immunotherapy.

Professor Bruce Whitelaw is Head of Division at The Roslin Institute and Professor of Animal Biotechnology at the Royal (Dick) School of Veterinary Studies of the University of Edinburgh. He is a molecular geneticist by training and his research focuses on the development of embryo manipulation and gene transfer technology in mammals. Bruce actively seeks to apply this technology in the field of animal biotechnology.

Special Thanks

The publishers would like to thank Rosie Wilkinson who acted as co-editor of this book during its early stages. The project would never have got off the ground without her dilligent work. We'd also like to thank the following scientists and ethicists who consulted on stories but didn't write afterwords themselves:

Professor Dek Woolfson, School of Chemistry, University of Bristol ('Dinner at High Table'),

Dr Mark Wallace, Department of Chemistry, University of Oxford ('Dinner at High Table'),

Dr Jan Deckers, Medical Sciences Education Department, Newcastle University ('An Industrial Evolution'),

and, Dr David Jones, Anscombe Bioethics Centre, Oxford ('Story Time').